# Summer Ball
# Weddings
## &
# Waltzing

De-ann Black

Paperback edition published 2025

Summer Ball Weddings & Waltzing

ISBN: 9798287676599

Summer Ball Weddings & Waltzing is the fifth book in the Scottish Highlands & Island Romance series.

Also by De-ann Black (Romance, Action/Thrillers & Children's books). See her Amazon Author page or website for further details about her books, screenplays, illustrations and artwork. www.De-annBlack.com

**Romance:**
Romance Dancer
Summer Ball Weddings & Waltzing
Quilt Shop by the Seaside
Embroidery Bee
Crafting Bee
Scottish Highlands New Year Ball
Ballroom Dancing Christmas Romance
Christmas Ballroom Dancing
Autumn Romance
Knitting & Starlight
Knitting Bee
The Sweetest Waltz
Sweet Music
Love & Lyrics
Christmas Weddings
Fairytale Christmas on the Island
The Cure for Love at Christmas
Vintage Dress Shop on the Island
Scottish Island Fairytale Castle
Scottish Loch Summer Romance
Scottish Island Knitting Bee
Sewing & Mending Cottage
Knitting Shop by the Sea
Colouring Book Cottage
Knitting Cottage
Oops! I'm the Paparazzi, Again
The Bitch-Proof Wedding
Embroidery Cottage
The Dressmaker's Cottage
The Sewing Shop

Heather Park
The Tea Shop by the Sea
The Bookshop by the Seaside
The Sewing Bee
The Quilting Bee
Snow Bells Wedding
Snow Bells Christmas
The Chocolatier's Cottage
Christmas Cake Chateau
The Beemaster's Cottage
The Sewing Bee By The Sea
The Flower Hunter's Cottage
Shed In The City
The Bakery By The Seaside
The Christmas Chocolatier
The Bitch-Proof Suit

**Action/Thrillers:**

Knight in Miami.                    Someone Worse.
Agency Agenda.                    Electric Shadows.
Love Him Forever.               The Strife of Riley.

**Colouring books:**

Summer Nature. Flower Nature. Summer Garden. Spring
Garden. Autumn Garden. Sea Dream. Festive Christmas.
Christmas Garden. Flower Bee. Wild Garden. Flower Hunter.
Stargazer Space. Christmas Theme. Faerie Garden Spring.
Scottish Garden Seasons. Bee Garden.

**Embroidery books:**

Floral Garden Embroidery Patterns
Floral Spring Embroidery Patterns
Christmas & Winter Embroidery Patterns
Sea Theme Embroidery Patterns
Floral Nature Embroidery Designs
Scottish Garden Embroidery Designs

# Contents

# CHAPTER ONE

The sea surrounding the beautiful Scottish island shimmered in the summer morning sunlight. The island was situated off the west coast of Scotland. A few boats bobbed gently in the little harbour beside the small town's main street where the quaint shops wrapped themselves around the curve of the bay. Cottages were dotted along the coastline, on the hillside sweeping up from the shore, and sprinkled across the patchwork of fields and countryside beyond. And the island's fairytale castle, a magnificent dark stone castle with spiralling turrets, was set in the heart of a large estate, and shielded by the nearby forest.

Finlay sat on the deck of his yacht. An expensive, full–size yacht, with an aquamarine hull, that was a fair match for his eyes, the sea, and the new sails he'd added that morning. Tall, lean and strong, he wore neutral tone classics — a light beige shirt and dark cream trousers. The yacht was anchored at the harbour.

The warm breeze blew through his thick, blond hair and he pushed it back from his handsome face, eager to read the feature in the magazine supplement from the daily newspaper that he'd just bought from the grocery shop. Finlay was pictured on the front cover, standing outside the fairytale castle, alongside his two brothers, Innis and Ean. And their three fiancées — Merrilees, Skye and Ailsa.

The brothers wore classic suits, made by a local bespoke tailor, while Merrilees, Skye and Ailsa opted for stylish tea dresses from the island's vintage dress shop.

The three engaged couples were due to be married in a group ceremony soon at the castle. The summer ball was part of the evening's celebrations after the weddings.

At thirty–three, Finlay was one or two years older than his brothers, and was in line to become the laird of the castle and estate when his father handed the title and responsibility to him.

The castle was run as a hotel, catering for guests and special events such as weddings and other celebratory parties.

Ceilidh nights and dancing were held regularly in the family–owned castle. The laird and his wife were away a lot on business and leisure time to the mainland, leaving Finlay, Innis and Ean, to look after the castle and the estate. The sons lived in the castle, having private quarters on the upper floor and a turret, and were happy to run it as a popular hotel.

The forest surrounding the castle and estate included thistle loch, a silvery river and the enchanting forget–me–not waterfall. Guests enjoyed the benefits of these and the nearby sea.

Barely twenty miles from the mainland, the island's nearest city was Glasgow, accessed by the regular ferry. The newspaper was based in Glasgow, and copies had arrived on the first ferry that morning.

Finlay and his brothers had taken part in the magazine feature to help promote the castle's hotel and function facilities. Finlay had paid to be featured before, months ago, and that's how he came to become involved with Merrilees. She was the photo–journalist the newspaper had sent from Glasgow to the island to write the feature.

Time had gone full circle, and the new feature, highlighting the weddings at the castle, was written by Merrilees. Her editor thought there could be no one better to write it as she was one of the brides–to–be.

Merrilees was now a romance novelist, and had moved from Glasgow to the island to focus on her books — and her romance with Finlay. But she still sometimes wrote freelance features for the paper. Especially the features for the magazine–style supplements that included plenty of editorial and pictures.

The newspaper was happy to do the castle's wedding feature as it would encourage other islands to take part in features. This had worked before for everyone. Now, with the three rich and handsome sons getting married in a joint ceremony, it was a feature the paper thought readers would enjoy. An insight into the wedding preparations, the bridal wear, and the excitement of the summer ball.

Finlay sat in the sunshine reading the feature in the magazine...

*...and the laird's three sons are getting married in the castle. All three couples will partake in a joint ceremony, and then there will be a lavish reception in the function room, followed by an evening of dancing at the summer ball.*

*Finlay, thirty–three, is in line to take on the role of the castle's laird. An expert yachtsman, winner of various sailing contests, he plans to use his yacht for the couples' honeymoon trip around the west coast of Scotland. The three couples will set sail the morning after the wedding, heading up north towards the Summer Isles, stopping at several islands and seaside towns and villages along the way...*

Alerts started pinging up on his phone.

Finlay read a message from Merrilees.

*Have you seen the feature in the magazine?*

*Reading it right now. You've written it well, and your photos are excellent.*

Before she could reply, Finlay phoned Merrilees, and her beautiful face smiled out at him.

Merrilees was in her late twenties. Her shoulder–length blonde hair was pulled back in a ponytail, and her lovely grey eyes looked keen to gauge his reaction.

'I'm pleased you like the feature.' Merrilees sat at her desk in stargazer cottage, situated on the castle's estate. It provided a secluded niche where she could write her books without being disturbed. Though when Finlay came knocking on her door, those were the intrusions she welcomed.

After they got married, they planned to split their time between living in the castle and the cottage. The best of both worlds.

The cottage got its name from the skylight window in the bedroom that offered a view of the clear night skies filled with stars. It was the perfect place for Merrilees to relax and gaze at the stars and let her imagination soar for the novels she was working on.

But on this sunny morning, Merrilees sat in the living room with the windows open to let the fresh air and the scent of the flowers waft in from the cottage garden.

She'd had a copy of the magazine delivered to her. 'Has Innis and Ean seen it yet?'

'Probably. They've both sent me messages, so I'm guessing it's about the feature.'

'Let me know what they think.'

'I will,' said Finlay.

'I'm going down to the vintage dress shop around lunchtime. We're all trying on our wedding dresses. I'll find out what Skye and Ailsa think of the feature too.'

Skye and her sister, Holly, owned the pretty vintage dress shop in the main street. It was near Ailsa's craft shop.

'I promise I won't go anywhere near the dress shop,' Finlay assured her.

'What are you up to today?' Merrilees said, taking the conversation away from letting slip any secrets about the wedding dresses.

'Preparing the yacht for the honeymoon trip. I know there's plenty of time yet, but I've added the new aquamarine sails, and I'm checking other things so that everything is ship shape.'

By plenty of time, he meant less than two weeks. Considering how fast the previous fortnight had gone in, the pace was quickening rather than stretching out.

'I have another two chapters to write.' Merrilees planned to finish her latest romance novel and send it off to her editor. The deadline was tight. The publishers wanted to have the complete manuscript before she set sail on the three–week honeymoon.

'I'll let you get on with your writing,' he said. 'See you later for dinner?'

'At the cottage or the castle?'

'The cottage. Things have been so hectic these past few days. Let's have a cosy, relaxing dinner for two.'

'I love the sound of that.'

'And I love you, Merrilees.'

'I love you too. See you tonight.'

Finlay continued reading the feature...

*...the laird and his wife will come back from dealing with business on the mainland to attend the weddings. But they will leave later that night on the last ferry.*

This part of the feature led on to the one thing Finlay and his brothers had an issue with.

Finlay glanced over at the cake shop wondering if Innis was reading it.


Innis owned the cake shop in the main street. The pale vanilla and pink exterior was enhanced by hanging baskets filled with yellow and pink roses that added to the floral pastel look.

A lovely mix of shops in the main street enhanced the picturesque quality of the island.

The pretty pink–painted knitting shop was sandwiched between Innis' cake shop and Brodrick's cafe bar, and beside that was Skye and Holly's vintage dress shop. Other nearby shops included Ailsa's craft shop, and Lyle's tea shop.

Perfectly iced cakes decorated with flowers made from fondant icing were displayed in the front window of the cake shop. And Innis' special chocolates.

The interior of the shop matched the exterior and had a modern vintage style. Elements of strawberry, lemon and cream added to the light and airy atmosphere.

Glass cabinets displayed a selection of cakes, lit with spotlights, and Innis' chocolates had a cabinet to themselves. Boxes of his luxury chocolates, ranging from truffles to fondant creams, sat on a shelf behind the counter and in the window display. A glass extension had recently been added to the back of the premises, like a small tearoom area where customers could enjoy a cup of tea with cake or scones. And sample Innis' chocolates. Silver cakes stands were on the tables, and the decor was pink and yellow, including the linen napkins.

Innis was icing an anniversary cake in the kitchen at the back of the shop. He'd smoothed royal icing on to the cake and was now piping the names on top.

His two shop assistants, Rosabel and Primrose, worked behind the front counter, wrapping orders and serving customers. The two ladies, sisters, both in their latter years, wore aprons and bakery caps with their silvery curls peeking out.

Innis was considered to be the most handsome man on the island. And there were a fair few other men worthy of that title, including his two brothers. He was tall, fit, thirty–two, with dark hair and a brooding nature.

Innis' amber eyes had given him the reputation of having wolf eyes. He was known to be a wolf in wolf's clothing. A man who suffered fools badly.

He wore a chef's collarless white shirt with short sleeves, black trousers and a chef's black apron. Everything unintentionally emphasised his fit physique.

His work kept him busy, and he liked to unwind after a long day at the shop by walking up into the hills, taking the hardest route to the top where he enjoyed his favourite view of the island, the glistening sea, and the castle where he lived.

Innis baked cakes, but he specialised as a chocolatier. He looked the epitome of an artisan chef as he finished decorating the anniversary cake.

His raw masculinity had attracted the attention of Skye, a beautiful and vivacious young woman, and their slow–burn romance had resulted in their engagement. He longed to marry her and have her move in with him. He lived in a substantial suite on an upper level of the castle. The long windows overlooked the front of the castle and had a wonderful view of the countryside and the sea.

The chatter from Rosabel and Primrose in the front shop jarred him from his faraway thoughts of marrying Skye. There had been a time, during the winter, when it seemed that he'd marry her before his brothers married Merrilees and Ailsa, but circumstances had led to the decision for the three weddings to be scheduled together in the summer.

While the shop was quiet for a few minutes, Rosabel and Primrose read the feature in the magazine. They loved the pictures, especially the front cover, and thought Merrilees' editorial was great. Until they came to the part about who was going to be in charge of the castle while the brothers were away on honeymoon.

Primrose adjusted her cap and sounded rather annoyed. 'Did you read who is coming back to the island to oversee the running of the castle while Innis and the others are off on honeymoon?'

Rosabel tied the ribbon on a cake box. 'No, I just skimmed it.'

Primrose read it to her...

'*While Finlay, Innis and Ean are away on honeymoon, their cousin, Roag, an expert chef, will be stepping in to take charge of the smooth running of the castle and estate.*'

Rosabel peered at the paragraph. 'Roag? That troublemaker!'

Primrose pursed her lips and nodded.

'I thought Murdo and Geneen and the other staff at the castle could hold the fort while they were away,' said Rosabel.

'So did I. Murdo and Geneen have worked at the castle long enough to manage the guests on their own. They already handle the bookings and deal with the functions and party nights.'

Primrose read another snippet from the feature. '*The laird wants a family member to take charge of the castle.*'

Rosabel flicked an accusing finger at Roag's picture in the magazine. 'There's going to be a stooshie when that troublemaker arrives.'

'It says he still owns a restaurant in Glasgow, but that his managers will look after it while he takes a working break on the island,' said Primrose. 'He's quoted as saying that he's looking forward to trying out Innis' kitchen area at the castle where he makes his chocolatier specialities.'

'Aye, and cause a rumpus while he's at it.' Rosabel sounded annoyed. 'Someone will have to tell the ladies not to swoon over his chocolate–box looks.'

'Or come to bed eyes,' Primrose added, looking at the picture of the troublemaking chef.

Roag was thirty–two, as tall and fit as Innis and the other brothers. His dark brown hair was stylishly–cut, with a few rogue strands falling sexily over his forehead, emphasising his intense blue–green eyes.

Merrilees had added a snippet regarding his name. Primrose read it out...

*'Roag was named after a sea loch up at the Isle of Lewis, on the west coast of Scotland.'*

Innis had heard enough. He carried the anniversary cake through and put it on a display stand in the front window.

The atmosphere was thick with the tension from the gossip and reaction to the news of Roag's visit.

'My father made the decision to invite Roag,' Innis told them, breaking the edgy silence. 'It's for business reasons too, having a family member look after the castle.'

Rosabel spoke up. 'There are a lot of folk that won't put the welcome mat out for him. And newcomers don't know of his flirtatious and philandering ways.'

'I'm sure the gossip will circulate soon.' Innis' deep voice sounded clear in the shop.

'I suppose so,' said Rosabel, and started to fold a cake box in readiness for the orders.

Innis adjusted the anniversary cake in the window display. The cake was a single layer of fruit cake, and iced with the names of the couple who'd ordered it. Nettie and Shuggie. Nettie was a keen knitter. Shuggie was the local taxi driver.

'Keep this in the display until it's time for it to be picked up,' said Innis. 'And take no payment for it.'

The women frowned.

'Shuggie has always been obliging when driving guests up to the hotel from the ferry,' Innis explained. 'The cake is with my compliments on their anniversary.'

Shuggie and Nettie were in their forties and were about to celebrate their tenth wedding anniversary by going on a cruise that they'd saved hard for. Their niece, Fyona, thirty, was due to arrive soon from the mainland to keep an eye on their cottage, and help assist the castle's head chef with the catering for the weddings. An expert in patisserie, she'd finished her latest training in cake decorating, and had worked in prestigious restaurants and hotels.

'I'll tell Nettie tonight at the knitting bee,' said Rosabel. 'She'll be delighted.'

'That's very nice of you, Innis,' Primrose added.

Innis nodded, and then looked out the window. He saw Finlay sitting reading the magazine on the deck of the yacht. Innis had a copy of the magazine for himself. He'd read the part about Roag. Maybe there was trouble brewing.

11

Customers came into the cake shop as Innis walked out and headed down to the yacht. But someone caught his eye...

Skye had seen Innis from the vintage dress shop window and hurried outside.

'Tell him,' Holly called after Skye, insisting urgently from the shop's open doorway.

Skye nodded and ran to catch up with Innis. Her long, strawberry blonde hair fluttered behind her, and the colourful seventies summer dress she wore suited her slender figure. In her late twenties, she'd always loved fashion and modelled part–time.

Skye and her sister, Holly, early thirties, had trained in fashion and design on the mainland, and had taken over the vintage dress shop from their mother when she wanted to retire to enjoy more leisure time with their father. Their mother had inherited the shop from their grandmother, and now they were happy to take it on. Their parents were away a lot, visiting family and friends in the nearby islands and on the mainland. Skye and Holly stayed in their parents' house on the hillside.

Bunting fluttered in the light breeze along the edge of the shop's sign — *the vintage dress shop*. Summery bunting hung outside various shops along the main street.

The shop sold pre–loved fashion, mainly dresses ranging from tea dresses to ball gowns and wedding dresses. Their online customers often made repeat orders and they'd steadily built up their business, especially the sales of the dresses. Local customers loved the vintage dresses too. Real bargains for the quality of the designs.

Innis watched Skye as she approached him. 'You've got that mischievous expression on your face.' His deep voice filtered into the warm air.

Skye's beautiful, wide blue eyes with their curious upswept tilt looked up at him. She was fairly tall, but Innis towered over her.

'Have you read the feature in the magazine?' she said chirpily.

'Most of it.'

'Did you read the part about the wedding dresses? Merrilees hinted at the wedding dresses we'll be wearing.'

'Not yet. Is there something wrong? Are you concerned it'll give away secrets?'

Skye had told him she was wearing a vintage dress, which was true. But she described it as a large, rose pink crinoline with lots of frou–frou. Innis had sucked up his reaction, wanting Skye to wear the wedding dress of her dreams. He didn't know much about bridal fashion, but the pink extravaganza wasn't quite what he'd pictured she'd wear. How was he even going to stand close to her? But, to him, Skye looked beautiful whatever she wore, so he'd kept any comments to himself.

'No, I...' She smiled and giggled. 'I was winding you up about the pink dress. I am wearing vintage. But it's a gorgeous white dress. A classic.'

Innis stepped closer. His sculptured features were lit by the sunlight that cast a shadow across half of his face. Neither side was smiling.

'Not a strawberry blancmange then,' he clarified.

Skye smiled sweetly. 'No. I was just having a wee bit of fun.'

Innis nodded slowly, taking this in.

Holly peeked out the dress shop window, her green eyes wide with anticipation, watching his reaction. Innis seemed to be taking it well, until he suddenly lifted Skye up in his strong arms and strode towards the sea.

'As you're in a playful mood,' he said, 'maybe you'd like a dip in the sea. It's a lovely morning for a swim.'

'Nooo!' Skye shrieked, clinging on to his broad shoulders as he approached the glistening sea.

Hearing the squeals, Finlay glanced up from reading the magazine. Seeing Innis striding towards the water carrying Skye, he smiled to himself, and then continued to read the feature.

Innis was now at the edge of the sea, with Skye clinging tight to him, giggling and shrieking.

'No, Innis! You'll ruin my dress!'

'I'm sure you've got a shop full of other nice dresses.'

Skye clung even tighter, feeling the strong muscles beneath the fabric of his shirt.

Pretending he was going to throw her into the sea, Innis relented, and instead pulled her close and kissed her.

'You're nothing but trouble,' he scolded her playfully.

His kiss made everything right again. She kissed him lovingly. 'But I'm your trouble.'

14

'Oh, yes,' he agreed, and then carried her back towards the dress shop before finally putting her down gently.

Skye's cheeks were flushed from the fun and the underlying passion. She ran into the shop.

'I told Innis,' Skye said breathlessly to Holly.

'I guessed that. I thought he really was going to throw you into the sea.' Holly's shoulder–length chestnut hair was pinned back from her lovely features with clasps. She wore a denim, button front, vintage skirt that skimmed just below her calves, and a yellow halterneck top from the seventies. The outfit suited her great figure.

Skye tied her long hair back in a ponytail and sat down at her pink sewing machine behind the counter to continue mending the hem of one of the vintage dresses. The repairs gave the pre–loved dresses a chance to be loved again.

They cleaned and repaired all the items they sold before listing them for sale on their website. Skilled in making repairs, this included invisible mending whereby the repairs were barely seen, and visible mending that became part of the design, such as embroidering floral motifs on the clothes. And they added sequins, beads, ribbons and other trims to upscale the clothes.

Holly went through to the kitchen, relieved that Innis knew about the ruse. 'I'll put the kettle on for tea.'

After his exciting encounter with Skye, Innis walked down to Finlay's yacht and stepped on board.

'Do you think we'll have trouble when Roag comes to the castle?' Finlay cut directly to the issue, rightly surmising that Innis was there to talk about this.

Innis leaned back against one of the yacht's edge rails. 'Roag's supposed to be a lot more mature and responsible these days.' He took a deep breath. 'But I sense a storm of trouble brewing.'

Finlay gazed up at the dazzling sunshine in the cobalt blue sky. Despite the cloudless summer sky that arched over the beautiful coastline and sparkling sea, he was inclined to agree with Innis.

'So do I.'

# CHAPTER TWO

Ean ran down the castle's staircase to the reception. Wearing his fitness gear for one of his regular runs, he cut an impressive figure, and his tall stature matched that of Finlay and Innis, but he was a little less strapping. He was lean and fit from his running through the castle's estate gardens, the forest, around thistle loch, making the most of nature's gym.

This morning he planned to go for a run down the shore, and stop by Ailsa's craft shop in the main street. He wanted to talk to her about the magazine feature, hoping she liked it as much as he did.

Ean owned a small boat that was anchored at the harbour, but art, painting watercolours, occupied most of his leisure time along with the running.

Murdo and Geneen were standing behind the reception desk having dealt with the arrival of new guests.

Everything about the castle's decor was plush and traditionally stylish. Tartan carpets, white and beige walls, oak beams and various wood furnishings. Chandeliers and table lamps cast a bright, welcoming glow. Oil paintings depicted landscapes, seascapes and views of the island. Several of the watercolour paintings were Ean's artistic work.

A framed array of photographs of the castle's laird, his wife and their three grown–up sons, were on the wall beside the staircase. Even in his mature years, the laird was a handsome man. His wife was very beautiful. Their sons were all heartbreakers. Finlay's looks were the nearest match to his father. Innis had his own particular look. Ean had an artistic air, and his elegant features, auburn hair and emerald eyes were like those of his mother.

An antique grandfather clock struck the mid–morning hour. Time to go for his run, Ean thought. He was already late, having become engrossed in reading the magazine feature.

Ean jumped the pleated red and gold cord at the bottom of the sweeping staircase that kept this part of the castle private. He landed on the dark tartan carpet and walked towards Murdo and Geneen. The tense expressions on their faces showed their reaction to the feature. They both had copies, and extras were piled on the edge of the reception desk.

Geneen was in her fifties, a trim and efficient member of the castle's main staff.

Murdo was a key worker at the castle, a sturdy man in his fifties, a handyman and builder and one of the castle's main assistants.

The front doors of the castle were open wide, letting in the warmth of the sunny morning. Instead of hurrying through reception and outside for his run, Ean walked over to the reception desk. He didn't even have to ask what they thought of the feature.

Geneen tapped an annoyed finger on the page where Roag's picture was featured. 'Everything about the weddings and the plans for the summer ball are great. But I can't believe you're inviting this scallywag to the castle to take charge while you're away.'

'Aye,' Murdo chimed–in. 'I think you know fine that you're inviting trouble to the castle.'

'My father made the decision,' said Ean. 'Initially, Finlay, Innis and I were inclined to agree with you. But then we discussed the practicalities of the whole situation. Nairne is well capable of handling the catering for a wedding. He's an expert chef. But this is three weddings. Plus the catering for the summer ball.'

Nairne was the castle's head chef, and although he had catering staff to assist him in the vast kitchen, he was responsible for creating the menus for the guests staying at the castle, and for special functions like the summer ball. He was also Ailsa's uncle.

Geneen and Murdo exchanged a resigned glance. It was a lot of work to organise, especially as the weddings and the summer ball were planned to be lavish.

'And, the guests have to be catered for at the same time,' Ean added. 'It's like having four times the catering work. And Roag is an expert chef with his own restaurant, and is well capable of helping Nairne organise everything.'

'Aye, I know,' Murdo agreed. 'But what about that lassie, Shuggie and Nettie's niece. She's supposed to be an expert in patisserie.'

'Fyona,' said Geneen. 'I met her briefly in the main street when she was here a while back visiting her aunt and uncle. She seemed nice.'

'We need all the help we can get,' Ean emphasised. 'It's not fair to put all the pressure on Nairne and his staff. Besides, we hear that Roag has changed his ways and become more mature. He's around a year older than me, Innis' age.'

'I heard that Roag has given up his aspirations to be a professional dancer, and concentrates solely on building up his restaurant business.' Geneen was a reliable source of gossip and news, so Ean was inclined to agree.

'I think so,' said Ean.

'Roag better concentrate on his cooking,' said Nairne, overhearing their conversation. Nairne was in his fifties, dressed in his whites and his chef's hat. He walked over to add his tuppence worth. 'I certainly don't want him leaping about in the kitchen, doing ballroom while he's baking and the tango while the tatties roast.'

Geneen laughed. 'I don't think Roag will be dancing in the kitchen.'

'Roag's a rascal,' Nairne reminded her. 'I wouldn't put it past him.'

'How long will he be here?' said Murdo.

'A month, give or take a bit of wiggle room,' Nairne explained. 'He should arrive in plenty of time before the weddings and the ball, then continue helping during the three–week honeymoon. But I'm very happy that Fyona is joining us for that time too. I'm fair impressed with her expertise in patisserie.'

Geneen spoke up. 'Nettie says that Fyona was planning to take a break after her last course in baking and sugar craft. And it's handy that she can cottage sit while she's here.'

'Well, I'm keen to see some of Fyona's recipes for her cakes and pastries. I know Roag is an expert in this too, but I like her style,' said Nairne and then headed back through to the kitchen.

Guests arrived, and Geneen and Murdo attended to them while Ean ran outside.

He felt the warmth of the sun as he jogged away from the castle, and then started to pick up speed down the forest road towards the shore. The scent of the sea air filled his lungs, and spurred him on.

Ean liked to run...fast, feeling the air whip by him. Running wild, enjoying the energy of the elements.

And more than anything, he was looking forward to seeing Ailsa.

He ran down the hillside that rose up from the main street and the sea. Several cottages were dotted around the hill, including Ailsa's cottage. Ailsa inherited the cottage when her grandmother moved away to Edinburgh to spend more time with her sister.

Knocking on the door, on the off chance she was there, he realised Ailsa wasn't at home, so he ran down to her craft shop in the main street.

Ailsa leased the shop premises. The crafts she sold were popular with local customers and tourists. She knitted shawls, hats and scarves. Her quilted items sold well, along with her handcrafted jewellery. Apart from the things she made herself, the shop stocked watercolour prints of the island, artist materials, craft kits and various other products.

Ean ran along the street and stopped outside her shop. Seeing the lights on inside, and Ailsa busy sorting items on the shelves, he opened the door and went in.

Ailsa's smile lit up his heart when she saw him.

His fitting T–shirt showed his lithe muscles, and her own heart reacted to seeing him. She was quite tall, but Ean's tall, fit physique towered over her as he leaned down to kiss her.

Ailsa was a classic beauty, with slender curves, dark hair that tipped the top of her shoulders in a long bob, a lovely pale complexion and azure blue eyes. As well as owning her own craft shop, she modelled knitwear and fashion, and used her modelling work to boost her income while she built up her craft shop.

She was born and raised on the island. Ailsa was well–travelled due to her modelling work taking her to various places on the mainland, but she couldn't imagine living anywhere better than the beautiful island in Scotland. And settling down with Ean, splitting their time between staying at the cottage and the castle.

Since Skye and Holly had now settled on the island, she'd become best friends with them, and loved the vintage fashions in their dress shop.

A copy of the magazine was on the shop counter. She'd read it, and left it there so customers could see it too.

'What did you think of the feature?' said Ean.

'I thought it was great.' She sounded sure, but her expression hinted at an underlying issue. 'I'm just slightly concerned about Roag coming here to help with the wedding catering and then take charge while we're away on honeymoon.'

He liked that she spoke her mind.

'Skye and Holly are fairly new to settling on the island, and they've never met Roag. Neither has Merrilees. She's only interviewed him on the phone.

But I remember him. He's a heartbreaker, and broke a few if I recall.'

'I understand, but we're hoping he's matured, changed his ways.'

Ailsa's expression showed she doubted this. She sighed heavily. 'But I refuse to have Roag put a dampener on our wedding plans.'

He pulled her close. 'Not long now.'

'I'm still in a whirl about the whole thing.' She glanced at her diamond engagement ring sparkling in the sunlight streaming through the window, picturing the wedding band that was due to be added.

'I want you to enjoy the planning. I won't put up with any nonsense from Roag,' he assured her. 'And Finlay and Innis certainly won't.'

His assurance lifted her doubts.

Kissing her again, Ean left and continued on his run, stopping to talk to Finlay on the yacht from the harbour's edge.

'Roag seems to be causing ructions before he's even arrived,' Finlay said to Ean.

'I've assured Ailsa that we won't put up with any trouble he stirs.'

'I spoke to Innis, and we're standing firm on that. Nairne won't put up with it either.'

'Or Murdo and Geneen,' Ean added.

'I think they'll all be able to handle Roag. He hasn't been here for four years, but surely he's matured, especially as he has his own successful restaurant business.'

Ean agreed. 'He's the same age as Innis, and look how he's matured, having his cake shop, and now wanting to settle down and marry Skye.'

Finlay nodded, and waved as Ean continued on his run along the shore.

Roag had seen the front cover of the magazine, but was too busy preparing the lunches in his Glasgow restaurant to read the feature. He wanted to relax and read it properly in private. Seeing Finlay, Innis and Ean pictured in front of the castle jarred him more than he'd anticipated. A feeling of them being familiar strangers.

Four years had sparked past in a whirlwind of events, from finally giving up his dancing aspirations in favour of giving his restaurant business a hundred percent of his energy.

He'd lied to everyone, including himself sometimes, that he was fine with hanging up his dancing shoes. No more ballroom dancing, contests, dance tours, or events sandwiched between his cheffing work.

As his restaurant business took off, he'd tried to shoehorn in a few performances, picturing he could have the best of both ambitions, with his chef work taking ninety percent of his time. But as the restaurant thrived, and his skills as a top chef, specialising in patisserie, were in increasing demand, it became clear than no less than one hundred percent would suffice. He made the hard decision that it was better to excel at one thing than be lesser at both.

He'd slipped into his chefdom without any fanfare. It was months before his restaurant staff realised he hadn't taken a weekend off to participate in any dance events. And by that time, he'd become accustomed to his new sole ambition.

But in his mind, while he prepared the new lunch menu, were the three faces he'd soon meet again. The laird himself had done the asking when it came to approaching him about looking after the castle while the sons were on honeymoon. And assisting Nairne with the catering. A brief email was exchanged between Roag and Finlay. The polite, but impersonal business message said little, and thereby spoke volumes.

Roag sensed the ripples of uneasiness from across the sea to the heart of the city before he'd even thought of sailing over to the island.

A storm was brewing. He felt it in his bones. But he could handle whatever culinary challenge they threw at him. Faint hearts didn't last long in his world, and he was thriving nicely.

'I see you and your restaurant got a mention in the newspaper's magazine,' one of his chefs remarked chirpily while working in the kitchen. 'Have you seen it?'

'A glimpse of the cover.' Roag played down the importance of it.

'It looks like a magnificent castle. I've never been over to the island to see it. What's it like? Old–fashioned? Bits crumbling behind the scenes?'

'No, it's as magnificent as it appears,' said Roag. The laird's business deals kept the castle solvent, and it was now a successful hotel. The family's wealth had thrived well over the years. Roag came from the moneyed part of the family too, and had invested a chunk of his own wealth in his restaurant.

'The men on the cover are so handsome,' another chef chimed–in. She smiled at Roag. 'And rich, but obviously they're taken now. Their fiancées all look beautiful, and happy. Maybe you'll meet a wonderful woman yourself on the island.'

Roag picked up a tray of pastry slices for the raspberry and cream delicacies, and put them in the oven, signalling that they should get on with their work.

His own romantic life was in tatters, again. When would he ever learn? Despite his roguish reputation, he was at an age now where he longed to settle down. But with no woman in his world that he could truly love, and trust, he had to help with the weddings and the summer ball, and look after the castle during the height of the summer. A working holiday, in a castle on the lovely Scottish island. And not be the troublemaker he knew they all anticipated.

As for meeting a wonderful woman on the island, he doubted this. But he was going to the castle to work, not have his heart broken. He hadn't met Skye or Merrilees, but he knew Ailsa, having made a play for her one evening during a ceilidh at the castle. Considered to be one of the most beautiful women on the island, Ailsa had politely refused his romantic advances. Obviously, she'd since found love with Ean, and he'd no wish to date Ailsa now. He'd overstepped that evening at the ceilidh, putting it down to the fun

26

and energy of the dancing. She probably wouldn't even remember that night, and if she did, Ailsa wouldn't want to make things awkward now.

'Roag made a play for me at one of the castle ceilidhs,' Ailsa revealed to Skye, Holly and Merrilees at the vintage dress shop at lunchtime.

Skye's eyes widened. 'Really? Does Ean know?'

Ailsa shook her head. 'I've never told him. And it was four years ago, before I started dating Ean. I don't want to rake up the past to cause trouble.'

Merrilees agreed. 'I'd keep that nugget of news to myself.'

'Does Roag still fancy you?' Holly said to Ailsa.

'Nooo, he was always flirting with the ladies. He thought he was the cock of the walk.' Ailsa looked at his picture in the magazine as they chatted about the feature. 'Roag was never my type. He was too...'

'Full of himself?' Merrilees suggested.

'And then some,' said Ailsa.

Skye studied his face. 'He doesn't look like Innis, Finlay or Ean.'

'No, Roag's got his own look,' Holly commented.

'Roag used to be described as double–handsome,' Ailsa confided.

The four of them evaluated his picture. None of them contradicted this.

'He seems to be a very successful chef.' Holly had looked up his website on the shop's computer. 'It's a stylish restaurant, and he's launched a new summer menu.'

There were other pictures of Roag on the website.

'His cheffing clearly keeps him fit,' Skye remarked.

'And his dancing,' Ailsa added.

'What dancing?' said Merrilees. 'When I spoke to him on the phone during the interview, he only talked about being a chef, not a dancer.'

'I guess he's not doing his dancing these days,' Ailsa surmised. 'But he used to be quite competitive in ballroom dancing. He performed on stage at weekends. Or so I heard from Geneen. She knows all the gossip.'

Skye picked up her phone and called Geneen.

'No,' said Holly. 'Don't go stirring up more gossip.'

'I just want to nosey about his dancing,' Skye insisted, and made a quick call to Geneen at the castle. She put it on speaker so they could all listen in while having their lunch.

'Apparently, he fell in love with two of the ladies he was partnered with for his dancing,' Geneen confided. 'They both jilted him for other dancers. Broke his heart, twice, or so I heard.'

'I thought he'd be the heartbreaker,' Skye said to Geneen.

'He made a move on Ailsa in the past, and she wasn't interested in him,' said Geneen.

'Ailsa is here in the shop. She's never told Ean this, so—'

'This is just girl–talk,' Geneen assured them.

'Thanks for the information, Geneen,' said Skye. 'We're all here at the shop to try on our wedding dresses.'

'Oh, how exciting! I saw that Merrilees hinted at the style of the dresses being vintage,' said Geneen.

'They're all vintage, but different eras. Sooo gorgeous,' Skye revealed.

The call ended on a cheery note.

'Right, let's try on the dresses,' said Holly.

The shop was a traditional converted cottage with a storeroom and kitchen at the back. They'd closed it to customers while they tried on the dresses. Then they planned to have lunch together in the shop.

A rail with the three wedding dresses and accessories was in the storeroom so the dresses wouldn't be seen by anyone else.

Holly and Skye carefully lifted the protective covering off the rail to reveal the gorgeous gowns.

Ailsa, Skye and Merrilees got changed into the dresses, and stepped into the shoes they planned to wear.

Skye's dress was a 1930s, white satin, full–length wedding gown, cut on the bias that skimmed her slender curves. Shoestring straps were due to be embellished with sparkling crystal beads, handsewn by Skye.

Ailsa dug into her bag. 'I brought plenty of crystal beads.' She stocked them in her shop and they glittered inside the small jar under the overhead lights.

'Thank you, Ailsa.' Skye clasped the jar and looked at the crystals. 'I'm going to sew them on the straps, and add a scattering on the neckline. Perhaps some on the bodice to add a wee bit of sparkle.'

A full–length mirror on a stand showed the colour and fabric of the dresses in the storeroom lights.

'Have you decided on a veil yet?' Ailsa said to Skye.

Holly lifted a light as air, chiffon veil from a hanger and handed it to Skye.

'I'm going to wear my hair down and attach the veil with diamante clasps,' Skye explained. The clasps were in a box along with other jewellery and accessories.

Merrilees twirled slowly, looking at her dress in the mirror. When she'd seen the dress in the shop, she'd initially no idea what era it was from as it felt timeless and traditional. The 1940's wedding dress was an ideal example of vintage bridal styling. The fabric was a heavier satin than Skye's, and the fitted bodice had a sweetheart neckline. The bodice was encrusted with crystal beads. Embroidered whitework was added by Skye and Holly. The dress had a fairytale quality and enhanced Merrilees' trim figure. From the bodice flowed a full layer of satin that draped beautifully to the tips of the court shoes she was wearing. They'd replaced the long satin sleeves with short cap sleeves in a lightweight chiffon lace.

A princess style was Ailsa's choice, selecting a wedding dress from the 1950s. It was more like a bridal ball gown. An off–the–shoulder neckline suited Ailsa, as did the pretty short sleeves. A confection of chiffon and silk, with beadwork on the neckline, bodice and around the hemline, it made her feel like she wanted to walk down a staircase in a castle and live a real life fairytale too.

'I'm going to wear my hair up,' said Ailsa. 'And pin floral diamante clasps in my hair. I'll attach the wisp of a veil to those.

Merrilees opted for a tiara to attach a short veil trailing down the back of her dress. She planned to wear her hair down, held back by the tiara.

The three dresses had been upscaled and restyled while keeping the heart of the original design. Beading and whitework embroidery had still to be finished, but the main work on the dresses was done. Their new shoes had been bought and kept in the shop, and all of them had decided to wear low heel court shoes that would be suitable for the wedding and adapt for the summer ball in the evening.

Merrilees wasn't skilled in dressmaking or crafting, but Skye and Holly had been happy to help restyle her dress for her. Ailsa had stitched most of the beadwork on her dress, but the structural adjustments were made by Skye and Holly.

'It's so exciting to see the wedding dresses coming together,' said Skye, taking hers off and hanging it back up again, knowing what she wanted to sew. 'Sometimes, I have to pinch myself that I'm marrying Innis. And that I'll live with him in the castle.'

'I feel the same about marrying Finlay,' said Merrilees. He'd been her first true love, the one she never forgot, even when she'd moved away from the island. Believing that he'd never even noticed her, and certainly never knew she'd a girlish crush on him. Now, all these years later, she was about to have her fairytale dream of marrying the laird–to–be in the castle.

Ailsa took her dress off and hung it up. 'I find myself thinking that soon I'll be splitting my time between my cottage, and the castle, moving into Ean's suite.'

Merrilees looked at her dress in the mirror, and then stepped out of it and added it to the others on the rail.

'Are your parents coming to the wedding?' Ailsa said to Skye.

'No, they're still abroad,' Skye explained. 'I insisted they didn't cut short their travels. We'll have a party to celebrate when they come home to the island.'

Ailsa's only relative attending the wedding was her uncle, Nairne.

Holly had planned to make them all sandwiches and tea for a snack lunch after the fitting. But before she'd even filled the kettle, a message came through on her phone from Lyle, her boyfriend, the owner of the local tea shop.

She read the message aloud.

*I have new tasty items on the lunch menu. Pop over if you fancy having lunch here.*

'Go,' said Skye. 'We'll make sandwiches.'

Holly was about to reply when a second message came through from Lyle.

*Bring the girls with you.*

Holly smiled at the others. 'Lunch at the tea shop? Lyle's treat.'

'Yes, please,' said Skye.

Ailsa and Merrilees were keen to go too.

Holly replied to Lyle.

*We're on our way.*

# CHAPTER THREE

The traditional tea shop, with its hanging flower baskets and bunting, was nestled in the heart of the main street. Lyle had made a success of his business, having taken it over when his grandparents retired. He'd had the upstairs floor of the two–storey shop converted to extend the premises. Customers could come in to buy cakes and other bakery delights, or sit down for morning and afternoon tea, or a full meal.

Lyle was in his late twenties, fairly tall and strong with light brown hair and hazel eyes. He'd trained as a patisserie chef, but his experience extended to catering for balls and large events, something that came in handy when Nairne needed help to cater for such occasions at the castle.

He changed his menus seasonally, and used his own recipes. His rich fruit cakes often had a dash of whisky added to the recipe, and the air in the tea shop sometimes had a hint of Lyle's secret ingredient.

Lyle wore a clean white shirt, black trousers and a chef's apron, and was adding Victoria sponges filled with cream and locally made strawberry jam to one of his display cabinets when Holly, Skye, Ailsa and Merrilees walked in.

Spotlights illuminated the delicious selection of cakes and scones in the glass cabinets, and the aroma of vanilla, strawberry, gingerbread and chocolate filled the air, outmatching the hint of whisky.

Lyle smiled when he saw the ladies. 'I've kept you a table for four at the window. The menus are on the table. Have whatever you fancy.'

Holly approached him, and without giving an inappropriate display of affection in front of the other customers seated in the tea shop, she gave him a quick kiss. 'Thank you, Lyle,' she whispered.

Lyle beamed, still in awe of his wonderful girlfriend. He loved her dearly, and although Holly was unaware of his plans, he aimed to propose to her after all the excitement of the weddings and the ball, and the honeymoon couples were back home at the castle. He wanted Holly to have her own special time without it being wrapped in with the others. He'd been planning the ring, everything, hoping she'd accept his proposal.

Holly joined the others and sat down at their table.

'Lyle's new summer menu looks so tempting,' said Skye.

'I'm having one of his chocolate pears with chocolate ice cream,' said Ailsa, working her way backwards from the sweets to the savouries.

He had a couple of staff helping in the kitchen and to serve customers, but Lyle baked all the cakes, scones and savoury flans himself.

Lyle came over to take their order. He chatted while they decided.

'What have you all been up to today?' he said, poised with his notepad to jot down the orders.

'We were having another fitting for the wedding dresses,' Skye told him.

'I read about them in the magazine,' he revealed. 'I'm sure the dresses will be beautiful.'

'We're busy with orders for ball gowns too,' Holly added. 'But I've got my dress picked and sorted.'

'I'm wearing my kilt, as are most of the men, especially the three grooms, or so I hear,' said Lyle.

'Yes, Finlay, Innis and Ean are wearing their kilts,' said Holly. 'Traditional kilted attire, and matching dark grey and black tartan.'

'My kilt is in shades of blue,' he said. 'Traditional style.'

'My dress will be vintage,' Holly revealed. 'We'll look like a well–matched couple.'

Lyle's smile brightened. Oh, how he longed to tell Holly his plan to propose, but he wanted it to be special.

'Can I have a slice of your summer quiche?' said Skye.

'With a mixed pepper salad?' he said.

Skye nodded.

Holly studied the menu. 'I'll have the same.'

Merrilees and Ailsa opted for the tomato quiche with a cherry tomato salad.

'I'll get the quiche for you, ladies,' he said. 'Then you can pick your puddings. Raspberry and bramble trifle is on the menu.' He glanced at Holly, knowing trifle was one of her favourites.

'Trifle for me,' Holly told him.

'Apple and apricot pie with cream,' Skye chipped–in.

Ailsa ordered the chocolate pear, and Merrilees was tempted by the strawberry cheesecake.

'And a large pot of tea?' said Lyle, jotting everything down.

'Yes, please,' said Holly.

Lyle went away to deal with their order. The kitchen was at the back of the tea shop.

Ailsa watched him walk away, and then smiled at Holly. 'You and Lyle are getting on so well. Do you think he's going to propose?'

Holly laughed. 'No, we're happy dating. We haven't discussed getting engaged. Lyle hasn't even hinted at it. I don't think he has any plans to propose.'

'He loves you to bits,' said Skye.

'And you've been dating for a wee while now,' Ailsa added.

'Another piece of romantic news on the island,' said Merrilees.

'Lyle doesn't have a castle, and I'm happy working in the dress shop,' Holly told them. 'We're not newsworthy.' Thankfully, she thought, but kept this to herself, considering that the others were front page of the magazine. And she didn't envy Skye going off to live with Innis at the castle. Holly much preferred a cosy cottage to settle down in when she got married. If and when that happened.

She'd fallen deeply in love with Lyle. His cheerful, easy–going nature was a breath of fresh air in comparison to some of the drama that had entwined around Skye and Innis, and Merrilees and Finlay. And to a lesser degree with Ailsa and Ean. Sometimes, love could be straightforward, sailing along on warmth and kindness, and learning to cook some of Lyle's special recipes.

36

Holly was happy for her sister and her friends, but there wasn't even a flicker of envy about them marrying into the wealthy and prestigious family who owned the castle. Lyle was quietly rich, but his warm–hearted and cheerful nature, within his tea shop world of baking, and cosy nights by the fire, or baking together when the shop was closed in the evenings, was more her cup of tea.

They were chatting about the weddings when Lyle came back and served up their lunch.

'I noticed that Finlay has changed the sails on his yacht,' said Lyle.

'He's getting everything ready for when we all sail off on our honeymoon,' Merrilees explained.

Lyle added a selection of sauces to their table to accompany their quiche and salad. 'Where are you sailing to, or is it a secret?'

'No, it's not a secret,' said Merrilees. 'Finlay has it roughly mapped out. We're sailing up north, towards the Summer Isles, but stopping at various places along the route.'

'We'll stay at different hotels along the way,' Skye added. 'If we're enjoying ourselves at any one town or island, we'll stay for a couple of days and relax.'

'Finlay is doing most of the sailing,' said Ailsa. 'But Ean can handle a boat, and he's going to help sail the yacht. As I'm sure will Innis. A lot of the time we'll be relaxing and having fun on various islands and wee seaside towns.'

'Well, it all sounds great,' said Lyle. 'Tuck in now, and I'll serve up your puddings when you're finished.'

'This is so tasty,' said Skye, enjoying her summer quiche, having added a scoop of mango chutney to her plate.

Merrilees nodded, and cut into her tomato quiche. Then something made her glance out the front window. And there was Finlay, casting off from the harbour, setting sail in the yacht.

'There's Finlay sailing away now.' Merrilees motioned out the window.

The others looked out, and saw the yacht leave the harbour and head out into the open sea. In the far distance was the silhouette of the outlying islands.

'He told me he was going to take the yacht out to make sure the sails and everything else is ready,' Merrilees explained. A wave of excitement washed over her at the thought of how close she was to sailing off on honeymoon with Finlay.

As the aquamarine sails of the yacht disappeared from view, they chatted again about their plans for the wedding, and the knitting bee. The weekly bee night was being held, as usual, at Elspeth and her Aunt Morven's knitting shop.

'Are you coming along to the knitting bee tonight?' Holly said to Merrilees.

'No, I'm working on my book. I've promised my publishers I'll have it finished before the weddings.' Merrilees was learning how to knit. She'd attended a couple of the bee nights, and Elspeth and others had encouraged her to try her hand at knitting. But her writing, and journalism work, plus plans for the wedding, had taken up her time recently, and the few rows she'd knitted of a scarf were still on the knitting needles tucked into the craft bag that the ladies had given her. Elspeth had given Merrilees balls of Fair Isle effect yarn that created a Fair Isle type pattern, to bolster her efforts.

'You can always pick it up when things quieten down,' Holly assured her.

'I liked what I learned. Rows of plain stitches,' said Merrilees. 'I'm determined to make a scarf that I can wear for the winter. And it'll probably take me until then to finish it.'

'Nonsense,' said Ailsa. 'You picked it up fine. It just takes practise.'

Merrilees brightened. 'I might take my knitting with me on the yacht.'

'I'm taking my craft bag with bits and bobs with me,' said Ailsa. 'Maybe there will be no time for any crafting, but I'm taking it anyway.'

'So am I,' Skye added.

Holly, Skye and Ailsa were going to the knitting bee that night.

'Elspeth says that Morven won't be at the bee tonight. She's away gallivanting with her boyfriend, Donall,' said Holly. 'But Elspeth is sharing samples of the new summer yarns with us all this evening.'

Skye sounded excited. 'The knitting shop has a new range of yarns in the front window. Lovely blues and pastel colours for the summer. I'll be tempted to buy some tonight. Though I've no idea what I'll knit with them.'

'I like the knitted softies Elspeth makes and puts in the window displays,' said Merrilees. 'I checked online. She sells the patterns too. I'd like to knit a robin, even if it takes me until the winter to knit and stuff it.'

The others laughed.

'Knitting a softie is another great way to learn how to knit,' Skye told Merrilees. 'Make something you can sit in your living room at the castle.'

Merrilees frowned. 'I don't think a knitted robin would suit Finlay's elegant decor. But I'd be happy to knit one for the cottage.'

'Elspeth's patterns are easy,' Holly said to Merrilees. 'I knitted her softie bumblebee. It's sitting in my bedroom.'

'There is a lot of joy and relaxation to be found in knitting and crafting,' said Merrilees.

'And friendship and fun at the bee night,' Holly added. 'Sometimes we're so busy chatting, laughing, gossiping and having tea and cakes we don't get much crafting done.'

'Other nights, I go home with something I've started and finished in a night,' said Skye. 'Like the cute wee egg cosies I knitted from one of Primrose's patterns. The only thing is, they're too nice to use, so I've got them sitting up on empty egg cups in the kitchen.'

'I can't resist buying the new yarn that Elspeth stocks,' Ailsa confessed.

'Be prepared to buy some more tonight,' said Skye. 'Have you seen the new colours in the window?'

'No, but I'll have a look on my way back to my shop. Although it's summer, folk are still buying my shawls and hat and scarf sets. I need to knit more. I'm trying to stock up on things before the wedding so that

I won't have a ton of catching up to do when we get back from the honeymoon.'

Skye looked thoughtful. 'Everything is going to be so different.' She sounded wistful. 'I'm actually going to be living in the castle with Innis.' Sometimes her stomach knotted realising she'd be moving out of the cottage, leaving Holly behind. The end of one happy era, and the beginning of a new one, hopefully just as happy, but in a different way.

Ailsa and Merrilees nodded.

'I just don't like having to leave you to handle the dress shop on your own while I'm away,' Skye said to Holly.

'I'm happy to deal with the dress shop,' Holly assured her. 'The biggest load of work is trying to get all the ball gowns and evening dresses finished and ready for sale for the summer ball. After that, things will quieten down again.'

'We got a load of vintage ball gowns delivered this morning,' Skye said to Ailsa and Merrilees. 'A fantastic bargain bundle. We've sorted through some of them, but we'll unpack them all after our lunch.'

'Geneen has bought a new dress for the ball,' Holly told them. 'I'm still making a few alterations to it, but she really suits it. She wanted something special for the wedding ceremony that she could continue to wear for the ball at night.'

'My heart flutters at the thought of the whole ceremony and the ball,' said Ailsa.

'I wish I was better at ballroom dancing,' said Skye. 'But my dress will hide a multitude of messing up my waltzes.'

41

Lyle arrived with their puddings. 'Roag used to be a competitive dancer. Maybe he can give you some tips.'

Skye blinked. 'Dance lessons from Roag?'

Lyle shrugged. 'Mind you, that could be asking for trouble. Forget I mentioned it.'

He served up Ailsa's chocolate pear. 'Enjoy it while the chocolate sauce is still warm. I melt the rich, dark chocolate just before serving and pour it over the pear.'

Ailsa scooped a spoonful of the chocolate sauce and nodded when she tasted it. 'The chocolate is delicious, but there's something extra in the flavour.'

'One of my special recipes,' said Lyle, and smiling, he left them to enjoy their puddings.

Skye tasted her apple and apricot pie with cream. 'I'm glad that Lyle is helping supply some of the food for the wedding buffet and the ball. I love his cooking.'

Holly smiled at Skye. 'Lyle's talent is underestimated. I'm learning a lot of handy tips from him in the kitchen.'

Lyle smiled to himself, overhearing snippets of their conversation as he refilled a cabinet with white chocolate cupcakes.

Holly, Skye, Ailsa and Merrilees finished their lunch and headed out of the tea shop, thanking Lyle for the wonderful meal he'd given them.

'I'm glad you enjoyed it, ladies,' said Lyle, walking them out and opening the front door for them.

Three kisses on the cheek, one each from Skye, Ailsa and Merrilees, made him smile. But the lingering kiss on the lips from Holly warmed his heart.

He waved them off, and then went back into the tea shop.

It was the afternoon before Roag had a chance to read the magazine feature in private in his office in the restaurant. The feature was well–written, and he noted that Merrilees had quoted him accurately. People had been phoning the restaurant having read the feature, and they'd taken extra bookings.

The pictures of the castle were like a glimpse of the past. Nothing much had changed. The traditional styling was as he remembered it, from the elegant chandeliers to the function room with its large dance floor where the summer ball would be held.

From discussions with the laird, a lavish buffet was to be created for the ball, doubling up as a celebration after the weddings. He thought this was an excellent use of the castle's facilities, and having the three weddings together made sense too.

One of the pictures showed a festive ball at the castle, and seeing the dance floor filled with couples wearing their finery and waltzing around the room, made him realise how much he missed dancing on a large floor like this. Since giving up his dancing, he'd made do with the floor space in the living room of his house in Glasgow. But it wasn't a sprung floor, and when he danced there on his own, often at midnight, after finishing work at the restaurant, it felt less than he was used to when performing on stage or competitive events.

Blinking out of his thoughts, he continued to read the feature. It mentioned the castle's excellent cuisine. He checked the castle's website to study their new summer menus, trying to get a feel for Nairne's catering. He also checked Innis' cake shop website, noting the range of cakes and baking available. And the chocolates. This was something he was particularly interested in.

Then he looked at the other local eateries on the island. Brodrick's cafe bar seemed popular and had a great range of ice cream.

Finally, he checked Lyle's tea shop, and was surprised by the quality and selection of the items that could be bought from the bakery counter, and that customers could sit down to enjoy meals there too. The photo of Lyle in his tea shop made him look like a cheery and amiable man.

There were no personal contacts that Roag could call and chat to about the local scene, so this concluded his research.

Now all he had to do was start preparing what he needed to take with him to the island, and try not to cause the trouble that everyone probably expected from him.

He knew what he wanted to pack into his car for his trip. This was the only guarantee. He wasn't looking to cause trouble. And he certainly wasn't looking for romance on the island.

His stay on the island was only for the wedding, the ball, and while the couples were away on honeymoon. No longer. Then he'd head home to the mainland. A summer romance wasn't in his plans. Two broken hearts was enough for now.

He'd be staying in the castle's left turret, part of the laird's private accommodation. The last time he'd been in one of the guest bedrooms, but the laird thought he should have one of the turrets, especially as he was standing in as a sort of make–do laird while they were all away.

There had been times in the past when he'd considered opening his first restaurant on the island. He'd eyed–up the commercial properties on the island's main street, and also viewed property on the other side of the island where a scattering of cottages were located, thinking he could convert one of them into an exclusive restaurant.

But the city was far more practical and lucrative for his type of business. And had worked out exceptionally well.

He'd been thinking about expanding his restaurant business in Glasgow, and maybe one day, to the island.

Roag enjoyed living and working in the city. He loved the theatres, entertainment, excitement, the buzz of it.

But deep in his heart was a love of the islands and the sea.

His gorgeous blue–green eyes looked at the castle in the feature, and then he closed the magazine, tucked it away in his desk drawer, and went through to the kitchen to get on with his work.

The summer menus he'd created were filled with his new recipes. His staff were currently ensuring these were popular with diners, and that each item could be made efficiently while Roag was away. New main courses for the lunches and dinners had been introduced recently, and the afternoon tea menus offered a wonderful selection of cakes, scones, pastries and chocolates.

# CHAPTER FOUR

A welcoming glow shone from the front window of the pretty pink knitting shop. The amber sunlight cast a lingering summer warmth over the shops near the harbour, and twinkle lights glittered in rows along the length of the main street where they were draped from the lamplights. Bunting fluttered in the mild breeze blowing in from the sea as Skye and Holly headed to join in the knitting bee night in the shop.

They stopped to gaze at the new yarn on display in the window, and two knitted softies.

'I love the light turquoise blue double–knit yarn.' Skye pointed to it. 'I'm going to buy a few balls. I've no idea what I'll knit with it, but that colour is sure to be snapped up.'

'It's lovely,' Holly agreed, then she noticed the new range of pastel pinks. 'These are so pretty. I'd like to knit a hat and scarf set for the colder months with those colours.'

'I'll probably do the same with the blue. I've got a great pattern for a set that Elspeth designed.'

'Leave some yarn for the rest of us,' Ailsa said as she hurried along from her craft shop to join them.

They all had their craft bags stuffed with yarn, knitting needles and sewing kits.

Chatting excitedly, they went inside. The shelves were neatly piled with an extensive range of yarn. Knitted jumpers, cardigans, shawls and scarves hung for sale from rails near the counter. Knitting needles and haberdashery items were displayed on two carousels.

The knitting bee nights were held in the room at the back of the shop. Patio doors opened out into the garden. The shop was a converted cottage, and Elspeth had lived in the flat above the shop until she'd met and married Brodrick, the owner of the cafe bar next door. They now lived in a cottage up on the hillside.

Elspeth welcomed them when they arrived. She was in her early thirties. Her blonde hair was pinned up, and she wore jeans and a lace weight cream top that she'd knitted from one of her own patterns.

Three long tables and folding chairs from the storeroom cupboard were set up, and lots of ladies were already seated and getting ready to knit, crochet, quilt or sew, or whatever craft they wanted to work on.

'Primrose and Rosabel have brought cakes from Innis' shop,' Elspeth told them. 'We're being treated tonight to fresh cream meringues, chocolate and cream layer cake, and whipped cream fancies.'

Primrose and Rosabel heard Elspeth and called through from the kitchen where they were preparing the tea and cakes. Other ladies were helping too.

'Innis told us to take a selection of the fresh cream cakes for our bee night,' said Primrose.

'So we'll have to force ourselves to enjoy two rounds of cream cakes and tea,' Rosabel added.

The ladies smiled, and chatter filled the air, along with the latest gossip.

Nettie sat down with her knitting. Taking the jumper she was knitting out of her craft bag, she shook her head at the tangled ball of yarn. 'Fluffy's been playing with my yarn again. The wee rascal,' she said, referring to her cat.

'Do you want a hand to unfankle it?' Elspeth offered.

'Yes, you're better at getting knots out of yarn than me,' Nettie admitted, trying to find where the knots started.

Elspeth relieved Nettie of the knitting and began to unravel it.

'Fluffy is going on his holidays too,' said Nettie. 'While Shuggie and I are away on our cruise, he's going to stay with my next door neighbour. She has a cat of her own. Fluffy already thinks she's his extended family, and spends as much time in her garden as he does ours. Luckily, he's a snuggler and a snoozer, so he'll be no bother, but I've told her to hide her knitting from his wee paws.'

The ladies laughed.

'He'll be spoiled rotten,' said Elspeth.

'Oh, you can be sure of that,' Nettie happily agreed.

'Any news about your niece Fyona?' Geneen said to Nettie, enjoying a night off from her work at the castle to join in the knitting bee.

'She'll be arriving on the island soon,' Nettie explained. 'Fyona shares a flat with friends in Glasgow, and she's recently finished another course in fancy cake making. She's become quite the expert, but she's worked hard to get where she is.'

'Is she working in Glasgow at the moment?' said Geneen.

'No, it was a temporary position with a restaurant so she could take another course in patisserie. She's worked for various restaurants and hotels to expand her experience. Her recipes are delicious. And her skills in making pastries, puddings, sweets and cakes are wonderful. Now she's hoping to have a working holiday here on the island. Cottage sit for us, and help Nairne with the baking for the weddings and summer ball at the castle.'

'Nairne says he's very impressed with her skills and experience,' Geneen revealed.

Nettie smiled. 'Fyona is very talented, and a lovely young woman. She's just turned thirty, and says she's not looking for romance this summer, and wants to concentrate on her career. After the summer she plans to work in Glasgow or Edinburgh, and one day open her own patisserie or tearoom.'

'It sounds as if Fyona has the skills, talent and energy to achieve that,' said Geneen.

'Fyona works hard, and it's paid off, but I hope that she finds time for fun and romance,' said Nettie.

'I'm sure she will,' Primrose chimed–in, carrying through a tray of cakes and putting it down on one of the tables for sharing.

Rosabel brought through a tray of tea. 'I wonder how Fyona will get on with Roag.'

'I tell you, Fyona has a sweet nature, but she used to be a wee bit wild when she was a young lassie,' said Nettie. 'If Roag challenges our Fyona, my money is on her.'

Elspeth handed Nettie the unfankled ball of yarn. 'I hear that Roag is quite a handful. I saw his picture in the magazine.'

'Oh, Roag's a looker.' Geneen shifted in her chair as if her feathers were ruffled. 'He has the reputation of being a heartbreaker. The type that sets women's hearts a flutter.'

'From the gossip in my shop today, he's been described by those that have met him as double–handsome.' Elspeth smiled as she said this.

'Aye, he is,' Geneen admitted. 'I'll give him that. And he knows it. Knows how to use his good looks to wangle what he wants. Well, fair warning, don't be taken in by him.'

'I'm sure Fyona won't be.' Nettie sounded confident. 'But wait until he sees her. She's quite beautiful. But not silly when it comes to men.' Nettie picked up her knitting where she'd left off.

Geneen was still working on a cardigan she'd started a while ago. 'Roag is the cousin of Finlay, Innis and Ean, but there's barely any family likeness.'

'Any gossip on his dancing?' Primrose said to Geneen.

'Roag gave it up, but when you love something as much as he did, I don't think you ever really put it behind you,' Geneen said thoughtfully.

'Well, he won't flummox Fyona with his dancing,' Nettie revealed. 'She trained in ballet when she was a wee girl, and modern stage up until she was in her mid–teens. She only gave up taking dance classes to concentrate on her patisserie training. But she says she still practises her ballet moves, especially the stretching.'

Merrilees and Finlay ate their dinner in the kitchen of stargazer cottage. The door was open to let the warm evening air from the garden waft in.

She'd worked on her book all afternoon, and stopped to make a tasty but easy spicy tomato pasta dish for dinner.

Finlay had brought the yacht back to the harbour in the afternoon, after sailing around the island, and then headed up to the castle, before joining Merrilees for dinner.

'This is great,' he said, enjoying his pasta. 'I've barely had anything since an early breakfast.'

She smiled over at him. 'Is the yacht ship shape?'

'It is, and I'm happy with the sails. Everything is ready to set sail for the honeymoon.'

A shiver of excitement went through her every time he mentioned this.

'How are you getting on with your writing?'

'I got quite a bit written this afternoon.'

'I have to help Ean with the guests at the castle tonight. So if you don't mind, I'll skedaddle after dinner.'

'That's fine.' She intended to write into the wee small hours. 'I'm working on writing the main romantic couple's happy ever after.'

Finlay's smile lit up his handsome face. 'It's not long now until the wedding, and our happy ever after.'

She blew him a kiss across the table.

'Without revealing any secrets, did your wedding dress fitting go okay today at the dress shop?'

'Yes, it's almost finished. I love it. I hope you like it too.'

'I'm sure I will. My kilted groom outfit is hanging ready in my wardrobe, so don't go peeking in my wardrobes.'

'I won't,' she promised.

'Nairne wants a menu meeting with us soon. He's finessing the details for the wedding cake and the buffet.'

'Okay.'

'I'll arrange a time soon. Innis and Ean, and Skye and Ailsa will need to be there too so we can all agree what we want. So it'll be an evening meeting.'

'That suits me.'

Finlay took a sip of his tea. 'Everyone's been talking about the magazine feature. They like it, though a few are dubious about Roag coming to the island.'

'When I interviewed him over the phone, he never once mentioned about his dancing.' Merrilees sounded mildly suspicious. 'I gave him every opportunity to include any other aspects of his work, his career. He said there was nothing of note, except being a chef. Now, apparently, he was a ballroom dancer, competing in competitions and performing on stage. Why would he want to keep quiet about that?'

'I won't pretend that I know him well. We were never close. As he was our cousin, and our fathers are brothers, he visited the island from time to time, especially during the holidays with his parents. They live abroad now. But Roag was very much his own man.'

'Does he envy your position as the laird–to–be? Would he have liked to have been in charge of the castle?'

'No, it was clear he didn't envy any of us. He didn't want the responsibility of owning and maintaining the castle. Roag loved living in the fast lane, the city, going to the theatre, clubs, a real social butterfly, and a moth to the flame with all the temptations that went with that lifestyle.'

'Including breaking a few ladies' hearts.'

Finlay nodded. 'Roag didn't seem like the settling down type.'

'What about his dance career? Was he an exceptional dancer? Or was it just a hobby–dream, and he decided his skills as a chef were more financially secure?'

Finlay became thoughtful. 'I remember seeing him dance once at a party in the castle's function room. People urged him to perform. I knew he'd taken dance lessons since he was a boy, and had ambitions to follow that type of career. I don't know what I expected from his performance, but it was exceptional.'

Merrilees finished her dinner, and so did Finlay.

'Do you want some fresh air before you go?' she suggested. 'I've been sitting for hours writing at the computer. Fancy a wee stretch of the legs? And not the dancing kind.'

Finlay stood up and they went outside into the garden, then meandered further into the lush

54

countryside for a walk, hand in hand, in the twilight warmth.

Merrilees breathed in the heady scent of the greenery and flowers. 'I feel so lucky to live in such a beautiful place.'

Finlay put his arm around her shoulders and pulled her close to him as they continued to meander. 'I'm the lucky one to have you in my life, and soon to be my wife.'

She rested her head against him, feeling that all was well with the world. It always was when she was with Finlay.


Geneen had a link to a video showing one of Roag's dance performances. She shared it with the other ladies at the knitting bee. He was ballroom dancing with an elegant woman and they were performing a classic waltz.

'The gossip is that two of the women who were his dance partners, jilted him to dance with his main rivals. This was his last dance partner. She's a lovely dancer.'

The ladies watched his performance on their phones, putting their knitting and crafting aside for a few minutes to view him.

'They dance well together,' Holly observed.

The others agreed.

'Oh, look, there are links to other clips of Roag dancing,' said Primrose.

'Check out his energetic freestyle routine,' Geneen advised. 'He can leap up into the air as if he's on springs.'

'He's like a strong, lithe gymnast,' said Skye.

'And double–handsome,' Holly chipped–in.

Geneen viewed him objectively. 'I suppose he has a sort of star–quality.'

'No wonder he's known as a heartbreaker,' Elspeth added. 'He's not my type, but I can see that he's a looker.'

Holly rewound part of his performance where he jumped up into the air, spun around, and then landed perfectly. 'I've a feeling the gossip is right. Roag is bringing trouble to the island. I just hope he won't disrupt the weddings.'

'We won't let him.' Geneen sounded determined.

Ailsa watched Roag, and saw a close–up of those eyes and achingly handsome face. But her heart was full with the love she had for Ean.

After watching his videos, the ladies turned their attention back to their knitting and crafting.

Finlay kissed Merrilees as they arrived back at stargazer cottage. 'Don't work too late.'

'I won't,' she promised.

His firm lips kissed her lovingly, and she felt her heart respond as strong as the first time. She couldn't ever imagine becoming accustomed to kissing Finlay.

Standing at the front door of the cottage, she watched him drive away, heading back to the castle.

Elspeth showed a couple of the ladies how she knitted bee stitch, and helped advise on a Fair Isle jumper pattern.

The evening went in, amid chatter, laughter and gossip.

'There's still cake left,' said Primrose. 'Does anyone want another quick round of tea before we tidy up?'

The ladies were happy to extend the evening, and a few of them helped make the tea and serve up the cakes.

'Have you decided what type of wedding cake you'll have?' Elspeth said to Skye and Ailsa.

'Yes,' said Skye. 'It's a large cake. Three tiers of rich fruit cake decorated with white royal icing. Nairne has already baked the cakes and is letting them mature for extra flavour. Then he's going to ice them. Fyona will probably help with the icing.'

'Fyona mentioned to me that Nairne wants her to give him a hand with the cake decoration,' Nettie confirmed.

'We're going for a traditional design,' said Ailsa. 'The laird and his wife got married in the castle. And their parents and grandparents before them. So there's a lot of history in the whole ceremony.'

'All three couples are getting married outside the function room in the garden,' Geneen was pleased to add. 'Murdo will set up the boughs that the couples will stand under to exchange their vows. These will be covered with flowers from the castle's gardens on the day of the wedding.'

'I know you've all got your invitations,' said Skye. 'So you're aware that we're getting married in the afternoon. That's part of the family tradition. I love the idea of taking our vows outside in the afternoon sunlight.'

'And then we'll all enjoy the buffet and the summer ball,' Ailsa added.

'Holly and I are working on finishing the dresses on order for the ball,' Skye assured them.

'We got a delivery of vintage evening dresses and ball gowns today,' Holly told them. 'Pop into the shop if you want to have a browse, though I know a few of you have dresses ordered with us.'

Rosabel smiled excitedly. 'The weddings are going to make the summer ball even more special.'

'It was originally Finlay's idea to marry Merrilees and hold a summer ball as part of the celebrations,' Ailsa explained. 'Then Ean and Innis decided we should all get married and make it one of the most memorable weddings the castle has ever had.'

'I couldn't be happier,' said Skye. 'Innis and I planned to get married fairly soon, so the whole planning got underway. And now...here we are. I feel the time has gone in so fast.'

'And picking up pace,' Ailsa added. 'But we're fortunate to have such a close–knit community helping with everything too.'

Elspeth, Rosabel and Primrose carried through the tea and the remainder of the cake. Elspeth had added a plate of shortbread petticoat tails.

The ladies tucked their knitting and sewing back into their craft bags, and relaxed for another round of tea and chatter.

A message from Ean popped up on Ailsa's phone. She read it aloud to Skye.

'Ean wants to know if we can go to the castle a couple of nights from now to discuss the menu and buffet with Nairne and the others.'

'Yes, that's ideal,' Skye confirmed.

Ailsa typed her reply to Ean.

*I'm at the knitting bee. Skye is here too. We'll both be there for the meeting.*

*Come up when you close your shops. Have dinner here at the castle.*

*We'll do that. xx.*

As the knitting bee evening finally finished, the ladies filtered out into the night, having helped Elspeth tidy away the tables and chairs and the tea dishes. With several of them helping, the task was done in no time.

Skye left with a bag of the turquoise yarn, and Holly had bought three shades of pink, planning to mix them to knit her hat and scarf set.

The bee nights started at seven and finished around nine.

Holly checked the time, pausing for a moment outside the knitting shop. The sea shimmered in the background, and the air felt calm.

'How tired are you?' Holly said to Skye.

Always bubbling with energy, Skye's reply was her usual bright response. 'I'm still fizzing with excitement. What do you have in mind?'

'An hour at our shop, sorting through the dresses. We could have the bulk of the unpacking done ready for the morning.'

'Let's do it,' said Skye.

They walked along to their shop. It was only two shops down, past Brodrick's cafe bar that was buzzing with activity.

Holly unlocked the dress shop door, and they went inside, flicked the lights on, and tackled the unpacking of the delivery of dresses. All the dresses had been cleaned before selling. Now they needed minor repairs and alterations to make each dress fit for the ball.

'These designs looked lovely online,' said Skye, holding up a deep blue chiffon evening dress that sparkled with silvery blue glitter around the hemline. 'But they're even lovelier than I thought. Look at this dress. It's not a ball gown, but it would be ideal for waltzing around the dance floor.'

Holly agreed, and held up another dress. 'This reminds me of a prom dress. Another winner for the ball.' Holly hung it up on a hanger. The sky blue dress had a fitted bodice that sparkled here and there with blue sequins, and the chiffon and silk skirt was full and perfect for waltzing at the ball.

For the next hour they unpacked all the dresses, divided them into those that required specific types of mending, such as a hem needing stitched, straps that had to be sewn back on, seams secured, and sequins added where the original ones had fallen off or were dangling by a thread from the dresses. A note of each repair was pinned to the hangers for easy reference.

Finally, they finished up, turned the lights off, locked the vintage dress shop for the night, and headed home to the cottage on the hillside.

# CHAPTER FIVE

Merrilees lay in bed gazing up at the stars through the skylight. She'd kept her promise to Finlay not to work too late.

After closing her laptop for the night, she'd made herself a cup of tea and sipped it outside in the cottage garden. Having lived in a flat in the city, she loved being able to step out of the kitchen into the garden and enjoy the night air. And the skies were so clear, she could see the stars.

The teenage crush she'd had on Finlay when she lived on the island as a young girl had been filled with daydreams that he'd feel the same way about her, and that they'd live happily ever after in the fairytale castle. But he hadn't noticed her then, and never knew how she felt, and she'd moved away to the city and grown up to become a journalist. The fairytale had seemed even further away. He lived on the island. She stayed in the city. Only through a twist of circumstances had she come back to do an interview with Finlay about the castle. And now the fairytale was due to come true.

Finishing her tea, she'd gone to bed, and now lay there gazing up at the stars. The sparkling engagement ring on her hand outshone the stars in every possible way, at least to her.

The old–fashioned clock on the wall, lit by a beam of moonlight shining in, showed it was a minute past midnight. Another day closer to the wedding.

Roag's expensive red car drove through the heart of the city. Having finished late, working at the restaurant, ensuring the orders for the deliveries were done, and other tasks, he headed home.

His mansion–style house was nestled in a large garden on the outskirts of Glasgow. Trees shielded the property from prying eyes, and he had to stop at the ornate gated entrance and enter a code that opened the gates and allowed him to drive up and park outside the front of the house.

The garden was tended to by a hired gardener to keep it tamed, unlike the owner of the house. Though he was less of a rogue these days.

Lilac and purple wisteria climbed across the front of the house, clinging to the original structure that dated back to the early 1900s. It was the family home his parents had left, with no plans to ever return, and although the trees surrounding the property were thicker and taller than when he was a boy, there was a comforting familiarity about living there. Little had changed except the decor. Roag had updated that long ago, and the neutral colour scheme throughout the house was livened up with splashes of colour from large watercolour paintings and vibrant cushions and throws.

He grabbed his briefcase filled with copies of the new menus that he liked to study outwith the restaurant, giving himself a clearer perspective of what was on offer and how it would be viewed by diners.

He picked up his laptop too, slinging the strap of the bag up on his shoulder, and locking the car that was lit by two lanterns outside the front entrance.

As usual, he didn't enter through the front door, but walked along the narrow path that edged the lawn, round to the kitchen at the back of the house.

In Roag's world, the kitchen ruled supreme.

He went in and flicked on the lights, illuminating his dream kitchen, one that he'd designed to suit his needs. No expense spared.

The kitchen was functional, and designed for speed and efficiency when he was cooking. But the functionality took second place to the impressive design and decor. White, cream and pale blue with hints of green. Pots and pans gleaming silver and copper. Glasses and jars glistening under spotlights that were a decorative descant to the main overhead lighting.

A dining table was set near the patio doors that opened out on to the garden. White–painted, ornate metal tables and chairs provided an outdoor dining setting on the patio. A fire pit ensured that he could dine outside even it if had been snowing. And it did during the winters. Though rain was more prevalent. A canopy shielded the patio when needed, folding back against the wall, and like a shop's canopy, it could be pulled out to allow him to dine in the rain if the notion took him. Sometimes it did.

A sturdy wooden table stood in the kitchen. The family table remained where it had always been. Another piece of his past he'd been reluctant to replace. This was where Roag ate most of his meals, seated on the wooden chairs that were softened by colourful cushions. No cooking for him tonight though. He checked that everything was in order, and on things needing restocked.

And then he turned the main lights off, leaving only the spotlights on, and went upstairs to his bedroom to change into casual clothes. A pair of tight–fitting black leisure trousers and a black vest that emphasised his lean–muscled physique.

Running back downstairs, he flicked on a couple of lamps in the living room, and pressed the buttons on the music system. His house was far enough away from his nearest neighbours not to disturb them with the music he used for his dancing.

Roag didn't dance too often these days, but tonight he felt compelled to dance beyond the midnight mark.

The dance trophies he'd won were displayed in a cabinet. A testament to his talent and tenacity to win. Two traits that served him well with his restaurant work.

As the music played, he limbered up, using the back of a chair as a ballet barre, stretching his muscles ready for the powerful moves he was about to do.

And then he danced — wild, free and strong, performing a routine from his past.

The song matched the power of the dance. Roag had the power to perform it. Of all the routines he was requested to dance on stage or impromptu, such as at a function at the island's castle, this was the most popular.

Not a missed step, not a beat out of time, Roag danced to the song, remembering the reaction from audiences when he'd performed it during a whirlwind two–week tour of various cities. Already established as a chef with his own restaurant, he'd taken a sliver of time off for the tour, hoping he could juggle both, not wanting to give up either profession or dream.

But fate had dealt him a rough hand, and ructions at his restaurant caused ripples of regret. The final note in deciding what to step away from. The dancing.

A hard decision, but a wise one, in hindsight.

Roag danced on as the next song began, changing to a melody from his ballroom days. No partner to waltz with, he danced alone, adapting the steps, moving with a freestyle economy, smooth and elegant.

He'd loved and lost his last two ballroom dance partners. When his first leading lady dumped him for his nearest rival, he'd told himself to march on. And he did, finding and falling for an excellent replacement. But endured a repeat performance of the first catastrophe. One dagger to the heart had slowly mended. Two left a wound that had only healed the previous year. He didn't love either of them now. Maybe he'd been a fool, thinking that the romance of the dance was part of his true feelings. But the shields were up on his heart these days, and nights where he burned off his excess energy with his dancing.

His physique was as fit as ever, stronger in some ways because of the long hours he worked as a chef. Some days it was relentless. But he'd no complaints. He loved his cheffing.

The muscles in his back stretched as he kept his core strong and held his ballroom posture perfectly.

A third song played, and the beat rose, increasing as the music reached a crescendo.

And the lone figure of Roag danced until the last note, and then switched everything off, went upstairs to his bedroom, showered in the en suite bathroom, then got a few hours of snatched sleep before his usual early start in the morning.

Skye's pink sewing machine whirred in the vintage dress shop the next morning as she stitched the rolled chiffon hem on one of the dresses that was a contender for the ball.

Sunlight streamed through the front window of the shop, brightening everything, including the crystal beads that Holly was sewing on to Merrilees' wedding dress. The beads on the bodice sparkled in the sunshine, and it let Holly see where any extras were needed.

'I think Merrilees' dress is almost finished,' said Holly. 'Take a look. See if you think I've missed any bits that need sparkles.'

Skye finished machining the chiffon hem and stood up.

Holly held the wedding dress up while Skye evaluated the sparkles.

'It's scintillating,' said Skye. 'I don't think it needs any other sparkles sewn on.'

Holly smiled. 'I'll hang it up.' She went through to the back of the shop and hung it on the rail with the others, carefully covering it to protect it from harm.

Skye sat back down at her sewing machine and picked up the next dress that was folded on the table beside her. 'I'll secure the seam on this one. It's a minor repair. Then I'll pop over to the cake shop for something tasty to go with our morning tea.'

Getting on with the work, making huge progress with the mending, they chatted about the wedding rings.

'Any news on the rings?' Holly said to Skye, selecting thread to match one of the pale yellow ball gowns, preparing to hand sew the shoestring straps to secure them to the bodice.

'Nothing yet. But they should be finished soon.' Skye sounded excited.

All six rings were being made by the local goldsmith using Scottish gold.

Each ring was different, particularly Skye, Ailsa and Merrilees' rings, that were designed to suit their engagement rings. But all six rings were of a traditional design. The three couples had gone together to the goldsmith's shop a few weeks ago when the weddings were first being planned. The goldsmith measured them for size and fit, and they'd tried on various styles of wedding bands before selecting what they wanted.

'I love that they're made from Scottish gold,' said Skye, as she repaired the dress seam with her sewing machine. 'It feels magical.'

'Perfect for weddings in a fairytale castle,' said Holly, smiling over at her, as she threaded her sewing needle with pale yellow thread.

Fyona was doing her homework. Not for any further exams. No, this was to find out information about Roag, his restaurant, his abilities. She'd soon be packing her things and taking the ferry over to the island to work with Nairne at the castle. And alongside Roag.

What better way than to have lunch at his restaurant in Glasgow. She lived in the city, so it made sense to venture into Roag's domain and try out the food for herself.

Tip–offs from Nettie and Geneen made her realise that she should do her homework. Roag's reputation preceded him, and it was a fair bet that they'd have different culinary methods that could clash at the castle.

Forewarned, forearmed, and all that.

Nettie had sent Fyona links to videos the previous night, the ones that Geneen had given her, showing Roag dancing. Fyona's heart reacted to seeing him, but she pushed her feelings aside, telling herself that he wasn't her type.

Sunlight shone on her silky, light copper, shoulder–length hair as she walked up to the restaurant for lunch. Her pale blue chambray dress matched the colour of her eyes, set in a lovely face. The porcelain tone of her complexion had a touch of summer sun, and she saw her slender figure reflected in the window of the restaurant as she walked by.

Glancing inside, she noticed that many of the tables were occupied, but she went in, taking a chance that there was a table available.

And there was. A member of staff seated her at a table in the heart of the stylish restaurant where she had a view of the whole scenario. The counter where a tempting array of cakes, pastries and desserts were displayed. And the door to the kitchen. As staff went in and out in organised efficiency, she saw a glimpse inside it.

Opulent, summed up the overall look of Roag's restaurant. Not her taste, but she admitted it was nice. Modern vintage was more her style, old–fashioned elements that the tearoom of her dreams would have.

Fyona looked at the menu, comparing it to the one she'd seen online. It was more or less the same, with only a minor change to one of the side dishes. Having studied the online menu, she knew what she wanted to order. Carrot and red pepper soup, followed by the summer platter offering a taste of Roag's culinary delights that included sorbets with fresh fruit such as orange and melon, minted salad, and cheese soufflé with fresh baked bread.

The staff were pleasant, and her soup was served up quickly without any fuss. As she tasted it, she relished the spices Roag had added to the recipe.

Enjoying her soup, she kept glancing surreptitiously around, wondering when she'd see Roag himself. From the snatches of chatter filtering through from the kitchen when the door was ajar, it was clear that he was in the kitchen orchestrating the lunches.

By the time she was on to the summer platter, she'd given up hope of the elusive chef venturing out of the kitchen. So she was taken off–guard when the tall figure of the confident chef strode through the heart of the restaurant, spoke to a member of staff at the patisserie counter, and then headed back towards the kitchen.

She hadn't expected to be so taken with his looks. But it wasn't just his handsomeness that jolted her senses. It was the feeling he brought with him, as if by walking through the restaurant his energy caused ripples in the relaxing atmosphere, making him a man that never went unnoticed, even if he wanted to.

Roag was clearly very handsome, Fyona admitted. No surprises there. She'd seen the feature, his website, and his half–naked physique dancing in one of his videos. But nothing could've prepared her for the actual experience of seeing him walk past her table. Those eyes of his glanced down at her, locked right into hers, then released the grip he had on her and disappeared into the kitchen again.

She let go of the breath she hadn't realised she'd been holding, and continued to sample the food.

Several minutes later, the kitchen door swung open and Roag emerged again, carrying a tray of delicate pastries filled with whipped cream and fruit and put them in the display counter.

Unless she was mistaken, he'd glanced over at her again, perhaps sensing her watching him, knowing she was more than just a random diner. Making her feel like a culinary spy, in to snoop on the competition.

Concentrating on her food, she steeled herself for the wave of energy that was due to walk by her again and into the kitchen.

If she'd only looked up, she would've seen that the kitchen wasn't where he was making a beeline for.

Roag approached her table in a few long strides. A heavy second ticked by as he stood there looking down at her while she focussed on her food.

'Hello, Fyona.' His rich, deep voice resonated through her, causing her to jolt.

Her cutlery clattered on the plate as she gazed up into his fabulous eyes that seemed to know exactly who she was and what she was up to.

# CHAPTER SIX

'When you've finished your summer platter, come through to the kitchen,' Roag said to Fyona.

Roag's invitation hung in the electrically charged air between them, and then he walked away and disappeared into the kitchen.

Fyona blinked out of her surprised thoughts, into deeper ones. He'd clearly done his homework too.

Was he inviting her into his kitchen to confront her about snooping on his cuisine? Or to give her a friendly tour of the kitchen and an insight into his methods? Friend or foe?

Unable to decide, and never one for shrinking from a challenge, she finished tasting the summer platter sampler, and then walked confidently into Roag's kitchen. Standing there, she immediately dug into her bag, took out a bobble, and tied her hair back in a ponytail. The chef in her never wandered around a working kitchen with her hair dangling near the food prep.

Roag sensed her before he saw her, feeling the watermark in the kitchen tip towards a challenging vibe. He glanced over his shoulder as he piped melted chocolate on pastries. Her gesture prompted him to nod towards the cupboard beside her near the door.

'My spare whites are in there. And you can wash your hands at the corner sink.'

Fyona opened the cupboard and saw the pristine white jacket, dark trousers, and white hat hanging up. Roag's name was embroidered on the left upper chest.

She hung her bag on a hook, and then put the jacket on.

It was long enough to qualify as a three–quarter length dress when she wore it, negating any need to embarrass herself trying to tackle the trousers. Rolling the sleeves up until they were of manageable length, she put the hat on and tucked the ends of her ponytail inside so that all that was visible was a glimpse of her silky copper hair.

Under the lights of the kitchen, her hair glowed fiery red, a fitting insight into Fyona gearing up to accept the challenge that Roag was about to throw at her. Fighting fire with fire.

The atmosphere in the kitchen sizzled with anticipation. Staff glanced at each other, none daring to make a comment. They sensed what was going down.

Roag prepared the sweet pastry slices, adding decorative lines of chocolate over the top layer of puff pastry that was smoothly coated with fondant icing. Pastry cream sandwiched the three layers together.

'Could you finish the mille–feuille while I prepare the chocolate ganache,' Roag said to Fyona.

His eyes challenged her to sink or swim.

Fyona washed and dried her hands and then dived in at the deep end.

Picking up the piping bag, she trailed straight lines of the melted chocolate across the iced surface, and then used the tip of a knife to create the decorative design.

Roag mixed the melted dark chocolate and cream into a glistening ganache and poured it over the top of a chocolate sponge cake that was sandwiched together with buttercream. Smoothing the silky mixture over the cake, he kept flicking glances at Fyona tackling the pastries with panache.

He expected her skills to be high, but the way she deftly created the finished look to the pastries highlighted her ability, and her calm determination not to be thwarted.

But seeing Fyona standing there, working expertly in his kitchen, affected him in ways he hadn't anticipated. He'd seen pictures of her on her website, and a couple of videos where she demonstrated her baking and cake decorating skills.

She'd had the temerity to waltz into his restaurant for lunch, clearly thinking he wouldn't recognise her. Then knowing he had, she'd accepted the gourmet gauntlet he'd thrown down at her without batting her pale blue eyes. Even having the confidence to take her time, finish her platter, and then walk into his kitchen.

Roag's sensual lips hid the smile that rose from the depths of his heart. Full marks Fyona.

But would she be a handful to work with at the castle? He watched her with the finished tray of pastries.

'Will I take these through to the display?' Fyona offered.

'Yes, thank you.' He saw her carry the tray out of the kitchen, and caught the impressed and mildly entertained looks that some of his staff threw at him.

No one commented. Neither did Roag. But if there was any point scoring going on, the first round went to Fyona.

Game on, Fyona thought to herself, sliding the tray of pastries into the spotlit glass cabinet. None of the diners noticed the extra member of staff wearing Roag's white jacket, or that the woman in the centre table wearing the blue dress had magically disappeared into the kitchen, and never came back out. They were all too busy enjoying their lunches. As it should be, she thought to herself.

It was her own fault for coming to Roag's restaurant and putting herself in the eye of the storm. Now she needed to see what else he'd challenge her with as she walked back into the kitchen.

But the game took another route, and as she walked in, Roag walked out, carrying a tray of glazed fruit tarts.

His eyes flashed a glance at her as they passed in the doorway.

She smiled to herself, surmising he'd left the ganache task and grabbed the fruit tarts as an excuse to see what she was up to.

Not a word exchanged between them. Fyona put a spurt on, knowing she had a couple of minutes in the kitchen while he was busy at the display. Taking the initiative, she'd noticed that a batch of cupcakes were half finished, and proceeded to swirl them with the vanilla buttercream. She was busy doing this when Roag came back in.

Another secret smile from Roag, and a tug on his heartstrings. Full marks again, Fyona.

She assisted with making savoury pastries, and then as the lunchtime rush was done, she decided to leave.

'I think we're done now,' Fyona said to Roag, taking off his jacket and hanging it back up in the cupboard along with his hat.

'Until we meet at the castle,' his deep voice reminded her.

She didn't need any reminder. Her heart was racing at the prospect of having to work with him soon. The glimpse she'd wanted into his culinary skills had turned into an adventure she hadn't planned on. Working in the hub of the kitchen alongside Roag stirred challenging feelings inside her. It was her own fault for stepping into his domain. He was hard to read, and she wasn't sure if the friend or foe question had been answered.

Unhooking her bag, he watched her walk out of the kitchen, her ponytail swinging, posture confident.

Roag hurried after her, surmising she'd be about to settle her bill for lunch before leaving.

And he was right. 'No payment is required.'

Fyona looked up at Roag. 'I didn't come here for a free lunch.'

'You worked for it. So we're even.'

'And I didn't even have to wash the dishes,' she quipped. Shrugging her bag up on to her shoulder, she smiled politely and walked towards the front door, inwardly wanting to make a run for it, to breathe, to think of the consequences of her actions.

Roag strode after her and opened the door. 'See you at the castle. Unless you decide to come back for dinner tonight.'

'I'm busy this evening.' This was true. She planned to do some packing to get ready for her trip.

'Dinner another night,' he suggested.

Was he toying with her? Playing games? She wasn't sure.

'I'm busy that night too.' She smiled, and walked away into the warmth of the day. She could feel him watching her, and then the connection was gone as he went back into his restaurant.

Heading home to her flat, Fyona couldn't shake off her encounter with Roag. Come on, she urged herself, don't be thrown off kilter by the handsome chef. And don't drop your guard when you meet him again at the castle.

Roag felt rattled, long into the evening, thinking about Fyona. Part of him smiled to himself picturing her wearing his jacket, sleeves rolled up, willingly tackling the challenge he'd thrown at her. Part of him wondered if he'd handled the situation all wrong. The indecision rankled him. He was usually the decisive type.

Forcing himself to concentrate on cooking the meals in the restaurant, the evening wore on, and he finished as usual working late in his office, tending to business matters, before locking up and driving home.

The lights of the city shone through the car windows, and he turned some music on, listening to the strong beat of the song. It had been quite a day. His unexpected visitor still flickered through his mind. Feisty Fyona. She wasn't his type. Clearly, he wasn't her type either. It was better this way. Romance wasn't part of his plans this summer.

Turning up the volume of the music, he continued to drive home, feeling the rhythm of the song sweep the tensions of the day away as he headed towards the outskirts of the city.

Finlay, Innis and Ean had breakfast together the next morning outside on the private garden patio at the back of the castle. The table was shaded under a turquoise and white garden umbrella from the bright sunlight.

The patio doors led through to the area of the kitchen where Innis made his luxury chocolates. The main kitchen was so large it easily accommodated Innis' chocolatier set–up.

They liked to have breakfast together most mornings outside on the patio unless it was pouring rain.

Finlay and Innis ate full cooked breakfasts of square slices of Lorne sausage, scrambled eggs, grilled tomatoes, mushrooms and tattie scones. Ean opted for tea and toast as he planned to go for a run.

Cutting into his slice of sausage, Finlay discussed with them their plans for the day, and the evening.

'I've invited Merrilees to have dinner here before our meeting with Nairne. Would you like to invite Skye and Ailsa to join us?'

Innis tucked into his tattie scones and nodded.

'I'll tell Ailsa,' said Ean.

Dinner agreed, they discussed castle business, and then the conversation went back to the plans for the wedding.

'Nairne has a selection of items that he wants us to approve for the wedding buffet,' said Finlay. 'He needs to plan what to order in, so I suggest we think carefully what we want before the meeting tonight.'

'Traditional food,' Innis stated. 'Make that the core of the buffet. It'll suit the whole grand occasion and be ideal for the ball.'

The others agreed.

Ean picked up another slice of toast. 'And you'll be making the chocolates,' he said to Innis.

'I will,' Innis confirmed. 'I've made a plan of what I'll make, and I'll do some of the prep work in a few days. White, milk and dark chocolate truffles are always popular.'

Nairne came out of the kitchen to the patio. 'Here are copies of the menu items I have in mind for the buffet.' He handed them a copy each. 'You'll notice I've included a few traditional dishes such as tipsy laird trifle and cranachan with fresh cream and raspberries. We'll cut down the list tonight.'

'This looks impressive,' said Finlay.

'Once we've got the savoury and sweet dishes planned, I'll talk to you about the wedding cake,' Nairne reminded them. 'I suggest we use the family skean dhu that your parents used for cutting their cake.'

The brothers nodded.

'I think that's a great idea,' said Innis.

'I'll take it out of the glass cabinet nearer the time,' Nairne explained. 'It'll be cleaned and polished.'

The skean dhu was a traditional Scottish knife, often tucked into the socks of those wearing kilted outfits.

'Merrilees, Skye and Ailsa should each make a first cut of one of the three tiers of the cake,' Nairne told them.

'I assume that Merrilees will cut first, as she's marrying Finlay,' said Innis.

'Yes,' Nairne confirmed. 'As the oldest and laird–to–be, his wife would be first, and then Skye, followed by Ailsa. Each groom will guide their wife's hands, and take a layer of cake each, with Merrilees starting at the largest lower tier. And remember, all the cake must be eaten by the end of the night. That's our tradition at the castle's family weddings.'

'I doubt that will be an issue,' Finlay said with a smile. 'At the festive parties there's never anything left but crumbs of the Christmas cake.'

Nairne smiled. 'Well, your cake is the same type of rich fruit cake, and I'm going to get Fyona to help me with the royal icing.'

'What about Roag?' said Innis.

'I'm hoping he'll make a few of his own specialities,' said Nairne. 'There's no value in having an expert chef like him and not letting him do what he excels at.'

'Any news of when Roag will arrive?' Ean said to Nairne.

'I got a message from him yesterday morning,' Nairne told them. 'No specific date. He's trying to tie everything up with his restaurant, making sure the staff are au fait with his new summer menu. But soon. The turret is prepared for him.'

'And Fyona?' said Finlay.

'She's arriving soon too and staying in Nettie and Shuggie's cottage,' Nairne added.

'Sorry to interrupt,' said Murdo, hurrying outside. 'The goldsmith is here with the wedding rings.'

Finlay put his napkin down and stood up. 'Great, I'll talk to him,' he said to Murdo. 'Finish your breakfasts,' he added to Innis and Ean.

Nairne went back into the kitchen, and Finlay and Murdo hurried through to the reception.

'I wanted to deliver the rings in person,' the goldsmith said seeing Finlay stride through. He handed him a dark blue velvet box where all three sets of rings were kept.

'I appreciate that.' Finlay couldn't wait to open it. Inside the box was lined with white velvet. The six rings, paired for each bride and groom, shone under the chandeliers. The yellow Scottish gold was polished to perfection.

'I'm confident that they'll all fit,' said the goldsmith. 'But I'm happy to make any adjustments.'

'This is exquisite work,' Finlay told him. 'I hope you'll be coming to the weddings.'

'I got my invitation. And my nephew is due to join me in my goldsmith work, so if he's here, I'll bring him as my plus one, if that's acceptable.'

'Your nephew will be welcome. And thank you again for making the rings.'

'My pleasure. I love working with gold, especially traditional designs.'

'Can I offer you breakfast before you go?' said Finlay, knowing he'd driven from the other side of the island where he worked from his cottage.

'No, it's fine. I'll be getting back to my work.' Then he looked thoughtful. 'I read in the magazine that Roag is returning to the island, holding the fort while you and your brothers are away on honeymoon.'

'Yes, we're expecting Roag to arrive in the next few days.'

'I remember a few years back when he had his eye on opening a restaurant near me. A few wee businesses have sprouted up in the past couple of years on the other side of the island. I wondered if Roag, coming back here, would be considering opening a restaurant there.'

'I don't think that he plans to stay on the island. He thrives in the city.'

The goldsmith smiled and nodded. 'Aye, maybe better for his business. But with the castle's hotel facilities bringing a lot more new guests and visitors to the island, everyone's wee businesses are benefiting.'

There had been an increase in visitors to the island with the castle's promotions and features in the press. Events such as the first fashion show at the castle had created a lot of interest in the island, and been highlighted in a fashion magazine. And now the current magazine feature added to the publicity effect. The castle had seen a marked increase in guest bookings. Guests loved the shops in the main street, and enjoyed exploring the whole island, resulting in the other side becoming busier.

'I'm glad, and I'll be sure to tell my brothers.' Finlay shook hands with the goldsmith. 'See you at the weddings.'

Giving a cheery smile, the goldsmith headed out of the reception, and Finlay took the velvet box through to show Innis and Ean the rings.

'Can we try them on?' said Ean.

'I think we should.' Finlay lifted his ring from the box and put it on with ease. 'Great fit.'

Ean picked up his ring and slipped it on. 'Perfect.'

Innis wiped his hands on a napkin before wearing his. He held his hand up and nodded. 'Expertly crafted.'

They glanced at each other, all sitting at the table wearing their wedding rings, knowing that soon they'd be married, and breakfasts out here on the patio with just the three of them would become a thing of the past.

Taking the rings off, they put them back in the box.

Finlay stood up. 'I'll put them upstairs in my suite for safe keeping.'

Breakfast finished, Ean got ready for his morning run, and Innis headed out to his car to drive down to start work at his cake shop.

Light flickered through the trees in the forest as Innis drove away from the castle and along the road, arched with trees, down to the shore.

The sea shimmered in the sunlight, and he smiled when he saw the familiar figure peddling towards the dress shop on her pink bicycle. The basket on the front was filled with packages of thread and other sewing items that she'd picked up from the post office.

'Skye!' Innis shouted out the window as he drove by, slowing down.

The light sea breeze blew through her long, strawberry blonde hair, and she wore a midi–length summer dress, a pre–loved design with a boho look to it.

The vintage dress shop's pink bicycle wasn't just for decorative effect when it was parked outside the shop. Skye and Holly used it to pop along the harbour road on errands that didn't require driving their car that was usually parked outside their cottage on the hillside.

'Morning, Innis,' Skye called to him with the brightest smile.

'The wedding rings have arrived at the castle,' he told her as he pulled up outside his cake shop. He got out of the car.

Skye stopped her bike beside him.

'Oh, I can't wait to try mine on.'

'Try it on tonight at the menu meeting. And Finlay and the others are having dinner at the castle before the meeting with Nairne. I'll drive you up after you close your shop,' he offered.

'I'll be ready,' Skye said, excitedly.

Innis leaned down and kissed her, and then went into his cake shop.

Skye parked the pink bicycle outside the dress shop, carried the parcels inside, and couldn't wait to tell Holly that the rings had arrived at the castle.

# CHAPTER SEVEN

It was a busy day for the shops at the main street. Later, as the early evening sun cast an amber glow along the harbour area, Holly watched Skye drive away with Innis for dinner at the castle.

Holly gazed out the window of the dress shop, happy for her sister, but feeling the change of circumstances sweeping into their lives. For the better, but Skye's mercurial nature handled change well, whereas Holly was more inclined to ponder things deeply.

Shaking off her thoughts, Holly continued to work on sewing and mending the ball gowns, enjoying stitching the lovely fabrics, using her sewing machine to hem one of the dresses.

The shop lights and the fiery glow shining in through the window from the fading sun made the fabric shimmer as she fed the hem through the machine. The pale yellow fabric glistened in the light.

When she finished it, she held it up and looked at herself in the mirror. She'd yet to select a ball gown for herself. Maybe this was the dress for her. Skye, Ailsa and Merrilees were wearing their wedding dresses for the ball. And as no bridesmaids were at the ceremony, Holly needed a dress she could wear for the wedding and the ball combined. This fitted the bill nicely. The fabric fell in soft waves from the fitted bodice. It would be lovely for dancing, and appropriate for the wedding.

She went through to the back of the shop and tried it on. A nice fit, and the floaty layers of chiffon felt wonderful. The length suited her too. Worn with comfy low heel shoes this was the dress for her.

Holly labelled it and hung it up on a separate rail beside the wedding dresses, adding a cover on top.

Another task done, and a tricky decision on what to wear to the wedding made, she went back through to her sewing machine to tackle one more ball gown before heading home.

Lyle locked the doors of his tea shop and started to clear up after all the customers had gone. Sometimes he kept it open for special nights, but he preferred to keep his schedule flexible. Besides, he needed the evenings to bake the cakes, scones and flans for the following day.

He'd just dimmed the lights in the front of the tea shop when he saw Holly walking by. So lost in thoughts of her own, she didn't notice him. Sensing something weighing down on her, he hurried outside and called after her.

'Holly! Are you okay?'

Lyle's voice snapped her back from her wistful thoughts. She stopped and looked over at him. 'Yes,' she lied.

He walked towards her. 'What's wrong?' he said gently.

Holly shrugged and glanced out at the sea, trying not to become an emotional wreck.

Lyle patiently gave her time to compose herself before she replied.

'It was just...seeing Skye drive away tonight with Innis. They're having dinner at the castle before discussing the wedding menu with Nairne.'

Lyle nodded, taking this in, and let her continue.

'I know I'm being silly, and I'm so happy for Skye and Innis, really I am.' Holly took a deep breath and again glanced at the sea, seeing Finlay's yacht at the harbour, all ready to sail away when it was time for the honeymooners to leave. 'It's just that there are times when it hits me that everything is going to change. I suppose I don't adapt to changes in circumstances as well as Skye.' Holly looked at Lyle. 'Please don't say anything about this to Skye.'

'I wont,' Lyle promised. 'This is between you and me.' Everything in his tone and expression showed he understood.

Holly wiped away the tears she'd tried to stem. 'I'm happy, but I'm sad. And it's a jarring mix sometimes.' Her lovely green eyes gazed at him.

Lyle's heart felt for her. 'Do you want to come in for a cup of tea, or a hot chocolate?' he offered kindly.

Holly shook herself, sweeping her hair back and took a calming breath of the mild sea air. 'No, thanks. I'm planning to have a night in at the cottage, relax, watch the telly.'

He didn't push her to accept, or overwhelm her with platitudes. Instead he gave her a reassuring hug. 'See you in the morning, Holly.'

She smiled and nodded, then started to walk away.

He walked back towards his tea shop.

'Lyle!' Holly's voice rang out in the evening air.

He stopped and looked round at her. She was standing nearby, looking totally lost.

'Can I change my mind?' she said, hiding the emotional resonance in her tone. But he'd come to know her so well, every nuance now familiar in his heart.

'Tea or hot chocolate?'

'Chocolate.' She started to smile as she walked towards him.

A comforting strong arm wrapped around her shoulders as he guided her into the tea shop. 'How about dinner, for two.'

Holly's smile brightened even further. 'Yes. But don't fuss to make anything special. You've had a busy day too.'

Lyle didn't correct her. He'd been busy since early morning until now.

He leaned close, still keeping a protective arm around her as he locked the tea shop door and guided her through to the kitchen. 'Let's have something tasty, that's totally not on the summer menu. Not a summer dish, but a hearty stew. I have some frozen that I can heat and spice up. Chunks of carrot, turnip and very tasty. I'll boil up a wee pot of tatties, and I've got fresh baked bread.'

Holly fought against her eyes welling up again, this time due to Lyle's kindness and the way he always made her feel better. This busy man always had time for her.

She took a steadying breath as they reached the kitchen. 'I'll peel the tatties.'

They worked together rustling up the hearty dinner, chatting about everything and nothing.

Holly giggled at Lyle setting one of the tables in the tea shop with napkins and a candle in a bottle, lighting it, and adding it to the table for a makeshift romantic dinner.

Finally, they sat down together to tuck into their meal. The candle flickered between them.

Holly tasted the stew and nodded. 'This is so delicious.'

Lyle smiled across at her. 'I don't have a castle, but—'

'I prefer this,' Holly cut–in. 'It's cosy.'

She realised that the weight of the day had gone, and all she felt was the warmth of the tea shop and the company of this wonderful man.

Picking up her mug of frothy hot chocolate, she took a sip. 'Stew and hot chocolate.'

'We're so bad.'

'But this is so good,' she said.

They tucked in as they chatted. This time about the weddings.

Holly sounded thoughtful. 'At least when the weddings at the castle are done, everything will calm down again. There won't be any other local marriages for a while. None that I know of.'

Lyle continued to eat his dinner. His silent response made her wonder.

'Have you heard of any other pending engagements?' she said, knowing a lot of gossip circulated in the tea shop.

'No.' His reply hinted that he did know, but wasn't telling her.

Holly studied his face. 'You look guilty. You do know something.' She leaned forward. 'Is there news of another proposal?'

Lyle's eyes connected with hers through the candlelight, and all of a sudden the penny dropped.

Holly tried to contain her smile, and continued to eat her dinner. 'I suppose I'll have to mend another vintage wedding dress for whoever the lucky bride–to–be is.'

Lyle's heart felt fit to burst with happiness. He hadn't proposed to Holly yet, but now he was sure of her response. He planned to make it special, and surprise her anyway with a beautiful diamond engagement ring, and a romantic atmosphere for the proposal.

They enjoyed the rest of their dinner, without discussing anything more about the proposal. Holly wanted it to be as much of a surprise as Lyle had intended.

The three engaged couples had dinner outside on the private patio at the back of the castle. It was a warm summer evening, and pleasant to dine outdoors. This was where the wedding ceremonies were scheduled to be. The couples would stand together there and exchange their vows.

No bridesmaids, no best men, just the couples and a registrar. He would conduct the traditional ceremony.

Family members, friends and those invited to the wedding would stand outside and watch the short ceremony.

Bagpipes would play to announce the arrival of the three brides as they stepped out of the castle to join the grooms. Later, once the rings were exchanged, and the couples were announced married, the bagpipes would play again, confirming the marriages.

After photographs were taken in the castle gardens, the couples would come back into the castle where the celebrations would begin in the function room.

'The buffet will be topped up during the evening,' Finlay told them. He gestured to the list that Nairne had given him. Copies had been given to Skye, Ailsa and Merrilees. 'Any preferences for the menu?'

'There are so many wonderful options,' said Merrilees. 'I'd happily have any of these.'

'I feel the same,' Ailsa agreed.

'So do I,' Skye added.

'Then I suggest we leave the decision to Nairne,' said Finlay. 'He'll know what dishes combine well, and what's needed to make and present them.'

Merrilees ate her haggis, mashed turnip and mashed potatoes encased in puff pastry. 'This is a lovely way to serve haggis with neeps and tatties.' It was served with a crisp green side salad. Scoops of horseradish, and Nairne's own mix of bramble and cranberry sauce enhanced the flavours.

Skye and Ailsa had opted for this too as Nairne had recommended they try it prior to the wedding.

The brothers had a selection of salmon dishes, including salmon en croute with broccoli and new potatoes.

Other items they tried and approved were rumbledethumps made from mashed potatoes, cabbage and onion.

They all started their dinner with soup — lentil soup, and scotch broth. Other soups were listed, but these were their choices.

After finishing their main course, Nairne joined them outside, sitting at a table beside them to take notes as they ate their puddings.

'We'll serve savoury tarts, pastries and vol–au–vents filled with a variety of cheeses, haggis, meat, fish, roast peppers, tomato and all sorts of tasty combinations,' said Nairne. He checked his notes. 'Finlay has requested Scottish tablet, so I'm hoping that Fyona or Roag will make this, or I'll rustle it up myself.'

'I can make the tablet when I make the chocolates,' Innis offered.

Nairne nodded and ticked this off his to–do list. 'Great. And we will be having the castle's traditional clootie dumpling.'

The menu planning continued as the sunlight faded to a warm twilight.

Nairne finally stood up. The whole process was easier and shorter than he'd anticipated. Smiling, he left the couples to enjoy their various puddings with scoops of ice cream. Nairne had ordered in several flavours from Brodrick's cafe bar. Butterscotch, vanilla, strawberry, and chocolate were picked for the buffet. A chilled counter was part of the buffet that would be set up for the weddings and summer ball in the function room.

'I love all the traditions we're including for the weddings,' said Merrilees.

'Cutting the cake with the skean dhu,' Aisla chimed–in.

'Is there something old, new, borrowed and blue?' said Skye.

'No, there's no record of that in any of the family weddings at the castle,' Innis told her. 'But you can include anything you want.'

Skye shook her head. 'I just wondered. I like the plan we have.'

'It seems easier somehow,' Merrilees commented.

'What about the dancing?' said Skye. 'Do we dance the first waltz?'

'We do,' Finlay explained. 'So we'll have to think of the song we want to dance to.'

'Usually the first waltz is danced after the cutting of the wedding cake,' Ean added.

While they chatted about the dancing, Finlay popped upstairs for the rings.

Joining them again, Finlay opened the velvet box and sat it on the table. 'Try them on,' he said, smiling.

Their faces lit up with excitement seeing the beautiful gold rings.

Skye picked up her ring and slipped it on her finger, as did Merrilees and Ailsa. Each band of gold was well–crafted.

'The wedding rings go so well with our engagement rings,' said Skye.

The others agreed.

'Try your rings on too,' Ailsa said to the men.

And they did. All of them sat for a few moments around the table wearing the rings, happy with the fit and designs. Then the rings were put back in the box and Finlay took it back upstairs for safe keeping again. But he came back down with a photo album and showed the ladies pictures of his parents' wedding at the castle, and his grandparents' wedding, though he only had a couple of pictures of the latter.

Merrilees looked around her at the exterior of the castle, the patio where the photos of the laird and his wife were taken. 'The castle looks the same as it did all those years ago.'

'The gardens have hardly changed either,' Ailsa added.

'We've hired someone to video the wedding and the ball,' said Ean. 'And he'll take our official photographs too. He's reliable, and we hire him to film various functions at the castle.'

'Is there anything else we need to discuss?' Innis said to them.

'Will there be speeches and toasts?' said Merrilees.

'No, unless any of you would like these to be part of the celebrations,' Finlay replied.

'I just want to enjoy the ceremony,' said Skye. 'And then dance at the ball and dine at the buffet.'

'I'm happy with that,' Ailsa agreed.

So was Merrilees.

As the night wore on, they had another round of tea, and chatted about what they'd need to pack for the honeymoon trip on the yacht.

'Pack things that are light and comfy to wear,' Finlay advised.

'Plus a waterproof jacket, just in case it rains,' Ean added.

'And your swimwear,' Finlay reminded them. 'The weather forecast says it's going to be a warm month, and we'll be stopping often to enjoy swimming in the sea, exploring other islands and coastal towns. Staying in hotels overnight. We've plenty to see and do, and go where the wind blows us.'

'I've never gone on holiday on a yacht before,' said Merrilees.

None of the women had.

'I think you'll love it,' Finlay told them. 'No storms are forecast.'

'Except for dealing with any mischief Skye whips up,' Innis teased her.

Skye swiped at him playfully. 'I don't plan to cause any trouble.'

'Speaking of trouble,' said Finlay, 'Roag sent me a message earlier saying he's planning to arrive in a couple of days.'

No sooner had Finlay said this, than the lingering glow of the twilight darkened, and although the deep inky sky made the stars sparkle brighter, storm clouds swept in from the sea, swirling in the darkness and taking some of the warmth out of the night.

They all went inside and the women got ready to leave.

Ailsa had driven up in her car, and intended driving herself back down to her cottage on the hillside. Ean kissed her and waved her off.

Innis followed in his car, taking Skye home.

Finlay spoke to Merrilees for a few minutes before she drove back to stargazer cottage.

'The meeting went well,' said Finlay.

'It did,' Merrilees agreed. 'I really do love the traditional theme of the weddings and I'm excited to dance at the summer ball. What other traditions are there?'

'Staying at the castle for the wedding night, before setting off on honeymoon in the morning. I thought we could sleep in the turret instead of the bedroom in my suite. Or should I say, our suite.'

'Our wedding night in the castle turret.' Merrilees smiled at him. 'That would be like a fairytale.'

'We'll do that,' he said firmly. Pulling her into his arms, he kissed her, and then she got into her car, waving to him as she drove away to stargazer cottage.

Holly turned the lights on in the cottage after having enjoyed her evening with Lyle. She'd just started to get ready for bed when Skye arrived home, having been dropped off by Innis.

'How did the menu meeting go?' said Holly.

Skye was still buzzing from the passionate kisses Innis had lavished on her before he drove back to the castle.

'Nairne has created an excellent selection of food for the buffet. We got to taste a few of the dishes for dinner.' Skye elaborated on what they had for their meal. 'Tradition is the main theme of the weddings. Old traditions from the castle's past.' She spoke about these too while they both got ready for bed, wandering from one bedroom to the other, chattering all the time, though Skye did most of the talking, clearly bubbling with excitement.

'Did you see the wedding rings?' said Holly.

'Yes, I tried mine on. It's a perfect fit and all the other rings are so lovely.' Finally Skye realised she'd been chattering almost non–stop. 'How was your evening? Did you work late at the shop?'

'I did, and I've decided on the dress I'd like to wear for the wedding. You know the pale yellow dress that I was mending?'

'Yes, it was a classic design.'

'I tried it on, and I think it'll be suitable for the wedding and the ball. I'll show you in the morning at the shop.'

Skye smiled, happy that Holly had selected a dress.

'And as I was leaving the shop, Lyle invited me to have dinner with him at the tea shop,' Holly revealed.

'Did you have something special from his summer menu?'

'No, we were scoundrels. Despite it being a warm summer evening, we had stew, potatoes that I boiled up for us, and chunks of bread. And hot chocolate.'

Skye laughed. 'Scoundrels indeed. Lyle is a wonderfully naughty influence on you. I think he's a keeper.' Her hint wasn't subtle.

Holly was so tempted to tell her about Lyle's equally unsubtle hint that he intended to ask her to marry him. But she aimed to keep that a secret until Skye came back from her honeymoon. She didn't want to steal any of Skye's thunder. There would be plenty of time to gush about another engagement on the island after all the excitement of the weddings and the fun of the summer ball.

# CHAPTER EIGHT

Roag stood on the main deck of the ferry, blinking against the morning sunlight that shone through the cobalt sky and reflected off the sea. In the distance was the outline of the island.

It had been a couple of days since he'd sent a message to Finlay telling him he'd be arriving, and now he was on his way as planned. He'd driven his car from Glasgow to catch the first early morning ferry across to the island, and it was parked on a lower deck.

Feeling a mix of anticipation and energy fighting to dominate his senses, he'd gone up to the deck to face the sea breeze and view where he was heading.

Four years had gone by in a blink of work and ambition, compressing the time. Seeing the island in the distance, it didn't seem so long ago since he was last there. His heart betrayed his steely resolve not to dwell on yesteryear, as flashes of the past flickered through his thoughts uninvited. The magnificent fairytale castle. The dark stone architecture with a rich history, surrounded by the warrior trees, the local name for the tall, dark pines around the edges of the gardens, that seemed to protect the castle.

Forcing his thoughts to change gear, the next image that shot through his mind was Fyona. Her lovely face and feisty attitude was harder to push aside than the images of the castle.

Taking a deep breath of the sea air, he stood forthright, facing the island as it came into clear focus. The harbour, shops along the main street, cottages dotted on the hillside, lush greenery and the deep aquamarine sea edging the white sand coast. The picturesque qualities of the island were on show in the dazzling sunlight. The castle was hidden from view, but he anticipated his cousins, and Nairne, awaiting his arrival. He hadn't specified an exact time, having needed to keep his schedule flexible, taking care of last minute tasks for the restaurant and business before finally sailing away from the mainland.

When the ferry arrived at the island, Roag was one of the first to drive off. The shops in the main street looked like they were thriving, and the bunting added to the summery feel of the whole pretty harbour area. He noticed the tea shop, the cafe bar, and Innis' cake shop as he drove past, having done his homework on the local businesses too. With all of them having websites, it was handy to take a glimpse of their menus and information about the owners.

Lyle impressed him the most, even though the tea shop looked quaint. The menus were excellent, and Lyle had extended the shop to the upper floor. A smart move. Innis had added a glass patio–style extension to the back of the cake shop, and he had his chocolatier set–up in the castle's kitchen, something he was keen to see. Brodrick's cafe bar was popular and his range of ice creams catered for all tastes. Roag planned to enjoy a night out at Brodrick's domain. And pop into the tea shop too. Plus he'd drop by Innis' cake shop.

Driving along the harbour road, he glanced at the sea, planning to go swimming down the shore soon. From the coast, the forest road took him along the familiar route leading up to the castle.

And there it was, as magnificent as he remembered, with the turrets outlined against the vibrant blue sky. A feeling of excitement charged through him at the prospect of living in the left hand turret.

Pulling up at the car park in front of the castle, he parked beside Finlay's white car in one of the private spaces.

Stepping out, he took a moment to breathe in the sense of grandeur.

'A red car has just pulled up outside,' Murdo said in a warning tone to Finlay. They were standing in reception discussing preparations for the weddings, while Geneen was behind the desk tending to the guest bookings.

Finlay saw the tall, well–dressed figure, wearing expensive dark trousers, a white shirt, tie and waistcoat, viewing the castle. There was no mistaking the new arrival.

'Roag is here,' said Finlay, his voice as deep a warning as Murdo's.

'Action stations,' Murdo hissed to Geneen.

She nodded and stood ready to meet him.

Murdo immediately sent a message through to Nairne in the kitchen.

Nairne was preparing pastries for the castle's lunch menu. He checked the message.

*Roag has arrived.*

Nairne hurried through to reception.

Murdo sent the same alert to Ean, then stood at the reception desk beside Geneen.

Finlay, as expensively dressed as Roag, went outside to greet him.

'The castle is as impressive as ever,' said Roag, thinking the same about Finlay.

They shook hands. The welcome was polite, but no more than that.

'I'll have your bags taken up to the turret,' Finlay told him.

'Thank you.' Roag lifted a couple of bags of personal belongings and his laptop bag.

Finlay led him inside to the reception where Nairne evaluated the man he was due to work with. He'd met Roag four years ago, but at that time Roag had only been a guest at the castle and wasn't part of the kitchen staff, so they'd barely conversed before.

Roag put his bags down and stepped forward. 'Morning, Nairne. I was just saying to Finlay that the castle looks impressive.'

'I'm preparing the lunches, but once you're settled in, I'll give you a tour of the kitchen's facilities,' said Nairne.

Roag's response took them all aback. 'I'll put my bags upstairs, get changed and come down to assist you.'

'Are you not wanting to settle in first before you get started with the cheffing?' Nairne said to him.

'No, I'm happy to start right away.' Roag then shook hands with Murdo. 'You're looking well, Murdo.'

'Aye, and so are you, Roag.'

'Nice to see you again, Geneen,' Roag called over to her.

Geneen smiled politely. 'Welcome back to the castle.'

The ice was broken, but the air had a distinct chill to it.

Roag picked up his bags and headed upstairs, stepping over the red and gold cord, hoping that by the time he came back down the atmosphere would've warmed up a bit.

Murdo and two other members of staff took charge of Roag's other bags and boxes with his personal cooking equipment, while Finlay went upstairs to show Roag to the turret.

'You're along here and up the spiral staircase,' Finlay said, overtaking Roag and leading the way. He would've offered to carry one of the bags, but the grip his cousin had on them indicated he preferred to keep his personal items to himself.

At the top of the staircase, Finlay opened the door, and they stepped into the main room, the living room, where sunlight streamed through the windows and offered a wonderful view of the front gardens, over the trees in the forest, and down to the shore where the sea sparkled in the distance.

'I don't think you've been in this turret,' said Finlay. It was situated above one of the private suites.

'I've never been in either of the turrets.' Roag looked around at the traditional styling that was decorated in light neutral tones that offset the dark wooden furniture. The chintz couch and chairs were comfy, and although the table lamps weren't lit, he pictured them giving a warmth to the room in the evenings.

Finlay didn't take Roag up on his insinuation that he'd never been invited to the turrets before, and gestured through to the bedroom. 'The bedroom is en suite. Phone down to reception for anything you need, including having your breakfast or other meals brought up here if you wish. Though you're welcome to dine in the guests' restaurant.'

'Thank you, Finlay.' Roag intended to dine mainly downstairs.

Murdo and the staff carried the luggage in, prompting Finlay to curtail his welcome.

'We'll chat later, and you'll meet Ean and Innis,' said Finlay. 'Ean is elsewhere in the castle. And Innis is—'

'In his cake shop,' Roag cut–in.

'Yes, he's busy there most days, but he's here in the evenings,' said Finlay.

Smiling politely, Finlay headed out, leaving Roag to get changed.

By the time Finlay was back down in reception, Ean came through from the function room, having read the message. 'What was the welcome like?'

'Polite, distant. Roag was always a hard man to read,' said Finlay.

Murdo and the staff went by with the last load of Roag's luggage.

'He's getting changed and coming down to assist Nairne prepare the lunches,' Finlay added.

'Diving right in at the deep end,' Ean commented.

A group of four ladies, sisters and friends that were guests, stopped to speak to Finlay and Ean on their way out to enjoy the sunshine and explore the estate.

'We're having a wonderful time at the castle,' one of them remarked.

While they were talking, Roag came bounding down the stairs. He wore his white jacket embroidered with the name of his restaurant, dark trousers, and carried his hat in his hand, ready to put it on when he went into the kitchen.

The ladies reacted, smiling, when they saw the tall figure of Roag.

'Oh, have you got a new handsome chef?' one of the ladies remarked to Finlay.

'This is Roag,' Finlay told them. 'He's joining us to help with the castle's catering.'

Ean gave Finlay a knowing glance. They'd seen women's reaction to Roag in the past. Nothing had changed in that respect.

Roag overheard the comments and came over to acknowledge them politely. 'I hope you're having lunch here today.' He wasn't flirting. He didn't need to.

'Oh, yes, we are,' one of the ladies said with a smile. 'We're going for a walk around the gardens, but we'll be back for lunch.'

'I love man who can cook,' another remarked.

'It's the way to a woman's heart,' a third added.

Finlay smiled politely at the ladies and guided Roag away from them. He spoke in a confiding tone. 'We don't fraternise or flirt with the guests.'

'No, only with beautiful newspaper journalists,' Roag retorted with a smile, and then walked through to the kitchen.

Finlay was fizzing.

Ean, having walked the guests to the front door, came over to calm him down.

'Don't let Roag rub your feathers up the wrong way before we've had a chance to become acquainted with each other again.'

Finlay nodded. 'You're right. Let's leave him to Nairne, and whatever they'll be cooking up in the kitchen.'

'Apart from trouble,' Ean joked.

Finlay smiled. 'That was always on the menu when Roag was around.'

Fyona found the key to the cottage stuck up the bahookie of an ornamental cat in the garden, beside the front door.

She'd arrived on the first ferry, but hadn't seen Roag in his red car. Her small hatchback was parked outside her aunt and uncle's cottage that was near the main street. Handy for popping to the shops, and for driving up to the castle.

Nettie and Shuggie had left the previous day to go on holiday, and Fluffy was living next door. Everything was going to plan.

Fyona unlocked the door and stepped into the homely cottage. It had a living room and two bedrooms, kitchen and bathroom. She smiled when she saw Nettie's knitting stash neatly tucked up on the shelves in the corner of the living room. Knitting needles, and items for sewing were there too. The colours of the yarn made Fyona's fingers long to knit something, even though she wasn't an expert knitter. She could create something like a scarf, but she'd never tackled knitting a cardigan or a jumper. She pictured herself relaxing in any spare evenings, knitting while unwinding after working at the castle.

She wandered through to the kitchen, immediately at home in the traditional cottage.

Nettie had stocked the kitchen cupboards with groceries, and the fridge had enough fresh food to keep her going for a few days without having to do any shopping. Except for buying a fresh loaf. Then seeing the bags of flour in a cupboard, she knew she could always bake her own bread.

Her bed in the spare room was covered with a patchwork quilt that Nettie had made, and there were various items throughout the cottage that showed her aunt's love of crafting, including a knitted tea cosy, quilted oven mitts, and a knitted throw over the back of the couch.

Bringing her bags in from the car, she put the kettle on for a cup of tea. She'd barely slept the previous night having worked late into the evening packing her things in the car, ready to catch the first ferry across to the island.

But now she was here, she could relax a little. Putting all her bags in the bedroom while the kettle boiled, she flopped back on the bed, and sighed with happy relief.

Hearing the kettle click off, she went through to the kitchen, made a mug of tea, and then opened the kitchen door and stepped outside into the back garden to drink it. The scent of the sea mingled with the flowers and greenery. It was something she missed while living in a flat in Glasgow — a garden that she could step out into. She planned to make the most of it during her stay. And swimming in the sea. That was one thing she was really looking forward to.

After enjoying her tea in the garden, she went in and started to unpack her bags, hanging her clothes in the wardrobe and folding the others into the dresser drawers.

As she unpacked the last item, she sighed to herself. She hadn't packed her swimsuit. That's if she still had one. Swimming wasn't part of her lifestyle in the city.

But she'd seen a swimsuit on one of the mannequins in the front window of the vintage dress shop as she'd driven by. It was a bright red halterneck with white polka dots, and frills to flatter and flaunt the figure.

The colour had caught her eye, and thinking it would do the same to others, she picked up her bag and headed out to buy it before someone else snapped it up.

Nairne finished introducing all the kitchen staff to Roag who had a knack for remembering people's names.

'I'll introduce you to Fyona once she arrives on the island,' said Nairne.

'Fyona is here,' Roag told him.

'Is she?' Nairne sounded surprised.

'I saw her this morning on the ferry. Her car was in another lane from mine, waiting to drive off. I waved, but she was concentrating on edging into her lane. I was one of the first cars off the ferry. I drove straight here.'

'She's probably unpacking at Nettie and Shuggie's cottage. She's cottage sitting while her aunt and uncle are away on holiday,' Nairne explained.

'I'm sure she'll make an appearance at the castle later today,' said Roag, sounding as if he was familiar with Fyona's ways.

'You know Fyona?' Nairne queried.

'She had lunch in my restaurant in Glasgow recently. And helped out in the kitchen with the cakes.'

Nairne's expression brightened. 'I didn't know you that you were friends with Fyona.'

Roag looked thoughtful. 'I'm not sure that we are. Not certain we're not. Or that we will be.'

Nairne wasn't in the mood to unpick Roag's confusing comments. 'Well, we'll see her whenever she arrives.'

Ean came into the kitchen and picked up the picnic basket he'd ordered.

'Off to enjoy the sunshine?' Roag called over to Ean.

The voice and the tone of it was a jolt from the past. Ean turned around and went over to reacquaint himself with Roag.

'I'm planning to surprise Ailsa with a picnic lunch down the shore.' Ean looked at his cousin, and extended a welcoming hand.

They shook hands, and although the kitchen was warm from the heat of the ovens baking cakes, an icy breeze wafted in the air for a moment, before the atmosphere warmed up again.

'Roag tells me that Fyona has arrived on the island,' Nairne said to Ean.

'I'll let Finlay know she's arrived safely.' Giving a polite nod and smile, Ean walked out of the kitchen carrying the picnic basket.

Finlay was behind the reception desk, along with Geneen, attending to guest bookings.

Ean told Finlay the news.

'Excellent,' said Finlay. 'Both our experts are here. We can forge on with our plans.'

Ean headed out to this car and put the picnic basket in the back seat.

Geneen confided to Finlay. 'Roag was always a clipe.'

Finlay laughed.


Fyona looked at the swimsuit through the window of the vintage dress shop. Up close, it was even nicer than she'd thought. She went in to enquire about buying it.

The whir of Skye and Holly's sewing machines filled the air, and they both looked up and smiled in welcoming seeing a customer walk in.

Skye was machining the seams of an evening dress, so Holly stopped sewing the minor repair on the ball gown she was stitching, and stood up to tend to the customer.

Neither of them had seen Fyona looking through the window.

'I noticed the red polka dot swimsuit in the window,' Fyona began. She wore light blue jeans and a blouse that was two shades darker.

'It's an original forties swimsuit.' Holly went over and started to take it off the mannequin.

Skye continued sewing, concentrating on finishing the seams neatly.

'A real bargain,' Fyona said, seeing the price tag.

'We try to offer our customers bargains, especially when items come in a bulk buy,' Holly explained. 'This swimsuit arrived a few days ago as part of a delivery of evening dresses and ball gowns from one of our reliable vintage wear suppliers.' After wrestling the swimsuit off the mannequin, she rechecked the suit for flaws and found none.

Skye stopped sewing and snipped off the threads at the end of a seam. 'There was a blue polka dot swimsuit along with it, but someone snapped it up for themselves.' She cast a playful glance at Holly.

'It was a perfect fit and I want one for going swimming in the sea this summer,' Holly explained. 'Are you here on holiday?' she said to Fyona.

'No, to work at the castle and cottage sit for my aunt and uncle.'

Skye and Holly's faces lit up as they realised who she was.

'Fyona!' said Skye, hurrying over to her. 'I'm Skye. Nairne says you'll be helping him ice my wedding cake.'

'I should've said who I was when I came in,' Fyona admitted. 'I read the magazine feature, and I'd seen your shop online.'

The excited chattering began, and Fyona was whisked into the little changing room. 'Try the swimsuit on,' said Holly.

'Then you must come and meet Innis,' Skye insisted. 'He's in his cake shop. And you'll meet Primrose and Rosabel too.'

Fyona started to take her jeans and top off and wriggle into the swimsuit while the chattering continued on the other side of the curtained cubicle.

'Do you knit?' Holly called through to her.

'A little bit, but Nettie's stash of yarn has made me want to knit a scarf,' Fyona admitted.

'We're knitting scarves and hats,' said Skye. 'There's lovely new yarn in the knitting shop.'

'That's where the local weekly knitting bee nights are held,' Holly explained. 'You'll have to come along and join in. You don't have to knit, you can sew or whatever, or just join in the chatter, tea and cake.'

'And gossip,' said Skye.

'I'll do that.' Fyona pulled the curtain back and stepped out, adjusting the frills around the bottom of the design that mimicked a scant skirt. The halterneck straps were dangling, and Holly stepped forward and adjusted them to fit.

Holly stepped back and assessed the swimsuit. 'Oh, yes, it really suits you.'

Fyona looked at her slender figure in the mirror. The style gave her curves in all the right places. Her hair glowed fiery red under the shop lights, but didn't clash with the red of the suit. 'It's the best style of swimsuit I've ever worn, and I love the bold colour.'

'What colour of dress are you wearing to the ball?' Skye said as Fyona disappeared to get changed out of the swimsuit.

'I don't have a dress for the ball. I probably won't be attending as I'll be helping with the catering,' Fyona reasoned.

'No, you have to come to the ball,' Skye insisted. 'Even if it's after the main buffet is all sorted.'

'I suppose that would be fun,' Fyona admitted. 'I've never been to a castle ball.'

'That's settled,' Holly said firmly. 'You have to come, and you'll need a dazzling dress. Luckily, we have those aplenty.'

Fyona stepped out wearing her clothes again, in time for Holly to gesture to one of the rails of ball gowns and evening dresses hanging on the rails.

'All great bargains,' Holly assured her.

'With a discount for anyone helping with the wedding,' Skye added with a giggle.

In a flurry of activity, Holly and Skye held up dresses in front of Fyona, assessing what colours she suited.

'Shocking pink...emerald...turquoise...' Skye wasn't entirely happy that they'd found the right dress.

Holly unhooked a red chiffon evening dress and held it up against Fyona. 'Oh, now we're talking. I think that red is your colour. What do you think?' she said to Skye.

'No one is going to miss you, Fyona,' said Skye. 'Not in a dress like this.'

Fyona clasped the dress, held it up and viewed herself in the mirror. It had layers of chiffon that created a full–length skirt that was shot through with glittering red thread. The bodice was fitting and, like the swimsuit, extremely figure–flattering.

'Can I try it on?'

And through they went, advising Fyona what shoes to wear with the dress that looked like it had been designed for her.

'I have a pair of low heel shoes that are comfy.' Fyona didn't mention that they were dance shoes. Pale gold, with cushioned soles for comfort, a single strap, and designed to be flexible.

'When you get back to the cottage, try them on with the dress,' Skye advised. 'If the hem needs altering once you've got the shoes on, bring it back, and we'll sort that easily.'

Skye put the dress in a bag, and then Holly held up another dress in the back of the shop.

'I'm wearing this one,' Holly said to Fyona. 'Skye will dance at the ball wearing her wedding dress, as will Ailsa and Merrilees.' They gave Fyona a peek at the three wedding dresses on the bridal rail.

'Wow! They're all beautiful,' said Fyona.

The excited chatter continued as they wrapped up the swimsuit. Fyona insisted on paying for the items. They insisted she accept the discount.

Ean walked into Ailsa's craft shop carrying the picnic basket and had a folded blanket under his arm. She'd just finished serving a customer and was planning to close for lunch.

He held up the basket. 'Fancy a picnic lunch down on the shore?'

Ailsa shrugged the tension of the busy morning from her shoulders. 'Yes, that would be wonderful.' She lifted her bag, and a couple of packets of glittering gems. 'I need to hand these in to the dress shop on the way. Skye and Holly ordered them for the ball gowns.'

'Here's Ailsa and Ean,' Skye said to Fyona, looking out the window and seeing them approach.

Ean stood outside holding the picnic basket and blanket, thinking that Ailsa was only going to hand in the gems.

'These were delivered this morning.' Ailsa put them down on the counter, seeing that they were busy with a customer.

'This is Fyona.' Skye introduced them excitedly. 'She's just arrived on the island.'

'It's great to meet you,' said Ailsa, and then waved to Ean. 'Come in and meet Fyona.'

The tall figure of Ean was familiar from the front of the magazine, and the online pictures Fyona had seen on the castle's website.

'Lovely to meet you, Fyona,' Ean said, smiling warmly.

'Nice to meet you too,' Fyona responded.

'Roag arrived this morning at the castle,' Ean revealed.

Fyona blinked. 'He's here?'

'Yes, he was on the same ferry as you. He said he waved but you didn't notice him,' Ean explained.

Fyona jarred at this information. She hadn't noticed him at all. And now Nairne and others at the castle would know she was on the island.

115

'We're going down the shore for a picnic,' Ailsa explained, short on time as she had to reopen her shop after lunch. And then they left, waving and seeming delighted to have met Fyona.

Skye clasped Fyona's hand. 'Now you have to meet Innis before you go. Come on.'

While Holly watched the shop, Skye happily hustled Fyona into the nearby cake shop where she was introduced to Primrose and Rosabel, before meeting Innis in the kitchen.

Innis was busy icing a cake. He stopped when Skye introduced him to Fyona.

'Meet Fyona.'

'I'm pleased to meet you.' His deep voice resonated in the kitchen, and those wolf eyes lived up to their reputation, as did Innis.

'Ean says Roag has arrived,' Skye told Innis. 'He's at the castle.'

'I'll phone Finlay and check that everything is okay.'

Keeping the introductions brief, as lunchtimes were busy for all of them, Skye whisked Fyona back to the dress shop where Holly handed her the bags containing the dress and the swimsuit.

'Remember to try your shoes on with the dress,' Holly reminded Fyona.

'I will, and thank you for the lovely welcome.'

They waved Fyona off and then decided what to have for their lunch too.

Fyona walked back to the cottage, rethinking her plans. If she didn't show face at the castle until the next morning, would it make her look tardy? And shine a bright light on Roag's eagerness to start work.

The sparkling blue sea tempted her to go swimming, and she saw Ailsa and Ean sitting on the sand having their picnic. But she could go swimming another day, she decided. It was important to make an appearance at the castle.

Fyona changed out of her casual clothes and tried on the red dress, wearing her dance shoes. The length of the hem was ideal.

She hung the dress on the outside of the wardrobe, and then put on a pair of slim–fitting black trousers, comfy court shoes, and a white, short–sleeve, collarless shirt. Sweeping her hair back into a ponytail, she refreshed her light makeup.

Locking the cottage, she put her four sets of clean chef whites in the car, and drove up to the castle, following the forest road that led to the impressive entrance. She'd seen the castle before, mainly from a distance while visiting the island, and had lunch there once in the restaurant with Nettie.

The pictures in the magazine and the website didn't exaggerate the castle's fairytale effect.

Parking outside the front, she clasped her bag, and her whites, and walked into the reception.

Geneen was at the desk and recognised her.

'Fyona, come in. I'll tell Nairne you're here. Finlay is busy with guests, and Ean and Innis aren't here at the moment.'

'I met Ean and Innis down at the main street.'

'That's handy.' Geneen phoned through to Nairne.

'Send her through to the kitchen, Geneen,' said Nairne, busy making the lunches.

'Nairne says to come through. That's the door right there.'

Smiling, Fyona walked into the busy kitchen and scanned the faces for Roag. He wasn't there.

Nairne noticed Fyona, and came over to welcome her with a warm smile. 'Come away in, Fyona.'

'I can come back when you're less busy. Or if you need a hand, I brought my whites,' she offered.

'Put a jacket on, and hang the rest in the big cupboard over there. They'll be laundered when necessary along with those of the other staff. Then help to plate the puddings. The menus are pinned up on the board.'

Accustomed to working in hotel and restaurant kitchens, Fyona stepped into the role she was familiar with. Wearing a white jacket, she tucked the ends of her ponytail into her chef's hat, washed her hands, and began plating the puddings, having checked the menus and incoming orders from the guests in the restaurant.

From the far side of the kitchen, where Innis had his chocolatier area, she heard Roag's deep voice speak in an authoritative voice to one of the staff, an assistant chef.

'Add a side scoop of vanilla ice cream to each plate,' Roag instructed, as he sprinkled grated chocolate over the portions of chocolate pudding.

'Do you want me to put a frosted raspberry on top of the ice cream?' the assistant chef said to Roag.

'Yes, thank you,' Roag confirmed politely.

118

Seeing Roag now heading her way, Fyona turned her back towards him, and tried to blend in with the other staff, all busy with their tasks.

Roag walked by, carrying a large bar of dark chocolate, ready to decorate other dishes.

She was relieved, thinking he hadn't noticed her working busily.

'Hello, Fyona,' Roag said, jarring her.

She continued to focus on plating the puddings. 'Hello, Roag.'

Nairne didn't miss the uneasy welcome they gave to each other. Roag's earlier comments started to make sense. But Nairne let the ripples settle by themselves without causing a fuss. Two expert chefs, especially a confident man like Roag, were probably going to jar each other until they settled into their respective roles.

Roag began to melt the chocolate in a double boiler, stirring the smooth mixture.

'Would you be able to make butterfly cakes for the afternoon tea in the restaurant this afternoon?' Nairne said to Fyona.

'Yes,' she said to Nairne. 'Just a classic vanilla sponge recipe?'

'Unless you have another variation,' said Nairne.

'Chocolate buttercream to secure the wings,' Roag suggested, joining in.

'There seems to be a plethora of chocolate puddings and chocolate cakes on the menu,' Fyona remarked. 'Vanilla buttercream would be better for the afternoon tea selection. I'll add a bit of strawberry jam to decorate some of them, and lemon curd for others.'

Nairne liked Fyona's suggestions.

'We'll have chocolate buttercream another day,' Nairne said to Roag.

For a few minutes the atmosphere could've been cut with a knife, then it faded as everyone in the kitchen became extra busy with requests for second helpings of dishes from the guests in the restaurant.

'They've got a great appetite today,' Nairne said, sounding happy.

At one point, Roag and Fyona found themselves working side by side in the large kitchen that somehow felt smaller with the two of them in it.

'I was surprised to see you here today,' Roag commented while continuing to make the meringues for the afternoon tea. 'I heard that you were fashion shopping in the main street.'

'I bought a swimsuit from the vintage dress shop,' she forced herself to sound unruffled by his remark. 'And a dress for the ball.'

'Do save a waltz for me,' he said.

'My dance card is fully ticked.' But not as ticked–off as Roag appeared to be at her rebuff.

They continued to work on their respective cakes. Fyona smoothed jam and whipped cream on a Victoria sponge cake.

'Not a single waltz for me?' Roag finally said, reluctant to give up.

'No waltzes, foxtrots, quicksteps, tangos or even a cha–cha–cha.'

Roag pretended to be disappointed. 'Not even a Highland Fling?'

'I save those for Hogmanay or other special occasions.'

His lips formed into a sexy smile that she was almost too close to him to handle without blushing.

'We're including a few traditional ceilidh dances at the summer ball,' Nairne told them, overhearing their conversation.

'Maybe I'll whirl you around during a fast–moving reel?' Roag suggested to her.

'Maybe you'll be too busy whipping your shirt off to give a bare chest performance of your expert dancing,' said Fyona.

'Ah, you've seen the video.'

'Hasn't everyone?' said Fyona, and then she concentrated on adding a light sprinkling of castor sugar to the top of the Victoria sponge cake.

Nairne cut–in. 'After lunch, I'd like to talk to both of you about the menu for the wedding. What we need to plan, including icing the wedding cake. I've baked the three tiers of traditional fruit cake. I'm looking for help with the royal icing.'

Roag and Fyona nodded to Nairne.

'What about the summer ball?' said Roag. 'I understand the focus on the wedding. But the ball seems to be relegated into the shadows. I'd like to ensure it receives its fair share of the limelight.'

'I agree,' Nairne acknowledged. 'We'll discuss the summer ball too.' Nairne looked thoughtful for a moment. 'Will you be considering performing a show dance at the ball?'

'No.' Roag's response was clear. 'It would be inappropriate to steal any of the newlyweds' fanfare.'

'Do you still perform these days? Or have you hung up your dancing shoes now in favour of your cheffing?' Nairne said to him.

'I haven't performed publicly in a long time. I'm sure you know that I split with my last two ballroom dance partners.' Roag didn't hide the harsh truth.

'I heard the gossip,' Nairne confirmed, glancing at Fyona to see if she knew.

She didn't chip–in what she'd read when doing her homework, and started assembling the next cake.

'Gossip always circulates the island,' said Roag. 'I'll clarify by saying that I loved and lost my last two ballroom dance partners. It was made quite public that my first leading lady dumped me for my nearest rival. Then the same thing happened with my last dance partner. Since then, I've not found, nor am I looking for, a new dance partner. I concentrate on my restaurant work.'

Nairne nodded, appreciating Roag's candidness. 'The dance world's loss is our gain. I'm pleased you want to boost the summer ball. I'll show you the schedule for the wedding and the ball when we chat later.' Nairne went over to check on a batch of cakes in the oven.

Fyona glanced at Roag, but he was now busy again making the meringues.

Ean poured the last of the tea from the picnic flask into Ailsa's cup as they sat on the blanket enjoying their light lunch and watching the glistening sea.

'It's tempting to go swimming, but I need to get back to the shop,' said Ailsa. She glanced over towards Finlay's yacht anchored at the nearby harbour. 'I'm sure we'll go swimming most days during our honeymoon.'

'We will.' Ean sounded excited. 'When we get back, we'll go sailing in my boat around the island, and swim often. The forecast is that this will be one of our loveliest summers in a while. A scorcher. The summers are always nice, but we picked a great one for our wedding.'

Ailsa smiled. 'It'll feel like an extended honeymoon even when we come home.'

'A summer to remember,' Ean said, and leaned over and kissed her, before packing up the picnic basket, folding the blanket, and walking her back to the craft shop.

'I've put a news post on my website telling customers I'm getting married, and that the shop will be closed until I get back from honeymoon,' Ailsa told him as they stood for a moment outside the front door. 'And I'm closing a few days before the wedding, so I can get myself ready, and hopefully unwind before our big day.'

Ean put the basket and blanket down, pulled her close and kissed her.

'Thank you for a lovely lunch,' she said.

'I'll phone you later.'

Ailsa stood there and waved as Ean put the picnic things in his car and drove away to the castle.

# CHAPTER NINE

'We held a Fairytale Christmas ball in the castle,' Nairne told Roag and Fyona as they had their meeting to discuss the menus. They sat in the kitchen at a table that Nairne used as his desk. 'It was a great success. That's why the summer ball was planned, and to add to the wedding celebrations. We have regular dinner dances for the guests in the function room. Guests are seated at tables around the edges of the dance floor having dinner, and get up to dance during the evening. But the Christmas ball was far more grand, with a lavish buffet. The summer ball will have a wonderful buffet too.'

Roag looked thoughtful, remembering the times he'd attended dinner dances at the castle. 'The function room has an excellent dance floor, and when it's lit with chandeliers it has an expensive ballroom quality to it.'

'I'd like to take a look at the function room,' said Fyona. 'I'm not really familiar with the castle, apart from a brief visit for lunch in the restaurant a while ago.'

'Come and have a look,' said Nairne, leading them out of the kitchen into the reception, past the restaurant, and through to the large function room. 'With the recent promotions in the newspapers and magazines, the castle has become busier than ever.'

'Is the wedding being featured in the press?' said Fyona.

'Yes, Merrilees says she's helping to write about the wedding dresses for a fashion magazine in the city. Merrilees knows the editor. She's promised them an exclusive story about the bridal gowns,' said Nairne. 'She told me she'll mention the wedding buffet and the cake. So this will be more publicity for the castle.'

They walked into the large function room that had patio doors leading out to the garden, a huge unlit fire, and a small stage.

'The wedding ceremony will be held out there in the garden in the late afternoon,' said Nairne. 'Some guests are invited to the wedding itself and the summer ball. Others will arrive only for the ball. The buffet will be set up all along one wall.'

The chandeliers were lit and the sunlight shining in from the garden added to the glittering effect.

'Will the wedding guests be required to wear ball gowns and evening suits?' said Fyona.

'Yes, ball gowns or full–length evening dresses,' said Nairne. 'And classic suits or kilted finery.'

Roag walked on to the large dance floor, feeling the well–sprung floor, tempted to try it again, remembering how much he'd enjoyed dancing on it.

Fyona sensed that he wanted to dance, but held himself in check. Then she saw Finlay walk in. She recognised him instantly, and Nairne made the introductions.

'We're pleased to have you join us, Fyona,' said Finlay. He flicked a glance at Roag.

'Don't worry,' Roag told him. 'I wasn't dancing, though this is an excellent floor.'

'Late in the evenings, when the restaurant is closed and guests have retired to their rooms, you're welcome to use the dance floor,' Finlay said, offering a token to smooth their relationship rather than ignite further ructions.

Roag reacted to the unexpected gesture. 'I'd like that, thank you, Finlay. I wouldn't play music. I'd use earpieces to avoid disturbing anyone.'

'Ideal,' said Finlay. 'The night porter will be on duty at the reception desk. I'll tell him what we're planning. He won't disturb you, but let him know when you're going to use the dance floor. He'll turn the lights on in the function room.'

Murdo called to Finlay from the doorway. 'Excuse me, Finlay. Guests have arrived, if you'd care to greet them.'

'Yes.' Finlay smiled at the others and headed through with Murdo to the reception.

Nairne had given copies of the buffet menu selection to Fyona and Roag, and wanted their input and suggestions. 'Take the copies away with you, and we'll chat about the plan again tomorrow.'

'You mentioned that Lyle had helped with the Christmas ball buffet, supplying cakes and pastries,' Roag prompted Nairne.

'He did,' Nairne confirmed. 'Lyle has past experience in catering for balls. His recipes are excellent. He originally trained as a patisserie chef. His skills have made his tea shop a success. Not a man to be underestimated. Lyle even makes his own butter for some of his baking.'

'Using a butter churn?' Roag surmised.

'No, he whips it up himself using fresh double cream.'

'Draining the buttermilk off as it separates?' Fyona clarified.

'Exactly,' said Nairne.

Roag checked the time. 'I think I'll pop down to the tea shop in the main street. I read the menu online, but I'd like to meet Lyle and talk to him about his menus.'

Agreeing that Roag and Fyona would settle into the island, and come back to work at the castle in the morning, Nairne went back to the kitchen. Roag and Fyona went with him to collect their things.

'Any ideas for the buffet menu?' Roag said to Fyona.

'A few, but I'd like time to think it over.' She took her chef's jacket off, and her hat, sweeping strands of her silky hair back from her face. It was still secured in a ponytail.

He reacted to seeing her lovely face and those beautiful blue eyes of hers looking up at him.

'I have a couple of ideas for the cakes,' he said. 'We'll talk tomorrow.'

While Fyona hung up her jacket and picked up her bag, Roag headed out of the restaurant. He ran upstairs to get changed out of his chef's clothing.

Fyona wandered through to the reception, admiring the grandeur of the castle's decor.

Finlay saw her, and after she was introduced to Murdo, and spoke for a moment to Geneen, he made a suggestion.

'Would you like a quick tour of the castle?' Finlay said to Fyona.

'Thank you,' she said, eager to have a look around.

Finlay showed her the restaurant, and then as he was walking with her through to the function room, Roag came back downstairs. Wearing a clean shirt, tie and waistcoat with dark trousers, he looked more like a stylish businessman than a chef. He stepped over the braided rope, and gave an acknowledging nod to Finlay and Fyona on his way out to his car.

Driving away from the castle, Roag took the forest road down to the harbour and the main street. The sea glistened along the shore, and there was a feeling of summer and fun in the air. But he found his thoughts drifting to Fyona. Neither of them had seen each other's full ability in the castle kitchen. But he sensed that she'd be ready with her ideas the following day, and he planned to be equally ready.

He pulled up outside the tea shop in the main street, and as he stepped out of his car he noticed the vintage dress shop.

Skye and Holly were working on the ball gowns, hand stitching the dresses and using their sewing machines.

Skye noticed the sleek and expensive red car through the window, and the tall, handsome, well–dressed man step out. 'I think Roag is heading our way.'

Holly stopped sewing and glanced at him approaching.

He walked in and introduced himself. 'I'm Roag. I wondered if I could talk to you for a few minutes?'

'Yes, I'm Skye, and this is my sister, Holly.'

'I recognised you from the cover of the magazine,' he said to Skye. 'And I saw your pictures on the shop's website,' he added to Holly, making it clear he knew about their business.

Skye stood up from working at her sewing machine. Roag was as tall as Innis, and had the same type of quality that made the shop feel smaller when he was in it.

Roag looked around. 'This is a lovely shop.'

'Thank you,' said Holly, coming over to chat to him too.

He noticed the rails of dresses, and then a pinstripe shirt caught his eye.

'We sell mainly dresses,' Holly told him, seeing his interest. 'But sometimes items of menswear are included in the bundles of dresses we buy.'

'Fyona said she bought a swimsuit and a ball gown,' he revealed.

'Yes, we sell the odd extra items that are part of the bundle purchases,' Holly explained.

He couldn't resist checking out the classic shirt. 'It doesn't even look like it's been worn.'

'Sometimes items have been stored in wardrobes and never worn, or worn once,' said Skye. 'I'm sure there was a silk back waistcoat that came in with the shirt delivery. Yes, here it is.' She unhooked it from a rail where it was hidden by the ball gowns.

'It's not unlike the waistcoat you're wearing,' Holly observed.

'Except it's new and not vintage.' He felt the quality of the waistcoat. 'I like this.' It was charcoal herringbone and grey silk.

'Try it on in the changing room,' Skye suggested. 'Try the shirt on too if you want.'

Roag nodded and took the waistcoat and shirt into the changing room.

Skye and Holly spoke in whispers as he stripped off and put the shirt on.

'He seems very nice,' Holly whispered.

'Double–handsome too,' Skye said with a giggle.

Holly hurried over to another rail. 'I think we still have that brocade waistcoat.' She found it and held it up. The front was deep red brocade, with a satin back that matched the colour of the brocade.

Skye checked it for flaws. 'It's maybe been worn once,' she estimated, and then called through to Roag. 'Would you be interested in a vintage brocade waistcoat, suitable for evening wear? It's a few shades darker than your car.'

Roag pulled the curtain back, keen to see it. He was wearing the pinstripe shirt but hadn't yet buttoned it up, revealing a strip of his lean–muscled chest and six–pack.

Innis had seen Roag's car and watched him disappear into the vintage dress shop. Unable to settle, wondering what he was up to, he left Rosabel and Primrose to tend to the cake shop.

When Innis walked in he was taken aback seeing Roag standing there exposing his chest and being fussed over by Skye.

'I think one of the shirt buttons is a dangler,' Skye said to Roag, unaware that Innis was watching. 'I'll sew the button on properly for you.'

Holly smiled tightly at Innis. 'Skye, Innis is here.'

Skye whirled around and saw the unsmiling expression on her fiancé's face. 'Innis! I was just helping Roag try on a shirt.'

'It might help if he actually buttoned it up to see if it fits.' Innis' deep voice resonated in the shop.

Roag didn't flinch, but buttoned up the shirt. 'It fits nicely. I'll take it. And I'd like to try on the waistcoats.' He smiled at Innis. 'Good to see you again.' Then he stepped back into the changing room and pulled the curtain while he put the red waistcoat on.

Skye went over to Innis, gauging his reaction. Clearly he was miffed that Roag was in the shop.

Seeing Skye smiling at him, Innis felt the tension in his heart melt. He wasn't overly jealous, just protective of her.

'I only came in to chat about the cakes for the wedding and ball buffet,' Roag said from behind the curtain. 'But these waistcoats and shirt are hard to resist.' He pulled back the curtain and was wearing his own shirt and the brocade waistcoat. 'I really like this. I'll take it, and the shirt.' He handed the shirt to Skye. 'I would appreciate it if you'd sew the button on for me.'

Skye took the shirt off him. 'I'll do that right now.' She went over to her sewing machine where she had needles and white thread and began to stitch the button on.

Innis stood where he was, unwilling to leave just yet.

Holly sensed the tension bubbling under the surface of pleasantries. 'I'll put the kettle on for tea. Would you like a cup?' she said to Innis.

'Yes, thank you,' came the reply from behind the curtain.

Skye tried not to giggle.

Innis shook his head.

Roag finally pulled the curtain back to show that he was wearing the grey waistcoat. 'I'll take both waistcoats and the shirt.' Then he disappeared again to take the grey waistcoat off and put his own one back on.

Holly busied herself in the kitchen making four cups of tea.

Roag finally stepped out, wearing his original clothes and put the two waistcoats down on the counter.

'What do you take in your tea, Roag?' Holly called through to him.

'Just milk, thanks, Holly.'

She carried the tea tray through and sat it down. 'Sorry we don't have any cakes or biscuits to go with it.'

'I'll pop to Lyle's tea shop and pick up some cakes for us,' said Roag, making a move for the door.

'No, I've got plenty of cakes,' Innis insisted, and headed out.

'Any chocolate truffles?' Roag called after him. 'I'd like to try those.'

The look that Innis gave him as he glanced back took the heat out of the sunny day.

Finlay walked Fyona to her car after giving her the tour of the castle. The sun shone brightly in the cobalt blue sky.

'The castle and the gardens look lovely,' said Fyona, breathing in the warm summer's day.

'We're fortunate to be shielded by the outlying islands. And the Gulf Stream with its warm winds help to create a temperate climate for the island.'

'I plan to make the most of it while I'm here.' Fyona got ready to leave. 'I'm going to take a drive around the estate and to thistle loch.' She got into her car.

'See you tomorrow.' Finlay waved her off and went back into the castle.

Fyona opened the car window, letting the warm breeze blow in as she drove away from the castle and along a road through the forest that took her to thistle loch.

The calm surface glinted in the sunlight, and as she got closer, she parked her car, stepped out and walked along the edge that was fringed with wildflowers and grass. And thistles. The Scottish thistles were growing in abundance. The varying shades of the purple and lilac contrasted with the colourful wildflowers that sprinkled the area with pretty pink, yellow and blue tones. She appeared to be the only person there. Farmhouses and cottages dotted the countryside in the distance.

Apart from admiring the scenery, feeling the calmness of the loch, and the warmth of the sun, she was looking for ideas for the wedding cake. Designs for the icing.

Unknown to Fyona, stargazer cottage was hidden somewhere in the trees, where Merrilees was busy writing her novel.

Merrilees finished writing another key scene in her novel, sitting outside under a garden umbrella. Her laptop was set on a garden table and she relaxed back on her cushioned chair, easing the tension from her shoulders.

Time for afternoon tea. The thought had just entered her mind when Skye phoned. Her smiling face beamed out at Merrilees. The call was on speaker.

'Do you have five minutes to chat? I don't want to disturb you if you're writing.'

'It's okay, I've stopped for a cup of tea.' She went into the kitchen and started making it while taking the call.

'Roag is here at the shop.' Skye turned the phone to show him eating a chocolate truffle. 'He popped in to chat about the wedding buffet menu. To see what flavours we like. Ailsa is here too, and Holly and Innis.'

Skye and Holly had invited Ailsa to join them. They'd closed their shops during the tea break chat. Innis stayed to have tea, while Rosabel and Primrose tended to the cake shop.

Taking a sip of his tea, Roag then spoke to Merrilees. 'I loved the feature you wrote. It was excellent, and the photos.'

'I'm glad you liked it,' said Merrilees.

Roag got straight to the point. 'I had a meeting with Nairne and Fyona today about the buffet menus. We're meeting again in the morning to discuss ideas. I'll work on the menus this evening, and it would help if I knew your particular tastes.'

'For the cakes or savouries?' said Merrilees.

'Let's start with the savouries. Skye and Ailsa like puff pastries with cheese, tomato and sausage rolls. Haggis vol–au–vents too.'

'These suit my tastes, especially the cheese pastries.'

Roag took a mental note of this and moved on to the cake options. 'Traditional cakes get the thumbs up and tie in nicely with the theme of the wedding. Victoria sponge cake with whipped cream and jam. Chocolate cake filled with chocolate buttercream. Chocolate cake covered with chocolate ganache. Carrot cake. And lemon drizzle cake.'

'Five of my favourites, especially the Victoria sponge and the chocolate cakes,' said Merrilees.

'Any other cakes you all like?' Roag threw the question out to all of them.

'I enjoy vanilla and buttercream,' said Ailsa.

'Anything with chocolate,' Skye added.

'I make white cake for my restaurant. It's popular,' said Roag. 'I thought it would be ideal for the wedding and the ball.

'Oh, yes,' said Skye. 'I'd like that.'

The others agreed.

'I'm going to talk to Lyle in the tea shop,' Roag told them. 'He's making some of the cakes. Brodrick is supplying various flavours of ice cream.' He glanced at Innis. 'I've yet to discuss with Innis what he's making, but I assume it'll include your delicious truffles and other cakes.'

Innis nodded. 'Once I see what's going to be on the buffet menu, I'll decide what to include. Certainly a chocolate cake, or cupcakes.'

'And your chocolate scones,' Skye chimed–in.

'Sounds great,' Roag concluded. 'Well, this gives me plenty of information about your tastes,' he said to all of them, including Merrilees. 'I'll not keep you back from your work any longer.'

The impromptu meeting was over, and Roag picked up his bag containing the shirt and waistcoats, smiled and headed out. He put the bag in his car and then went over to the tea shop.

'We'll speak soon,' Skye said to Merrilees, waving at her.

'Yes.' Merrilees finished making her tea and carried it out to the garden and sat down. She sipped her tea and gazed out into the far distance, over the garden's lush greenery and flowers, towards the trees and countryside beyond, relaxing before starting to write again.

Lyle was pleasantly surprised when Roag walked into the tea shop and introduced himself.

'I was in the vintage dress shop, talking to the brides, and Holly, about the wedding buffet,' Roag explained. 'Innis was there too, and I wanted to talk to you about your menus, especially the cakes you'll be supplying.'

Lyle gestured to the cakes on display in his glass cabinets, and handed him a menu.

The tea shop was fairly busy with customers, but it always was these days, so he was happy to chat to Roag and made him welcome.

'Can I offer you a cup of tea and a tasting of some of the cakes and pastries?'

'If you've time. I see you're busy. I know what it's like when someone comes into my restaurant and wants a natter.'

'Ach, take a seat through in the kitchen. We'll get a chance to talk there and I'll show you some of the things I have in mind. I've made a list of what I think would be tasty, and appropriate for the wedding buffet.'

Roag followed him through to the kitchen. 'You've got a great tea shop. I like the atmosphere and the decor. A classy mix of traditional and modern.'

'Thanks, and now I've extended the premises upstairs. I'll show you later.'

Roag sat down at the table in the kitchen where Lyle kept his notes.

'But I'm keen to offer things for the summer ball,' said Lyle. 'I understand that the wedding gets priority, and Nairne is concentrating mainly on that. But folk are buying ball gowns galore from the vintage dress shop. Holly's stitching extra to meet demand. So is Skye. I want to add items that will boost the summer ball buffet. Brodrick's ice cream certainly will. But I

137

was thinking of classic cakes — lemon drizzle, Victoria sponge, chocolate cake, as I'm sure you've already got planned.'

'Yes, but we need to decide on who supplies what.' Roag skim–read Lyle's list. 'I see you've included white cake.'

'Do you want to try a piece?' Lyle offered.

'I certainly do. It's one of my favourites, and difficult to get just right.'

'I have my own recipe. I'll be back in a minute.' Lyle went through to the display, cut a piece and brought it back in time to pour Roag a cup of tea to go with it.

'This is perfect,' Roag mumbled, tasting a forkful. 'And white, not off–white or cream, which some white sponges are.'

Lyle looked pleased. 'I'll show you my recipe.'

While staff tended to the tea shop customers, Lyle took a well–earned break for tea and white cake with Roag.

'Have you met Fyona yet?' said Roag.

'No, but I've heard all about her being an expert in patisserie. Holly says she bought a ball gown today in the dress shop.'

Roag nodded. 'I've bought two waistcoats and a shirt from the shop.'

Lyle laughed, and they discussed the menus. And then something else that Roag wanted to plan.

'Don't go muddying the water with this,' Roag urged Lyle. 'I want to get the buffet menu sorted out before I discuss my plan with Nairne.'

'I can keep a secret.' Lyle ate his cake while Roag revealed his plan.

# CHAPTER TEN

'I'm helping Nairne with the buffet for the weddings and the summer ball,' Roag said to Lyle. 'But the main reason I'm here is to oversee the running of the castle while Finlay, Ean and Innis are away on honeymoon. I promised the laird that I'd do my utmost to ensure that the hotel guests were happy and enjoyed their stay. I aim to keep that promise.'

Lyle nodded, taking this in, and drank his tea as Roag continued.

'I've been looking at the castle's website since I agreed to do this, checking the news updates that show the dinner dances in the function room. They seem to be popular.'

'They are,' Lyle confirmed. 'Sometimes I supply cakes and pastries if Nairne is busy with other things.'

'So, here's what I'm planning. When it's Christmas or New Year, my restaurant is extra busy, then it takes a dip afterwards. But now I up my game, put on new menus, keep the buzz going afterwards.'

'I do the same. And not just at Christmas. Sometimes there are events on and the island becomes busy, or it's the summer, or an autumn fair. I change my menus after the busy days too. It keeps the tea shop thriving.'

'Well, I'd like to do the same after the excitement of the wedding and the summer ball are over,' said Roag. 'I'm planning to have one or two dance party nights at the castle for the guests, and make it available for those locally.'

'Dance party nights? Like the dinner dances in the function room?'

'With bells on. Waltzing, ballroom dancing and other popular dancing. A buffet rather than a dinner. A fun, but classy party atmosphere. Something special, and a delicious buffet.'

'That sounds great.'

'Nairne and his staff could handle this themselves, but I don't want to cause them more work when they've already been so busy with the preparations for the weddings. So I thought that I could help to cook the buffet, and get you involved, as you're involved with the wedding catering already.'

'I'm up for doing it,' Lyle agreed.

'By all accounts, the castle has become busier, due to publicity and the excellent food and facilities. With this great summer weather, I think it'll be even more popular, and holding special party nights could really boost the castle's popularity.'

'Are you thinking of staying on after Finlay and the others come home?'

'No, I'll be heading back to my restaurant in Glasgow. I've no plans to move to the island. Though I did consider opening a restaurant on the other side of the island a while ago.'

'So did I,' said Lyle. 'But I love my tea shop premises here in the main street.'

They continued to discuss menu ideas for the party buffets.

'Fyona will still be here, and I'm sure she'll help too,' said Roag.

'I haven't met her yet, but I've heard she's an expert in patisserie.'

'She's very talented. Totally different in style to me, but that's what we need. Different recipes, a variety of items on the menu.'

Lyle picked up on Roag's admiration for Fyona. 'You seem to like her.'

Roag smiled. 'She's lovely, but I'm not looking for a summer fling.'

'What about a permanent fling?'

'Ah, now that's a whole different topic. Right now, all my energies are focussed on the castle, and then getting back to my restaurant.'

'Is Fyona planning to stay on the island? I know she's looking after her aunt and uncle's cottage. Maybe she'll stay and continue working at the castle.'

'I don't know, but Nairne was talking to her today in the kitchen. She said she's concentrating on her career, and after the summer here on the island, she's planning to work in Glasgow or Edinburgh, and eventually open her own patisserie or tearoom.'

Fyona drove back down to the main street after enjoying exploring the area around the loch and taking pictures of the thistles.

Ideas for the wedding cake icing, and other recipes for the buffet, filled her thoughts. Tradition was the theme, she kept reminding herself. The castle was in the heart of everything too. Decorating the cake with white royal icing was at the core of the plans. She pictured adding white fondant thistles around the edges. Traditional. Scottish. Beautiful.

And she had another idea. Unsure if it would work, it was something she'd discuss with Nairne the next day.

The sea glistened in the late afternoon sun, and instead of driving to the cottage, she pulled up in the main street and went for a walk along the shore. Taking her shoes off and putting them in her bag, she enjoyed the feeling of the soft, warm sand, soothing and relaxing after the hectic day. She let her hair down from the tidy ponytail and shook it free. The fiery red lightened well in the summertime and she liked the highlighted effect it created.

'Hello, Fyona.'

She stopped and looked round to see Roag striding towards her. The only man down on the seashore wearing a shirt, tie and waistcoat. Her heart took a double hit — surprised that he was there, and how sexy handsome he was in the sunlight. Seeing him outdoors, not in his restaurant or in the castle, made her view him in the bright summer sun. Those blue–green eyes of his looked like the colours of the sea. His dark brown hair was highlighted in shades of molten bronze.

'Can I talk to you for a moment?' he said.

Without her shoes on, he was even taller than usual, and she looked up as she replied.

'Yes, I was just going for a walk along the shore.'

'Let's walk,' he suggested, and they fell into step as he accompanied her.

'I saw you when I came out of the tea shop,' he explained. 'The only young woman down the shore dressed smartly for business.'

She eyed his attire. 'You should talk.'

'At least we match.'

She relented, seeing his sensual lips give her a sexy smile.

'I was talking to Lyle about cakes for the buffet,' Roag explained. 'And I can thoroughly recommend his white cake.'

'I love white cake, so I must try it. I'm interested in seeing the tea shop.'

'Lyle's menu is excellent, and he was happy to share ideas for the buffet.'

'I'll pop into the tea shop soon.'

Roag broached on the subject of her plans. 'Lyle was wondering if you'll decide to stay on the island. I said that I overheard you telling Nairne that you're planning to work in Glasgow or Edinburgh. Maybe open your own tearoom one day.'

She sensed he was fishing for information, but she had nothing to hide. 'That's right. After my work here is done, I'm leaving the island. I'll try to find a suitable position with a hotel or restaurant. As for the tearoom, I've been saving, and aim to start small, leasing a wee shop, and turning it into a tearoom. If it works, I'll then move to larger premises.'

'That sounds like a sensible business plan.'

'I flat share in Glasgow, and I'm not averse to moving to Edinburgh. It'll depend on where I find a suitable position after I go back home to the city.'

'I'll be heading back to run my restaurant in Glasgow,' said Roag.

Fyona gazed out at the sea as the late afternoon sun cast a golden glow over the shore. 'The island is beautiful,' she said wistfully. 'I went to thistle loch earlier. It was so relaxing and the scenery is idyllic. I took photos of the thistles. I'm thinking of using them as part of the design for the wedding cake icing. White fondant thistles.'

'Traditional, classic.'

'Exactly. I've a few other ideas that I'll work on this evening. One idea for the top of the wedding cake...I'm not too sure about.'

'Want to run it by me?' he offered.

'I've made and decorated wedding cakes before. This is the first cake where the couples will be living in the castle where they're getting married. I wondered if I should add a tasteful castle look to the top of the cake. Not a topper,' she clarified. 'Two turrets made from white fondant icing incorporated into the top layer of the cake.'

Roag considered this, and then nodded. 'The cake is going to be shown on the castle's website. It is a unique opportunity to create a castle theme.'

'But not make the cake into a castle. A nod to the castle, while keeping the whole cake traditional, classic white icing, and adding the white thistles. No sparkles or falderals.'

'I think that would be great.'

'I'll draw a few sketches tonight to show to Nairne. I think he'll at least approve of the fondant flowers being thistles.' She glanced at Roag. 'Any ideas you've come up with?'

'I spoke to Skye, Ailsa and Merrilees about their favourite cakes and flavours.' He listed the cakes they liked. 'Chocolate cake, Victoria sponge, carrot cake

145

and lemon drizzle came out tops. I mentioned that I make white cake for my restaurant and they liked that idea.'

'All popular classics.'

'Yes. But I was thinking we could make miniature versions of these, cupcake size, to serve at the buffet,' he said.

'That's what I was thinking — mini cakes. They work so well for buffets.'

'Okay, we're in agreement so far.'

'I'd also like to suggest a sheet cake. A large, rectangular, single layer cake. A vanilla sponge cake mix. I'll cover it with white icing. Easy to cut and serve, and it'll offer an alternative to the wedding cake for those that don't want fruit cake.'

Roag nodded. 'Great suggestion.'

Fyona turned around and started to walk back along the shore. Roag walked beside her, revealing the plan he'd told to Lyle.

'Dance party nights sound wonderful,' she said. 'And you're right about things taking a dip after all the excitement of the weddings and the summer ball. This would keep the pot boiling.'

'Would you be up for helping me if Nairne, Finlay and the others agree to this?'

'I would. When would you plan to hold the first one?'

'Soon after the wedding and summer ball. Instead of the next scheduled dinner dance, I'd like to make the evening more like another ball with a buffet. Guests would dress up, waltz around the dance floor.'

'It sounds exciting, and romantic.' She swept her hair back from her face as she smiled at him.

His heart took a hit this time, seeing her beauty shine in the golden light.

She sighed heavily. 'I suppose I'll have to force myself to buy another dress from the vintage dress shop,' she joked with him. 'Though it won't need to be a ball gown. An evening dress would do fine for waltzing at the party night.'

Roag fought the urge to tell her that whatever she wore she'd look beautiful. But he didn't want to overstep.

They'd arrived back to where they'd started, and Fyona headed up to the shore to where she'd parked her car.

'It's been quite a day,' she said, planning to go and relax at the cottage, and prepare the sketches for the cakes.

'I'll see you in the morning, Fyona.' Roag smiled and walked away to his car.

They drove off in the same direction for a moment, and then Fyona headed for the cottage, while Roag's red car continued along the harbour road and up towards the forest.

The feelings that charged through him took him aback. He hadn't felt like this in a long time, not since he'd met and become involved with his last dance partner. And even then, the intensity now was much stronger. He didn't believe in love at first sight. Attraction yes, but he'd be lying to himself if he denied that Fyona stirred him to the core. Turning on the music in his car, he hoped it would drum out the thoughts that played in his mind. Romance with Fyona would never work. He warned himself not to get involved, not to be the troublemaker his cousins and others thought of him. And maybe rightly so, in the past. A past long gone.

It was his own fault for approaching Fyona when she was clearly walking along the shore to relax. Now he had the images of her hair, like fiery gold, framing her lovely face, as she smiled at him.

He turned the music up as the fading light flickered through the trees, shining through the windows like copper fireflies.

As he drove towards the castle, shaded in the amber glow, he flicked the music off, and parked outside in a private bay.

The reception was so busy that his arrival went unnoticed by Murdo, Geneen and Finlay as they tended to the guests.

Stepping over the rope across the staircase, he hurried up to the turret and closed the door. The windows were still open, and he went over to take in the view of the sea shimmering in the distance. The sunlight was taking its time to fade, and he wished it was already midnight so he could burn off his excess energy on the dance floor.

Instead, he noted down the ideas he had for the buffet menu to show to Nairne in the morning.

Twilight finally cast shadows through the turret, and he flicked a lamp on as he continued to make notes. Not just about the buffet menu, but ideas for the dance parties, topics to discuss with Nairne.

Hunger pangs eventually reminded him that he should have dinner. He was tempted to order something to be brought up, then changed his mind, and headed downstairs to serve himself in the kitchen.

The delicious scent of the food increased his appetite, and Nairne noted his arrival.

'Help yourself to whatever you want for your dinner, Roag.'

'Thank you, Nairne.'

Roag was about to plate a roast dinner for himself when he heard Innis' voice coming from the other side of the kitchen. He went over and saw Innis packing dark, milk and white chocolates into boxes, and talking to one of Nairne's assistant chefs.

'There's a spare bag of chocolate chips that you can use,' Innis said to the assistant. And then Innis glanced at Roag, seeing him approach.

'It's a nice set–up you've got here for your chocolatier work,' Roag told him. Shelves were stacked with boxes ready to be filled with chocolates, and the facility had a butler sink, ovens and a worktop where Innis made his specialist chocolates. Everything gleamed under the lights, and the air was rich with the aroma of chocolate, vanilla, butterscotch and other flavours.

'Are you into chocolatier work yourself?'

'I dabble, but nothing like this,' Roag said with admiration.

Murdo came hurrying in and spoke to Innis. 'Skye has arrived with some more of her things. Staff are helping her carry them upstairs.'

'I'll be right there,' Innis told Murdo. He wiped his hands. 'Skye is starting to move her belongings into my suite so everything is ready for when we get back from our honeymoon.' Then he hurried away.

Roag served himself dinner and sat at a small table out of the way to eat it, taking in the busy but efficient running of the kitchen.

After dinner, Fyona finished the sketches for the thistle design and the turrets. She put them in her bag ready to take with her to the castle in the morning.

Some of her belongings needed organised, and she went through to the bedroom to tidy them away.

While sorting the last of her things, she found the portable ballet barre she'd brought with her. It was lightweight, freestanding, easy to erect, and she set it up in the bedroom. Daily ballet movements and stretches kept her limber and helped ease any tension from her working day.

Changing into a pair of leggings and a comfy top, she practised one of her barre routines from her ballet days, feeling the benefit of it. The flexibility, strength, posture and balance.

Fyona loved her ballet from the past and enjoyed exercising, using her dance methods in the comfort of the cottage. Holding gently on to the barre, she began with plié movements.

It only took ten minutes, and afterwards, she wandered outside into the garden to breathe in the calming night air and gaze up at the stars glittering in the sky.

She thought about Roag, and wondered if he would stay on the island. And would she? But they both seemed determined to leave and go back to the mainland.

Gazing up at the vast sky, she saw the North Star, and made a wish, hoping it would come true, and help her to find her own way back home, to where she'd find true love and happiness, wherever that would be.

Innis had added another wardrobe to the large bedroom in his sumptuous suite in the castle.

Skye hung up the last dress she'd unpacked from the bags she'd brought with her. She stepped back and closed the wardrobe doors.

'I can officially say that I now have more of my things here in the castle than I have left at home in the cottage,' Skye announced with a flourish.

Innis stood in the open doorway, watching her, his imposing stature almost filling it. Inclined to keep his thoughts to himself, he understood why he'd earned the label of being a lone wolf who rationed his smiles.

Since Skye gave him her heart, the sweetest he'd ever known, and accepted his proposal, he sensed that he had become a better man. And all because of her. The mercurial woman he used to fool himself into believing wasn't his type. When deep in the night he knew she was his perfect match.

Any previous hesitation in dating her was due to nothing more than him heeding the warnings he'd been given by others. *Don't break her heart.* He'd unintentionally broken a few in his time, but Skye's heart was safe now with him.

Skye ran over to him, and on her tiptoes kissed him and ruffled his black chef's jacket. 'What's that serious face for? Are you worried my vintage clothes will overtake the bedroom and you'll be smothered in frivolous frou–frou?'

His deep thoughts lingered longer than the vivacious Skye was prepared to wait for a reply.

'Are you concerned you'll wake up in the middle of the night and have to fight your way through the fashion decades from the thirties Art Deco to the dazzling disco era?'

'I'd fight through anything just as long as I'm with you.' His deep voice resonated in the bedroom.

Skye wrapped herself around him, and smiled, causing him to smile too.

'Phew! It's a warm night. I should've opened the windows in the living room.' She ran through, opened them wide, and breathed in the air that wafted up from the shore.

Innis came over and stood behind her, wrapping his strong arms around her. She leaned back against his broad chest.

'Look at the thousands of stars sparkling in the sky.' She gazed out the window at the sky arching over the forest and the sea.

Innis pulled her even closer and murmured lovingly to her. 'You make my world sparkle.'

She turned her head and her soft lips welcomed his sensual kisses.

Skye was looking forward to the wedding, and the honeymoon, but most of all to coming home to the castle to start her married life with Innis.

# CHAPTER ELEVEN

The grandfather clock in the castle's reception showed that it was well after midnight.

The night porter manned the front desk. He was so steeped in reading a book, he didn't notice Roag walking down the stairs and deftly stepping over the cord.

Roag's footsteps were unheard as he stepped on to the tartan carpet. No one else was around. The restaurant was closed for the evening, and the guests had retired to their rooms. Deciding not to disturb the porter from his reading, Roag headed towards the function room.

The doors were open, and the room was cast in shadows and light from the nightglow shining through the patio doors, illuminating the dance floor in bands of silver moonlight.

Everything around it was cast in semi–darkness. The atmosphere reminded Roag of stage performances he'd given when he toured theatres, performing as part of a dance show tour. The stages were lit for specific effects, such as a fairytale forest. Without the burden of theatrical scenery, the atmosphere on stage was created from the lighting, music, the costumes, and the ability of the dancers to perform for the audiences.

Looking out through the glass doors, here he was in a wonderful castle, seeing the trees silhouetted at the edge of the forest. Ambient light shone through from the reception, doubling up with the nightglow pouring in. The crystals in the chandeliers sparkled like starlight.

He could've asked the porter to switch the lights on, or done it himself, but he preferred the atmospheric privacy where he could perform. He had the large dance floor all to himself. There was something wonderfully exciting about dancing in the silvery shadows.

To the untrained eye, Roag's appearance was that of a well–dressed guest. A long–sleeve white shirt, unbuttoned at the neck, tucked into the waist of his stylish black trousers. On closer inspection, these were part of his dancewear. The shirt looked like crisp cotton, but was made from fabric with stretch in it. As were the trousers. He could dance, stretch, spin, do all sorts of movements unrestricted by his clothing. His black, shiny shoes looked traditional, but felt soft as butter.

He'd brought a suitcase of dance clothes with him, including a classic suit for ballroom dancing. The stretch in the fabrics provided ease of movement, and a stylish appearance.

His phone was tucked into his trouser pocket, loaded up with music, and he started playing the first song, a dramatic ballad, hearing it via the wireless earphones.

Having done his warm up stretches upstairs in the turret, he was ready to dance.

Roag remembered the feeling of the performance, not only the dance movements. Combining the two created the spark needed to entertain an audience, and enjoy himself. There was no audience here, but in his mind were the sights and scents of the theatres, forged deep in his memories of times long gone that he would never forget.

The steps were light and fast, travelling across the floor in a swift diagonal. With a single but powerful leap in the air, he turned around and repeated the steps in the opposite direction.

He didn't realise that he was smiling until he was halfway through the song and the routine.

The joy of dancing was in his heart. He'd left the dance world behind, but his love of dancing hadn't faded, and shone as brightly as the well–lit stages where he used to perform.

The first song finished and the next one began, merging musically.

Roag danced another routine, more sexy in style, a mix of classic ballroom, modern stage, ballet moves and pirouettes that surprised him in their perfect balance.

He hadn't lost his touch. Hopefully he never would. If anything, he'd gained inner strength and power from his long working hours, that were at times both mentally and physically challenging.

Roag had always been up for a challenge. That was one of the main reasons he'd accepted the laird's offer to help run the castle. And the reason he couldn't get Fyona out of his thoughts. Feisty Fyona was a challenge.

He concentrated again on his routine.

It felt marvellous to dance on the well–sprung floor, having it all to himself.

Finally, the song list finished, and he ended with a flair, extending his strong arms out to the side and spinning to a close.

The grandfather clock had moved on one hour as Roag headed back up the stairs. The night porter was having a cup of tea in the reception and still reading his book, and never noticed the stealthy dancer disappear upstairs.

Roag planned to tell Finlay in the morning that he'd used the function room to practise his dancing.

Back in his tower, Roag stripped off and showered.

Stepping out of the shower, his well–exercised muscles gleaming wet, he dried himself and put on a pair of red silk boxers. He wandered through to the bedroom, opened the window wide and breathed in the heady scent from the trees that edged the forest. The warm night air drifting in reminded him of past summers at the castle.

He could still feel the energy from the dancing pulsing through him, and stood there unwinding, pushing his damp hair back from his face.

Fyona had slept well, and drove along the harbour road, heading to the castle. The sea glistened in the morning sunlight, and she was all set for her meeting with Nairne.

The sea air blew in through the open window, and was replaced by the scent of the greenery from the forest as she approached the castle's estate.

The castle's gardens bloomed with flowers, and Skye had mentioned to her that the three bridal bouquets would be made on the day of the weddings, using freshly picked flowers from the gardens and tied with white ribbons.

Fyona parked her car and headed into the castle. The reception was buzzing with chatter. Geneen and Murdo were behind the desk, and Nairne, Finlay and Ean were there too. They were watching the computer screen. Clearly something was going on, and she could only surmise from the snippets of the overlapping comments that Roag was at the heart of the matter.

'Look at him leaping up and twirling across the floor...' said Geneen.

'Dancing in the dark...' Murdo sounded surprised.

'Roag's a fine dancer...' Nairne remarked.

'I told him he could use the function room, but he should've spoken to the night porter...' said Finlay.

'Are you going to tell Roag he was caught on the security cameras?' Ean added.

Geneen noticed Fyona and waved her over to view the footage on the computer. 'Roag was dancing in the midnight hours. Come and have a peek.'

Fyona went over and watched the recording, blinking as she saw his powerful performance. She'd seen the online videos from his past, but knowing that he'd given up dancing, she somehow expected he'd be less impressive. But Roag appeared to have upped his game.

'Wow! He's fit,' Fyona said, letting slip her reaction.

The others smiled at Fyona, and starting to blush, she quickly tried to explain. 'What I mean is, for a man that has given up dancing, his performance is great.'

Roag came down the stairs in time to hear Fyona praising his dancing. From the top of the staircase he'd heard them talking, and surmised that he was the cause of the furore.

'You've been caught on the function room's security camera,' Finlay told him.

Roag walked up to have a look at the video, smiling as he saw what the fuss was about.

'I told you to tell the night porter that you were there,' Finlay said to him. 'It wasn't just so he could turn on the lights, but to turn off the cameras.'

'I didn't want to disturb him when he was working at reception,' said Roag. 'There seemed to be no need.'

'You'll have to add music to the video when you put it up on the castle's website,' Murdo joked with Finlay.

'Guests will want dance lessons from Roag for the summer ball when they see his performance,' Nairne added, joining in the joke.

'I'll book a ballroom dance lesson from you, Roag,' said Ean. 'Ailsa and I need to practise our first waltz for the wedding.'

Roag smiled, knowing they were winding him up. 'Sorry, I don't have a dance partner to help me demonstrate the ballroom dancing.'

Geneen spoke up. 'Fyona is a dancer.' She smiled at Fyona. 'Nettie told us at the knitting bee that you trained in ballet and modern stage dancing.'

'I didn't know you were a dancer,' Roag sounded surprised as he looked at Fyona.

'I used to take lessons when I was a wee girl, but I stopped to concentrate on my patisserie training,' Fyona explained.

'Do you still practise?' said Roag.

'I practise my ballet moves. I use my ballet barre. I brought it with me. But it's only to keep me supple and strong. I don't dance these days.'

Roag's eyes widened. 'You have a ballet barre?'

'A portable one. Nothing fancy.' She saw Roag looking at her with extra interest. She wasn't sure she liked this. She wasn't convinced she didn't.

Geneen and Murdo exchanged a glance, sensing a spark between Roag and Fyona. The others noticed too.

Fyona felt it intensely, and hoped to hide it behind a professional smile.

'I'll get ready for our meeting. I've brought sketches of icing ideas for the wedding cake,' Fyona said to Nairne, and walked away to the kitchen.

Nairne went with her, eager to see these.

Roag wanted to join them, but was still caught in the conversation about his dancing.

'Ailsa mentioned that she's slightly nervous about dancing our first waltz at the wedding,' said Ean. 'Especially as it's going to be on the video. We're hiring someone to film the whole event.'

'Maybe we could all use some ballroom waltz lessons,' Finlay agreed. 'I think Merrilees would like that. I know that we can dance, but for the wedding waltz, it would be great to dance something special.' He looked at Roag.

'I'd be happy to give you a lesson in waltzing,' said Roag.

A group of guests coming out of the restaurant after having breakfast overheard him.

'Dance lessons!' exclaimed one of the ladies. 'Can I put my name down for those?'

'I'd like to join in too,' said another guest.

'Count me in as well,' another added.

Finlay glanced at Ean and Roag, and then spoke to the guests. 'We weren't actually planning to have ballroom dance lessons at the castle.'

The disappointment showed on the guests' faces.

'I've always wanted to learn how to waltz well,' a guest said. 'The dance floor in the castle is lovely.'

'We'll talk to Roag and see if we can organise something,' said Finlay. 'A ballroom dance lesson in the function room.'

Roag smiled tightly. He didn't mind giving private lessons to the three couples for the wedding waltzes. But he hadn't planned on teaching the guests.

As the guests moved on, Roag shook his head. 'I don't teach dancing.'

'Surely you could give a few basic tips on waltzing,' Finlay reasoned.

'Okay,' Roag agreed, wondering if Fyona would be willing to partner up with him to demonstrate how to waltz around the dance floor.


Merrilees was in the vintage dress shop to take pictures of the three wedding dresses so that she could use these for the feature in the fashion magazine.

Skye, Holly and Ailsa were there.

'The magazine want me to take pictures of the dresses hanging on the rails, showing some of the vintage shop in the background,' Merrilees told them. 'Celia is planning to have a pre–loved theme for the issue. It'll be published in the next edition of the magazine, but she's going to put it up as a fashion news feature on their website after the weddings.' They all knew Celia from a fashion show that had been held at the castle.

Skye and Holly organised the dresses on the rails, and Ailsa helped sort out the background while Merrilees peered through the camera.

'Ailsa's dress looks lovely,' said Merrilees, taking pictures of it. 'Now, can you hang Skye's dress up?'

Merrilees had just finished photographing all three dresses when a message came through on her phone from Finlay. She smiled when she saw that he'd sent her a copy of the video showing Roag dancing in the function room at night.

'Take a look at this,' Merrilees said to them.

Skye, Holly and Ailsa watched him dancing.

'When did Roag do this performance?' said Holly.

'Last night. The security cameras filmed him,' Merrilees explained from Finlay's message.

Merrilees phoned Finlay. 'I'm at the vintage dress shop. Skye, Holly and Ailsa are watching the video too.'

Finlay explained about Roag's dancing, and wondered if she'd be interested in the waltz lesson.

Merrilees told the others, and then spoke to Finlay. 'I would. And Skye and Ailsa want to go to the dance

161

lesson. Holly wants to go too, and bring Lyle. Would that be okay?'

'Yes,' Finlay agreed. 'And Roag hopes that Fyona will be his partner to demonstrate the waltz. She has a background in dancing.' He mentioned the details.

After the call, Merrilees discussed this with the others. Merrilees had attended Scottish Highland and country dance classes on the island when she was a young girl, but she'd never done ballet or modern stage dancing.

'Nettie said that Fyona still practises her ballet, especially the stretching. She certainly had a fit and trim figure when she tried on her swimsuit and her dress,' said Holly.

'I've always wanted to try a ballet routine,' Skye added excitedly, lifting her arms up and attempting a twirl.

They laughed as she twirled into Innis as he walked into the shop, bringing them a bag of fresh baked scones for their morning tea break.

Skye giggled as he caught her. 'I'm practising my ballet moves.'

Innis listened as they told him all the gossip.

'I know you're really good at waltzing and dancing at the ceilidhs,' Skye said to him. 'But I'd like to learn a special waltz for the wedding and the ball.'

Seeing Skye's enthusiasm, and the smiling faces of Ailsa and Merrilees, Innis agreed to go.

Fyona sat with Nairne and Roag in the kitchen discussing the buffet menus. She showed them the sketches of the fondant thistles for the wedding cake.

'The sketches are rough, but it'll give you an idea of the size and design of the thistles,' said Fyona. 'I'll ice four thistles around the side of the bottom tier. Three on the second, and two on the top tier.'

'The thistles would be perfect,' Nairne told her.

Roag admired her sketches. 'These are lovely designs.'

Fyona then showed Nairne the design for the turrets.

'Oh, yes,' Nairne said, sounding keen. 'Perfect for a castle wedding. And your design is classy.'

Fyona smiled. 'I'll start work on icing the wedding cake today.'

The sheet cake and other suggestions were agreed on for the buffet.

Nairne took the list of items and Fyona's sketches to confirm these with Finlay and Ean.

Roag and Fyona started to bake cakes ready for the current lunch menu.

Those gorgeous eyes of his glanced over at her a few times, causing all sorts of thoughts to run through her mind. Stop it! She scolded herself. Since first meeting him she'd known the effect a man so handsome could have on her, and on most women. Her reaction wasn't unusual. But she needed to focus on her work, not Roag's kissable lips when he spoke to her.

Carrying a tray of cupcakes to the oven, he cast a comment to her. 'I'd like to talk to you later, in private.'

The way he said *private* hinted at personal rather than business, and a shiver of anticipation went through her. 'About what?' she said to his retreating figure.

He put the tray of cakes in the oven, and came back to her. 'Being my ballroom partner.'

'For the waltz lesson?'

'No, to team up with me and go on a dance tour,' he teased her. 'Take the dancing world by storm.'

His sexy lips couldn't hold back his smile.

'Be careful,' she warned him. 'I love a challenge.' And resisting Roag for the next few weeks was going to be a secret challenge.

'I love a challenge too,' he countered. His mind fought against the attraction he felt for her. On one hand, he wanted to ask her to have dinner with him. Make his feelings known. But playing with fire was expected of him, and he was determined not to live up to his roguish reputation.

'On the dance floor, or the kitchen?' she shot back at him.

In that moment, he admired her attitude, seeing the defiant look in those blue eyes of hers as she gazed up at him.

'Both, when it comes to you,' he said. This was true.

Thinking he was daring her, she nodded her acceptance. 'Let's start with the kitchen.'

He picked up a hand whisk and held it as if wielding a short sword. 'Daggers at dawn?' He checked the time. It was an hour until the lunches began in the restaurant. 'Correction, at midday.'

Fyona took him aback as she tipped the long spatula she was using against his whisk. 'Game on.'

'Want to bake Victoria sponges or white cakes?' he suggested.

'White cakes.' Her game face was smiling while challenging Roag.

His blood stirred, enjoying her playfulness and baking skill.

He selected what he needed. They'd agreed that both their cakes would be about the size of a Victoria sponge.

While he worked, Roag watched her deftly measure out cake flour, sugar and other ingredients and begin making a sponge cake. Fyona worked fast, though this seemed to be her natural speed rather than hurrying to beat him.

Fyona glanced surreptitiously at Roag. His methods were measured, making hers look hasty, but this had always been her style.

They both separated their eggs, using only the egg whites for the cake mix.

'Can I have your egg yolks?' Nairne said, seeing what they were up to, and planning to use them for his quiche.

'Yes, we're making white cakes,' said Roag.

'I can see that.' Nairne smiled. 'It'll save me making lemon drizzle cake for the lunch menu. This will be today's cake special.'

'Mine will be ready in time,' Roag assured him in case Nairne was comparing their swiftness of skills.

Fyona concentrated on her baking, letting them chat, and added clear vanilla extract to her mixing bowl. Soon she was pouring the mixture into two cake tins, popping them into the preheated oven and setting the timer.

Leaving Roag to eat her sugar dust, Fyona went over to Innis' chocolatier area. Seeing what she needed, she quickly phoned Skye and explained what she was up to.

Skye looked out the window of the vintage dress shop and saw Innis unloading a delivery for his cake shop from the back of his car. She ran outside and called over to him.

'Innis! Fyona is fighting off Roag in the cake stakes at the castle. Can she steal some of your white chocolate buttons to decorate her cake?' said Skye.

'Tell her to take whatever she wants.' It was clear who Innis was backing.

'Go for it!' Skye told Fyona, running back into the dress shop.

'Thanks,' Fyona whispered, and then helped herself to the white chocolate buttons.

Next up, she thought, was the buttercream. They'd also agreed not to fill the cakes with whipped cream. They'd sandwich them with buttercream, and use this as the decorative toppings too.

Roag poured his cake mix into two tins as Fyona walked by him and took a block of the whitest butter she could find from the fridge.

The challenge continued, with Nairne and the other staff enjoying the fun while they worked on cooking the lunches.

The cakes were now cooling on racks.

Fyona carefully cut the golden edges off her cakes, revealing how white the sponge was.

This was Roag's method too. He was keeping up with her quite efficiently, though it was hard to tell which sponge was the whitest. Probably Fyona's if he was being fair.

Fyona beat her buttercream until it was a lovely white texture and began slathering it on as the filling. The remainder was smoothed over the top of the cake, leaving the cut edges revealing the white sponge cake. She added the white chocolate buttons to decorate it.

Roag had to admit that his buttercream had a pale yellow colour to it. Delicious, and when not in comparison to Fyona's cake, white enough. His buttercream topping was swirled up into peaks and needed no further decoration.

Nairne saw that he didn't have to step in as it was a decisive win for Fyona.

The two cakes were sliced and plated for the lunch.

Fyona handed Roag a piece of her cake.

Roag gave her a slice of his.

Forks at the ready, they tasted the cakes.

Roag was the first to nod. 'This is excellent. Obviously a different recipe from Lyle's but wonderfully light and white.' He gave an exaggerated bow, conceding the win to her.

Fyona smiled, happy to have won the challenge, but when she tasted Roag's cake she wasn't so sure that she was the outright winner. 'Oh, the taste and texture of your cake is sooo delicious. I'd call it a draw.'

Roag was having none of this. 'No, you won. But maybe next time I will.'

'There's going to be a next time?'

'We're a competitive pair,' he reasoned. 'In the kitchen, and I'll bet on the dance floor too. Will you partner with me for the wedding waltz?'

Fyona's heart jolted for a moment, thinking he'd said *their* wedding waltz. And in a flash she'd pictured marrying Roag. The thought shocked her, rattling her to the core. What a silly thing to imagine. It would only ever be in her imagination. She wasn't the woman for a man like Roag. And he wasn't the man for her. He needed a beautiful woman, probably a model, not a chef like her. She needed a man who was the marrying kind and wanted to settle down. Fyona doubted settling down was in Roag's current plans. Or hers for that matter.

And a sizzling hot summer romance with the double–handsome Roag, although enticing, would only end in a broken heart for her.

# CHAPTER TWELVE

Fyona drove away from the castle as the amber glow of the fading sunlight flickered through the trees along the forest road. In the distance, the sea glistened like liquid gold, and she headed along the shore to the vintage dress shop. Fifteen minutes until it closed, and she needed a dress because she'd agreed to partner with Roag for the waltz lesson.

Parking outside the shop, she went in to find Skye and Holly sitting at their sewing machines mending ball gowns and evening dresses. They stopped stitching when they saw her and smiled.

'I was hoping you were still open,' said Fyona. 'I need a ball gown for tonight.'

Neither of them seemed surprised.

'Roag phoned us,' said Holly. 'He said that you're helping him demonstrate the waltzing, and that you're going back to the castle this evening to practise with him.'

'And you want a ball gown,' Skye added.

'I do, but—'

Holly cut-in. 'Roag wants to pay for the dress.'

'I'm quite capable of buying the dress myself,' said Fyona. 'Especially as they're such bargains.'

'Roag insists,' said Holly. 'He doesn't want you to be out of pocket because you're helping him.'

Skye was already looking through a rail of ball gowns and evening dresses. 'What type of dress did you have in mind?'

'Something like the red chiffon. I love the floaty feeling of the chiffon, and the style needs to be suitable for demonstrating how to waltz while wearing a full–length ball gown or evening dress.'

'How about this?' Skye held up a pale blue silk and chiffon dress.

'Oh, I like that.' Fyona stepped forward and lifted up the layers of chiffon, feeling the lightness of the fabric.

Holly came over to help. 'There was a dress I mended that was pink chiffon. Yes, here it is.' She held it up in front of Fyona. 'It would fit you too.'

'Try them on,' said Skye, ushering Fyona into the changing room.

Fyona put the blue dress on and pulled the curtain back. 'What do you think?' she said to Skye while Holly looked through a rail in the back of the shop.

'The colour is perfect on you. Turn around so I can see the back.' Skye frowned. 'The straps need adjusted to make the bodice and neckline a better fit, but I could do that right now.'

'I'll try the pink on, and see if it's a better fit,' said Fyona, disappearing into the dressing room again.

By now, Holly had found another ball gown. The fabric was the palest gold and was shot through with gold thread. 'We forgot about this beauty.'

Skye smiled and nodded at Holly and then called through to Fyona. 'We've found another dress. It's very sparkly.'

Fyona stepped out wearing the pink dress. 'This fits nicely.'

Skye and Holly agreed that it suited her.

Fyona swished the full skirt back and forth. 'I can picture myself sweeping around the dance floor in this.'

Holly leaned down and checked the hem. 'It's a good length. What shoes will you be wearing? Flats like the ones you're wearing?'

'Probably, but I have a pair of proper dance shoes that would be ideal for ballroom dancing.' said Fyona. 'And I have my ballet slippers, though they wouldn't be ideal for waltzing.'

Skye smiled at Fyona. 'I'd love to learn some ballet moves from you. Is it true that you've got a ballet barre?'

'It is. I use it for ballet barre routines. Short routines, about ten minutes, stretching and various movements.'

'Are the ballet moves difficult?' said Skye, attempting what she imagined was a plié.

Fyona stepped over to one of the rails of dresses and clasped hold of the end, using it as a makeshift ballet barre. 'This is an ideal height, waist height. Stand to the side and place one hand on the barre.'

Skye hurried to the opposite end, and joined in.

'This is a demi–plié,' said Fyona, demonstrating the exercise slowly, heels together and feet pointing outwards in first position, bending her knees, keeping her posture upright, and extending her other hand gracefully out to the side. 'It's a half bend.'

'This feels great,' said Skye. 'Am I doing it right?'

'Keep your core strong, your heels on the floor, and maintain your posture. You're doing well,' Fyona said encouragingly.

By now, Holly had clasped on to another rail and was joining in.

'I find that my routines help with my flexibility, core strength, and improve my balance and posture,' said Fyona.

'I can feel this working,' Holly remarked.

'I feel like a ballerina,' said Skye, extending her arm to match Fyona's movements.

'And this is a grand plié.' Fyona demonstrated a full bend.

For the next few minutes, Fyona showed them part of her ballet barre routine, and then she tried on the third dress.

'It's really sparkly,' said Fyona, moving back and forth, seeing it glitter in the lights.

'A fairytale dress,' Holly assessed.

Fyona sighed. 'I don't know which one I like the most.'

They were trying to decide when Roag phoned Skye.

'Did Fyona buy a dress?' he said.

'She's here now, wearing a lovely sparkly ball gown,' said Skye. 'But she likes a pink dress too.'

'Tell her to take both of them.' He insisted on paying.

Fyona shook her head. 'I can't let him buy two ball gowns.'

Roag overheard her. 'Yes you can, Fyona.'

Skye dealt with the payment and chatted to Roag. 'Fyona showed us some of her ballet barre exercises. We used the dress rails as barres.'

'You were all doing ballet in the dress shop!' He sounded surprised.

Skye elaborated on the moves. 'We learned a demi–plié and a grand–plié.'

'We really enjoyed it,' Holly chimed–in.

After Roag's call, the ball gowns were folded carefully into two bags and Fyona left the shop and drove to the cottage, wondering which one she'd wear that evening. Wondering too if Roag planned to challenge her on the dance floor. Ballroom or ballet? Or both.

In her bedroom she tried on both the dresses and decided she'd wear the pink one that evening. The pale pink chiffon was light as air, and she wore it with her dance shoes.

She took the dress and gold shoes off and put them in a bag as she'd no intention of arriving at the castle dressed for a ball.

Opening the wardrobe doors, she decided what to wear. Her love of dancing showed in her clothes. Not the chef whites, or the smart trousers and shirts she wore for work. But the wrap skirts made from soft silky fabrics, reminiscent of the midi and maxi–length chiffon ballet wrap skirts she used to wear, and still wore, but only for her ballet barre routines. Picking a georgette floral print wrap skirt, she teamed it with a pale blue, crossover wrap top with three–quarter–length sleeves, like the tops she wore over her leotards.

Stepping into a pair of pumps, she then refreshed her makeup, brushed her hair silky smooth, picked up her handbag and the bag with the dress and shoes, and headed out to her car.

173

It was a warm night as she drove along the shore, but the sea air prevented it from being muggy.

Arriving at the castle, she went inside and looked around. The reception was quite busy, as was the restaurant.

Roag bounded down the stairs to meet her, wearing black trousers, a white shirt, tie and waistcoat. He suited the look so well, and her heart took a hit just seeing him.

'Do you want to come up and get changed?' Roag said to her, unhooking the staircase cord.

Fyona nodded and followed him up the staircase, and then up more stairs to the turret.

She looked around the turret, sensing the historic background of it, while taking in the mix of traditional and modern furnishings and decor.

The windows were open and she went over to gaze out. 'What a wonderful view. The sea, the coast, the forest, and I think that's thistle loch shining way over there.' In the distance, it looked like a streak of silver.

Roag came over to join her, standing so close she could pick up the clean scent of him that had a hint of cedar.

'It is thistle loch,' he said. 'I'm planning to explore the whole area, the loch, the coves along the coast, and go swimming while I'm here.'

'So am I. And I want to see forget–me–not waterfall, especially at night, as it's lit with solar lights.'

'The lights must be a new addition. The last time I was at the waterfall, there were no lights, but it still felt magical,' said Roag.

Being with him felt magical, especially standing beside him in the turret. But Fyona kept these thoughts to herself and held up her bag. 'I brought one of the dresses you bought me. Thank you, by the way. I was prepared to pay for them.'

Roag shook his head. 'I've inveigled you into my plans to teach ballroom dancing, waltzing, so it's only fair I buy the dresses.'

'Circumstances resulted in you agreeing to show Finlay and Merrilees, and others, how to dance their wedding waltzes.' She glanced around. 'Where can I change into my dress?'

Roag gestured through to his bedroom. 'I won't disturb you. Shout if there's anything you need.'

Fyona smiled and went into Roag's bedroom. Obviously, he was staying there as a guest, so nothing showed his personal taste. But the room was tidy, just like his methods in the kitchen. Neat and clean.

Wasting no time, she changed into her pink ball gown and dance shoes.

Roag expected Fyona to look nice in her dress, but he wasn't prepared for the elegant beauty stepping out of his bedroom wearing a pink ball gown and gold shoes.

'You look beautiful.' The words were out of his mouth before he could restrain himself. 'The dress,' he said. 'It's a beautiful dress.'

'The vintage dress shop has a lovely selection of pre–loved ball gowns and evening dresses.'

'It suits you,' he said, trying to sound calm when his heart was pounding just looking at her. 'Do you want to do a warm–up here before we go down to the function room?' He checked the time. 'It'll be available for us in about half an hour.'

'Okay.' Fyona had no qualms about warming up in front of Roag, and began with a few of her favourite exercises, ballet moves to gently stretch her body.

The elegant stretches and graceful moves showed her ballet ability.

Roag started to stretch too, more to take his mind off the beautiful young lady standing in the turret. He was so tempted to invite her to have dinner with him. 'Do you dance at all these days?'

'Only at the odd party or ceilidh. The last time was at a Christmas party in a hotel that I was working in. I wore an evening dress, nothing as lovely as this.' She smoothed her hands down the fabric of the dress.

The heat of the night poured in through the window, but it was no match for the warmth in his heart that he felt for Fyona, especially as she'd been so willing to help him demonstrate how to waltz.

'Are you trained in ballroom dancing?' he said, finishing his warm–up.

Fyona looked poised as she completed her warm–up too. 'No, but my modern stage training included waltzing and other versions of ballroom classics. I can waltz, though I'm sure you'll show me the proper hold.'

Roag stepped close, and took her in hold, adjusting the fingers of her left hand to rest lightly on his right shoulder. His elegant fingers clasped her right hand with his left hand.

'Keep this frame while you waltz,' he said, gazing down at her, causing her to feel a blush form across her cheeks.

'Should I look over your right shoulder?' she said, averting her gaze, and trying not to blush.

'Yes, or you can look at me. As romantic couples do when they're in love.'

Fyona made the mistake of looking up into his fabulous eyes as he held her in his arms.

'It is a warm night,' he said. 'The function room will be more airy. I'll open the patio doors.'

She wasn't sure if he knew she was blushing because of the effect he had on her. But she welcomed the excuse.

'The forecast of a scorcher of a summer is true.' Especially when she was up close and in ballroom hold with Roag.

Her fingers could feel the lean muscles of his shoulders beneath the fabric of his shirt. They hadn't even danced a step, and here she was, all a flutter. Scolding herself, she paid attention to his instructions.

'When we waltz around the dance floor, let me lead, you follow.'

'I understand,' she said.

Roag hesitated, and adjusted his hold slightly. 'Dance with feeling as well as technique. Pretend you're in love, let that feeling shine through in your waltz. That's what helps elevate a standard performance into something special.'

Sensing sparks igniting between each other, they both stepped back.

'Shall we go downstairs to the function room?' he said.

Fyona smiled and followed him out of the turret and down the stairs to the reception. Murdo was at the desk.

'You go on through to the function room,' Roag said to Fyona. 'I'll talk to Murdo, tell him we're about to start dancing.'

Fyona's dress gained a few admiring glances from guests in the reception, and she hurried along to the function room. The doors were closed, but not locked, and a sign said it was in private use.

She went inside and closed the doors behind her. The lights were on, and she was the only one there. Having the large dance floor all to herself, that wild, mischievous streak took charge, and she began to spin and twirl, combining ballet dancing with modern stage moves.

The floor was well–sprung, and made her dancing feel even lighter and more energetic. She moved with fluidity and grace, and included a couple of perfect pirouettes, before stopping instantly when she heard the doors click open.

Standing in the middle of the dance floor, Fyona smiled as Roag walked in and approached her, totally unaware of what she'd been up to.

Expecting him to start organising the music, she was taken aback when he revealed what he'd planned.

'You can say no if you want to, and that's fine,' Roag began.

'No to what?'

'I've told Murdo to turn the security cameras on in the function room,' Roag revealed.

'Why? We're going to be rehearsing.' She looked puzzled.

'Because I thought it would be handy to have a recording of our dancing. It'll be helpful to see ourselves, gauge our strengths and weaknesses. Take the short course, as if we've been ballroom partners for years.'

Part of her saw the sense in this. To view themselves dancing would be of immense use, not only to correct things, like her posture in hold, but to work on their strengths.

'There are no mirrors like some dance studios have to see ourselves waltzing together. But this would enable us to watch the video later,' he reasoned. 'The music will be picked up on the video recording, but our conversation isn't loud enough unless we really raise our voices.'

'Okay,' she agreed. 'Tell Murdo to turn the cameras on and let's get started.'

Roag blinked. 'The cameras are on. I came through to get your approval. If you didn't want to be filmed, I was going to tell Murdo to turn them off before we'd danced a step.'

Fyona's face told a story that Roag couldn't read.

She looked around, wondering where the cameras were, but her mind was buzzing.

'What's wrong?' he said.

'I didn't know they were on,' she said. 'I tried out the dance floor, having it all to myself, while you were talking to Murdo.'

He read her reaction now. 'You've been dancing?'

Fyona nodded.

'Waltzing around?'

She wished. 'No, I went for it. Ballet turns, pirouettes, a grand jeté.'

Roag frowned, recognising the names of some of the moves, especially the last one. 'You did a huge leap, like the splits in the air!' The astonishment in his tone was clear.

'It's a great dance floor.' It took all her resolve to keep her voice steady. Inside, she was squirming. 'I wasn't putting on a show like you did.'

He jolted.

Realising she'd mildly insulted him, she reworded her comment. 'It was just a private few moments, enticed by having the dance floor all to myself. As I'm sure your unintentional performance was.'

Roag stepped closer and gazed down. 'Apology accepted.' A smile formed on his lips, easing the tension.

Without looking directly at any of the cameras that were in the four corners of the room, Roag spoke to Fyona in a confiding tone.

'I can tell Murdo to erase the beginning of the recording, but I think we should keep it. The entire recording is for our eyes only, unless we choose otherwise.'

'I don't have any recordings of my dancing,' she confessed. 'So yes, we'll keep it. One for the archives for me to look back to remember when I danced in a fairytale castle wearing a pink ball gown.'

Roag held out his hand to her. 'Shall we dance?'

Fyona placed her hand in his.

Music started, as if on cue, filtered through the sound system.

'I gave Murdo a copy of my music line–up. He's playing it via the system in reception so as not to interrupt us. I told him to give me five minutes and then start it playing.'

'I know this song,' she said as Roag took her in hold, and she placed her fingers gently on his shoulder as he'd instructed her upstairs. 'It's a popular romantic ballad.'

Roag's voice stirred her to the core as he said, 'The waltz is the most romantic dance.' They started to waltz slowly.

Fyona followed his lead. She could waltz, not to a professional standard, but her years of ballet and modern stage, and social dancing, made her a fitting partner for Roag. Dance partner, she corrected herself.

'Turn to the left, reverse turns,' he instructed. They danced a full circle of the floor.

Her dress felt magical. No other word for it. Light as sparkling pink champagne, and under the chandeliers, the touches of diamante glittered beautifully.

'Now change direction and turn to the right,' he said. 'Natural turns.'

Memories of her modern stage routines flooded back, easing her learning process, and she found herself sharing the same internal rhythm as Roag. Despite their different backgrounds in dance training, in height and proportions, strength and flexibility, at the core they were a perfect rhythmical match.

'Our timing is in sync,' he remarked, sounding as surprised as she was. Neither of them having to adjust to the other's beat. 'Only one of my former ballroom dance partners was like that with me. The other, we had to work, to learn our joint timing, but that's usual.'

'It's handy for us. We need to take the racing line to partner up for the waltz lesson.'

'Finlay, Ean and Innis are very capable dancers,' he said. 'They were brought up in the castle, and danced at the parties and events since they were boys. But their wedding waltz is something they'll each treasure forever, dancing with Merrilees, Ailsa and Skye. I'd like to help them create something memorable. A traditional wedding waltz fit for a grand room in a castle like this.'

Fyona gazed around as they waltzed. 'Nairne says it'll be all done up with twinkle lights, as well as the chandeliers. It'll be ideal for the summer ball after the wedding.'

Roag nodded.

'I'm helping with the buffet, and then getting changed into my red ball gown to join in the dancing at the ball.'

'I've told Nairne I'll work with him, and you, making a wonderful buffet.' He glanced at her pink dress. 'You suit pink, but the red will be outstanding, and sort of matches me. I bought a red silk waistcoat from the vintage dress shop. I plan to wear it for the wedding and the ball.'

Fyona smiled. 'I now have three dresses that I hadn't planned to buy, even though you bought two of them. I need to not be enticed into the vintage

182

wonderland again. Half the items on the rails, I'm tempted to buy. I don't even know what I'll do with three ball gowns once this summer trip is over.'

'Keep them to wear at balls and parties in the city when you go back home,' he suggested.

'I don't think I'll have the time or the inclination to do this. My working holiday on the island is something I'll look back on, a memory of a magical summer and dancing at the ball. When the summer is over, I'll be leaving and planning my future.'

'No fairytale endings for people like us.' His words faded as the first song came to a close.

Fyona kept her head turned to the left, looking over Roag's broad shoulder. 'No, but we're here to help the bridal couples create their happy ever afters.'

The next song began, a more upbeat tune, one she knew, and listened to the lyrics.

*We're celebrating a wedding on a summer's day*
*Romance, love and flowers*
*I waltzed with you at the wedding ball*
*Wishing it was ours...*

As they danced, she felt sparks charge between them. Although she was supposed to gaze over his shoulder, towards the end of the song, she looked up at Roag. She wasn't sure what she saw reflected in his eyes, apart from her. Under other circumstances she would've been sure she sensed that he liked her, more than liked her. But it was probably her silly imagination, or maybe he did like her. They were getting on fine. Even their challenge in the kitchen had concluded on a friendly note.

Had she found an unexpected friend in Roag? Or was the romance of the wedding and the ball at the castle stirring up feelings that were no more than wishful dreams?

*When the summer's gone*
*And so are you*
*Will you remember me?*
*Will I remember you?*
*Waltz with me now*
*Hold me close, hold me strong*
*Make me believe this is where I belong...*

After the song finished, Roag showed her other moves for the waltz.

'I think you're ready to learn some variations for the wedding waltz,' he said.

# CHAPTER THIRTEEN

'The three couples will dance their first waltz together,' Roag told Fyona. 'I'll show them how to improve their hold, and learn the contra check.'

Fyona knew how to waltz and include contra check movements, stopping and changing direction. Roag helped her refresh her technique, and they danced this well together.

'I've suggested to Finlay that each couple will perform one special move during the waltz. He likes the idea, and discussed it with Ean and Innis. They like it too.'

'What type of moves are you thinking of?'

'Something that suits each couple. When I think of Finlay, he's traditional, elegant. Merrilees trained in Scottish Highland dancing. I picture them incorporating pivots, maybe even a fleckerl.' Roag demonstrated these moves.

'Innis is drama, edged with power,' Roag added. 'Skye is mercurial. I think they could perform underarm turns or a ronde.' He clasped Fyona's hand and showed her how to do underarm turns.

Roag continued to tell Fyona his ideas. 'Ean is artistic, stylish. Ailsa is classy. A sway would suit them, or face–to–face and back–to–back moves.'

Fyona found herself enjoying the variety of steps and movements.

'You pick up the dance steps fast,' he said.

She smiled. 'How long will the couples have to learn their wedding waltzes?'

'One private lesson here in the function room. Finlay suggests tomorrow evening as it will give them time to practise on their own before the wedding. The lesson will be recorded, like we're doing now, so they can replay it and learn.'

Fyona agreed to come back the following night to partner Roag.

'A few guests will be coming along tomorrow afternoon for a waltz lesson,' he added. 'I hope these times are suitable.'

'They are.'

'The dress you're wearing is perfect to show how to waltz while wearing a full–length ball gown or evening dress.'

'It feels wonderful to wear a dress like this.'

'So we're agreed on this schedule,' he said.

'We are.'

'Will we have our last waltz of the evening?' He held out his hand.

Fyona accepted it, and began to waltz around the room. He'd opened the patio doors earlier, and the evening air wafted in. The night was calm, unlike her heart as she waltzed with Roag under the chandeliers and had the whole floor to themselves.

But like most fairytales, it came to an end, and as the song finished, so did they.

'Thank you for going along with the dancing, Fyona.' He sounded genuinely appreciative.

'I love dancing. And now I'll have a record of it, something to watch and remember this summer dancing with you at the castle.' She gazed around and smiled. 'I expected to be icing cakes and baking pastries, not waltzing the night away with you.'

'I like when life throws us wonderful surprises. I certainly didn't think I'd be waltzing with you either.' And he never imagined having to force himself not to fall in love on the island this summer. 'I thought you might have prejudged me due to my past reputation.'

'I did,' she confessed. 'You had quite the reputation as a troublemaker.' And a heartbreaker.

'And now?'

'I realise the gossip is true.' She smiled and walked away, hearing Roag's laughter trail behind her as they left the function room.

Fyona picked up the hem of her dress and headed up the stairs.

Roag ran over to Murdo. 'Can I have a copy of the video?'

'I'll make sure you do,' said Murdo.

Hurrying after Fyona, Roag caught up with her as she walked along towards the suite that led up to the turret.

There was laughter in Roag's voice as he spoke to her. 'I'm not the only troublemaker in the castle.'

She felt him glance at her accusingly, but playfully.

'I don't think you're in a position to point the finger at Finlay or Innis.'

Roag guffawed. 'I wasn't meaning them, and you know that.'

They stopped as he unlocked the turret door. At the top of the narrow winding staircase they were so close his smiling lips tempted her to show him he was right.

But the trouble she could cause would reverberate throughout the castle. So she smiled back at him and behaved herself. No wild abandonment this evening. She was surely filled with too much excess energy and excitement from all the dancing and fun she'd had with Roag.

Adrenalin coursed through his veins, and his body reacted to Fyona in all sorts of ways that were totally inappropriate. Her soft lips were so kissable, and her playful defiance ignited feelings he'd long thought wouldn't arise this summer. Not on the island. Not when he had to be the responsible one and take charge of the castle when his cousins were away. In Glasgow, he thought he'd prepared for every eventuality when he went to the island. But he hadn't accounted for meeting a woman like Fyona.

He stepped inside the turret, and she followed him into the living room where the windows were thankfully still open and letting in the fresh air.

'I'll make you a cup of tea while you take your clothes off,' he said. 'You can have a quick one before driving home.'

Fyona tried not to laugh. 'I think you might want to rephrase that kind offer.'

For the first time since she'd met him, Roag's face burned with embarrassment.

Her laughter trailed behind her as she went into his bedroom and closed the door.

Striding over to the window, he ran his hands through his thick hair, pushing it back from this troubled brown. Unbuttoning his waistcoat, he took it off, along with his tie, cast them on a chair, and undid the top two buttons of his shirt, feeling his own stupidity choking him. What a thing to say. It sounded so bad. Luckily, Fyona had made light of it, and in the process, showed him up for the fool that he was. At least when he was around Fyona. And it was getting worse. He could feel himself falling for her in ways that tormented him and threw his entire plans into turmoil. He definitely hadn't accounted for that either.

Fyona came out of the bedroom wearing her skirt and top, carrying the dress and shoes in a bag, and looking for the cup of tea he'd offered.

Roag's face showed he hadn't even put the kettle on.

'It's fine,' she said. 'I'll have a cup when I get home.' Which would be less than ten minutes if she left now. 'Will you give me a copy of the video,' she added, walking towards the door.

'Don't go. I'll rustle up the tea,' he insisted, taking the bag off of her and gesturing towards a chair. 'Unless you're in a rush and have something to do when you get back to the cottage.' He hurried over to where a tea tray was set up and flicked the kettle on. A mini fridge was stocked with cold drinks and fresh milk.

'No, nothing in particular.' She sat down while he prepared the tea. 'I've had my eye on the balls of yarn that Nettie has in her knitting stash. Folders of patterns too, and needles galore.'

'Are you a keen knitter?' He welcomed making polite conversation to take the heat off his earlier faux pas.

189

'Not at all, but it's hard to resist when the living room has such a tempting selection of lovely yarn. And I've been invited to join in the next knitting bee night. I plan to go along. Perhaps I'll knit a scarf. Nothing too fancy.'

'Hand–knitted items are nice.'

'Maybe I'll knit a scarf for you too,' she said lightly.

He carried two cups of tea over and sat them down on a table beside her chair. Then he seated himself opposite. 'An early Christmas gift.'

'It won't be early as it'll take me until Christmas to finish it. That's if we're still friends by then.'

Such a casual remark made his heart react. She'd said they were friends. He would accept her friendship warmly. If it didn't lead to anything more than that, he'd go back to Glasgow with a friend he truly liked and trusted.

'I'm sure we will be.' He lifted his tea and took a sip.

Fyona raised her cup. 'Cheers, to friendship and fun. I really enjoyed dancing with you tonight. I feel I learned so much about the ballroom waltz.'

Roag tipped his cup against hers. 'Cheers, Fyona.'

'And those were handy tips on how to dance while wearing a ball gown.'

'I've advised Finlay to tell Merrilees, Skye and Ailsa to wear evening dresses or a ball gown for their waltz lesson. It'll let them practise how it feels to waltz when they're wearing their wedding dresses. Guests are similarly advised.'

'I'll bring my ball gown with me tomorrow.'

'Leave it here,' he suggested, getting up and going through to the bedroom.

Fyona went with him, taking her bag.

He opened a wardrobe and gave her a hanger. 'You can hang it up in my wardrobe, or perhaps it would be better on the outside of it.'

His wardrobe was quite full of clothes, particularly his suits, so Fyona hung her dress on the outside of it. 'I'll leave my shoes too if that's okay.' She put them beside the dresser.

And there she was, standing in his bedroom, and for a moment he wondered what it would be like to have Fyona in his life, like this, sharing things together.

She went back through to finish her tea, and they chatted about the wedding cake she'd been icing earlier in the day.

'You've iced the bottom layer beautifully,' he said. 'The white thistles are a lovely design.'

'Thank you. I'll ice the second layer in the morning, maybe even part of the top layer and make the turrets.'

They discussed the buffet menus, the cakes, pastries and chocolates, and while chatting found out that they'd both skipped dinner that evening.

'I could order us supper from downstairs,' Roag offered. 'It's not that late.'

'I'm fine. I should've had something to eat before coming up to the castle, but I got caught up buying the dresses and then getting ready.'

'Dinner another evening then,' he took the chance to say.

191

Fyona hesitated.

'As friends. We could try out the castle's restaurant.'

'Okay.'

He couldn't tell from her one–word reply whether she was being polite or feeling awkward, not wanting to refuse an invitation to dinner.

'But if you'd rather not—'

'No, I'd like to have dinner in the restaurant.'

'Obviously we'll be busy tomorrow night with the waltz lesson. Maybe the following evening,' he suggested.

Fyona smiled and nodded, wondering what she was getting into, and yet unwilling to refuse what she truly wanted to do. Besides, she told herself, it was only dinner.

'I've been meaning to dine in the restaurant since I arrived,' he explained. 'To enjoy sitting down and having dinner there, to better understand how the guests feel. I'd like your company as we can discuss the menus and exchange ideas.'

This seemed reasonable. 'Yes, let's do that.'

'I'll book us a table for two.'

Fyona finished her tea. 'I'd better get going. I'm planning an early start in the morning so I can work on the wedding cake.'

'I'll walk you to your car.'

'There's no need.'

Roag insisted, and they went downstairs and stepped out into the warm night.

Fyona gazed up at the stars and breathed in the scent of the roses growing near the front entrance and the jasmine and night–scented stock flowers. 'No wonder Skye is looking forward to living in the castle. She was telling me that she's moved most of her things in already.'

'Would you like to live in a castle like this?' he said, as they walked towards her car.

'No, I'd prefer a house with a garden. I like the idea of the castle, but to me, it wouldn't feel like home. It's too grand. And it would be like living in a hotel, albeit a wonderful one. I like my privacy, to come home to a house where I could relax after a busy day.'

'I have a house on the outskirts of Glasgow, and it has a large garden and trees surrounding it. Very private. So I understand what you mean.' He glanced at the castle and up towards the turret. 'I've designed my kitchen so that I'm able to dine outside on the patio, even on rainy days, as it has an awning, and heaters for winter.'

'It sounds lovely.' She opened her car door.

'Yes, it is. Come over for dinner sometime, maybe, when we're both back in the city.'

'Maybe when I'm dropping off your Christmas scarf.'

He laughed. 'A hand–knitted scarf deserves a fine, festive dinner.'

'At least you can cook. I'm not certain I can tackle the knitting.' Fyona got into her car, preparing to drive away. She smiled. 'See you in the morning.'

He waved her off. 'Goodnight, Fyona.'

As her car disappeared into the night, Roag went inside, and as he was walking through reception,

Murdo waved him over to the desk. 'I've sent you a copy of the video.'

'Thank you, Murdo.' Roag sounded eager to watch it.

'I'd a wee peek. That was some jumping and twirling Fyona was doing, like a ballerina. What a talented young lady. Ballet, baking and ballroom dancing.'

'Yes, she is,' Roag agreed, and then hurried upstairs to view their dancing.

He sat down at the dresser he used as a desk and watched it on his laptop.

Seeing them dancing together, waltzing around the floor, made him realise what a great match they were. Fyona wasn't a ballroom dancer, but the elements she brought to their partnership raised the bar to a level where even he could feel the strong connection between them. Others would too, no doubt.

He didn't envisage them competing on the dance circuit. Those days were gone for him. If only he'd known Fyona back then...

Sweeping aside such thoughts, he watched himself instruct her in some of the ballroom movements, impressed by how quickly she picked up his methods. Her years in dance training showed through, and her willingness to give things a go.

Closing the laptop, he finally went to bed.

The bedroom window was open, letting in the fresh air. He lay there for a few moments, rewinding the day. And there, hanging on the wardrobe door, was Fyona's pink dress, sparkling in the nightglow.

His heart ached like never before, and then he fell sound asleep.

# CHAPTER FOURTEEN

'Your turrets look great,' Roag complimented Fyona.

She was icing the two turrets on to the top layer of the wedding cake. She'd been working on the cake all morning, icing the second layer and the top with white royal icing.

Piping white icing along the bottom edges of the turrets, she secured them in place, carefully adding details to the design.

Fyona stepped back and sighed, releasing the tension. The icing was precise work, and she wanted the turrets to be perfect.

'Thanks,' she said. 'I'll work on the thistles for the two tiers tomorrow.' It was almost lunchtime and she'd only had a cup of tea in the castle all morning.

Roag had been equally busy helping Nairne, learning the process of running the kitchen and other aspects of the castle. Finlay had shown him how the bookings for the guests and orders were done. Roag didn't want everything to be left to Murdo, Geneen and Nairne when the honeymooners went away. He planned to step in strong and capable as the temporary replacement in charge of the running of the castle.

'Your table is booked in the restaurant for dinner tomorrow night,' Nairne called over to Roag.

'I appreciate it,' Roag said to Nairne. 'We're keen to experience dinner as the guests would.'

'I'm sure you'll both enjoy it,' said Nairne.

Clearing up her icing equipment, Fyona carried the top layer of the cake through to where the bottom layer was being stored in the kitchen out of harm's way. Roag picked up the second layer and followed her through.

'Do you want to grab a light lunch?' he suggested. 'The guests are expected to turn up for their waltz lesson around two–thirty this afternoon. That would give us sufficient time to digest lunch, do a warm–up and practise for half an hour or so before they arrive.'

Fyona liked that plan and went over to wash her hands, expecting they'd sit in a corner of the kitchen to eat lunch.

'Finlay said he was having lunch at stargazer cottage with Merrilees,' said Roag. 'Ean is down at the main street with Ailsa, and Innis is working at the cake shop. So would you like to dine outside on the patio. We won't be disturbing them.'

'I'd love some sunshine and fresh air.' She sighed, longing to enjoy the summer day.

Roag rubbed his hands together in anticipation. 'What would you like for lunch?'

She glanced around. 'We're spoiled for choice. But I'd like to try the vegetable and cheddar cheese frittata.'

'Excellent choice.'

Roag served up two portions of the frittata, while Fyona added a side order of mixed salad with tomatoes and courgettes.

Working efficiently together, they soon had their lunch sorted and carried it outside to sit down at the patio table.

'This feels almost like being on holiday,' Fyona said with a sigh, enjoying the food, the company and the summer's day.

Roag tucked into his lunch. 'We sort of are. A working holiday.'

Fyona agreed. 'We both love cooking, baking, and dancing.'

'Precisely. It means that I'm always doing what I love.'

'I certainly don't consider waltzing this afternoon as work. And I love icing cakes, especially wedding cakes. Though it would be nice to run off and go swimming down the shore one day.'

'We'll do that,' he said firmly.

'Yes, there will be plenty of time after the wedding and the summer ball.'

'Maybe time before those too.'

Fyona ate her salad and nodded.

They continued to enjoy their lunch, chatting about menus, cakes, recipes, making the most of the castle's estate and surrounding countryside.

After lunch, Roag took the dishes inside and then came back out to take a walk through the castle's gardens with Fyona before starting to get ready for the afternoon waltzing.

Guests turned up suitably dressed for their ballroom waltz lesson, and more couples arrived than Roag had anticipated.

'When word got round that you were instructing them how to waltz for the summer ball, other guests decided to join in,' Murdo said to Roag.

'The more the merrier,' said Roag. 'It'll help create a busier dance floor and they'll learn how to waltz with lots of other couples.'

Geneen came over to chat to Fyona. 'You look lovely in your pink ball gown.'

'It's from the vintage dress shop,' Fyona explained.

'Skye and Holly sell such stylish dresses,' Geneen enthused. 'I got my ball gown from them.'

Leaving Roag and Fyona to demonstrate the waltz, Geneen and Murdo went back through to the reception.

Roag had organised the music, selecting songs he thought would be popular.

Taking Fyona in hold, Roag began instructing the couples, showing them how to improve their posture and waltz smoothly around the function room floor.

The afternoon lesson went by quickly, and when it finished, the guests were happy with what they'd learned, and left in a cheery flurry of chatter to go back to their rooms.

Fyona and Roag went upstairs to his turret.

She changed out of her dress and put on a wrap skirt and blouse.

Roag took his waistcoat and tie off, and made them a cup of tea.

They sat in the living room relaxing until it was time for the evening lesson. They discussed plans for the menus, recipes, and plans for the dance party nights. Fyona realised that they were never stuck for conversation.

Holly locked the vintage dress shop up for the night, and put on the amber and gold dress she'd worn to the Christmas ball at the castle. She had it hanging up on a rail ready to wear for the waltz lesson.

She looked at herself in the mirror, remembering how much she'd enjoyed the festive ball. But she hadn't imagined she'd be wearing the dress again to practise waltzing with Lyle. He'd tried to show her how to waltz at Christmastime, and although Lyle wasn't an expert, he'd seen plenty of waltzes when catering for balls during his time in the city.

Holly's pale yellow dress for the summer ball was hanging up on a rail, but she wanted to keep it special for the wedding day.

Skye, Ailsa and Merrilees had kept their Christmas ball gowns too, and planned to wear them that evening.

Lyle drove up and parked outside the dress shop. Holly grabbed her bag and hurried out. He looked immaculate in his dark suit, shirt and tie, and got out of the car to open the passenger door for her.

'You look lovely,' he said.

'And you're very smart in your suit.'

'I didn't want to let the side down.'

Lyle drove them along the harbour road. The amber sunlight shone through the windows, and the gold in Holly's dress shimmered in the early evening glow.

'Skye is already up at the castle getting changed in Innis' suite,' she said. 'Ean helped Ailsa take a lot of her belongings from her cottage to his suite today. She's getting ready at the castle too. So is Merrilees.'

'Well, I'm looking forward to dancing with you.' Lyle smiled at Holly and then drove them away from the coast up to the forest and the castle.

Skye smoothed down the layers of pink organza on her ball gown and walked into the function room with Innis. He wore his kilt, not the one he was wearing for the wedding, but one he wore to the ceilidhs. The laces on his ghillie shirt were untied at the neck, anticipating it would be a warm night for the waltzing.

Music played in the background, and Holly and Lyle were chatting to Roag and Fyona as the other two couples arrived.

Ailsa wore her royal blue gown and walked beside Ean. Her dress had a velvet bodice and layers of tulle with blue sequins. Ean wore a kilt, white shirt and tie.

Behind them, Finlay walked in clasping Merrilees' hand. He was wearing his kilt, shirt, tie and waistcoat. Both Finlay and Ean wore kilts they used for more casual events, and had kept their kilted finery for the wedding. Merrilees ice blue crystal ball gown shimmered under the light from the chandeliers.

With everyone there, Roag began the lesson. It was being recorded for them to study later.

All the men were capable dancers and waltzed well. The ladies were slightly less confident, but Roag thought they danced well too. Improving their hold and posture added to their confidence. He advised them on how to dance while wearing the ball gowns, demonstrating this with Fyona.

Soon, all the couples were waltzing smoothly around the room. Then it was time for Roag to introduce their individual choreography.

The song they were dancing to was the one the wedding couples had selected for their first waltz. A classic, romantic ballad.

Roag showed Finlay and Merrilees how to incorporate pivots into their waltz during the chorus.

While they practised this, Roag taught Innis and Skye to perform underarm turns.

Then he showed Ean and Ailsa the face–to–face and back–to–back movements.

'There are other moves, such as a sway you could include,' Roag said to Ean and Ailsa, and they wanted to try this too.

'Would you like to learn a fleckerl?' Roag offered to teach this to Finlay and Merrilees. 'It's a combination of steps where you turn around on the spot. Turning one way, a natural turn clockwise, and reverse turns, counter–clockwise.'

'Let's try it,' Finlay said to Merrilees, and after Roag demonstrated the steps, they practised on their own. Merrilees' Scottish Highland dance training helped her pick up the steps quite quickly.

'I'd like to include these with the pivots,' Merrilees said to Finlay.

'Yes, we'll practise,' Finlay agreed. 'I like Roag's choreography.'

Holly and Lyle tried the various moves, and particularly liked the underarm turns, and attempted a fleckerl. She laughed as Lyle lifted her up as he danced a fleckerl when she messed up the steps.

'We'll replay the video and keep practising in our own time,' Finlay said to Roag as the lesson finished.

They all thanked Roag and Fyona for taking the time to teach them.

Skye and the other women chatted to Fyona while Roag explained his plan for the dance party nights to Finlay, Innis and Ean.

'Holly and I did our ballet barre moves in the shop today,' Skye said to Fyona. 'Ailsa joined in as well.'

'I enjoyed the ballet exercises,' said Ailsa.

'I've seen ballet barre routines, but I've never tried them,' Merrilees chimed–in.

'Come down to the shop one day and we'll show you,' said Skye. 'We use a sturdy clothes rail as our barre.' Skye held on to the back of a chair at the side of the dance floor and proceeded to demonstrate a plié. 'Fyona taught us how to do a demi–plié. Try it,' she encouraged Merrilees.

Holding on to a chair, Merrilees joined in the fun, and so did Ailsa and Holly.

'Underneath my ball gown my plié moves are perfect,' Skye said playfully.

There was a lot of giggling and cheery banter between the ladies.

Lyle left Roag talking to Finlay, Innis and Ean, and came over to see what they were doing.

'We're practising our ballet barre moves,' Holly told Lyle. 'The ones I told you about.'

'Ah, very elegant,' said Lyle.

'Try a plié,' Holly encouraged him.

Ever willing to give things a go, Lyle tried to fathom the movements, even though the ball gowns disguised most of the technique.

Fyona adjusted Lyle's stance and posture. 'Keep your core strong, that's it, Lyle. Bend down halfway.'

'That's all I can manage in these trousers,' Lyle joked.

By now, Roag's plan for the dance party nights had been approved by Finlay, Innis and Ean.

'While we're away, you're welcome to schedule dance evenings at the castle,' Finlay confirmed to Roag. 'Be sure to take photos so we can put them on the website.'

'I will,' said Roag, pleased that his plans had been accepted.

'Roag!' Holly called to him. 'Come and see Lyle's new moves.'

'This is as far as I can bend in these trousers,' said Lyle.

Going over to join in, Roag demonstrated a few ballet–like moves, stretching one leg high into the air while keeping his balance on the other.

'Are those stretchy trousers?' Skye said to Roag.

'Dance trousers. They have a bit of stretch in them,' Roag confirmed.

'I should've worn my kilt,' said Lyle, playing along with the fun.

'Do you want to give this a go? Skye called over to Innis.

He shook his head. 'I'll watch from the sidelines.'

The jovial atmosphere continued until they all started to head out having enjoyed their waltz lesson and the extra fun.

Lyle drove off with Holly, heading back down to the shore to drop her off home.

Skye, Merrilees and Alisa went upstairs with their respective fiancés, leaving Roag and Fyona in the function room.

'They all loved the choreography for their wedding waltz,' Fyona said to Roag.

'It was fun teaching them, and again, thanks for helping me demonstrate the dancing.' Roag then checked the time. 'What are you planning to do now?'

'Change out of my ball gown and then drive home,' said Fyona.

The patio doors were open. Roag walked over and peered outside. 'It's a fine night. Do you want to go on an adventure?'

'Where?'

'To the waterfall. You've mentioned a few times that you want to see it all lit up at night. It's quite safe there, but I'm happy to go with you.' His offer hung in the warm air wafting in, along with the sense of adventure igniting between them.

'Okay. I'll get changed,' she said, and headed upstairs to the turret.

Roag followed behind her.

Fyona went into his bedroom, took off her ball gown, and changed into her wrap skirt, blouse and pumps.

Roag removed his waistcoat and tie, and undid the top buttons of his white shirt that he wore with the black trousers.

'All set for a night–time adventure?' said Roag.

Fyona picked up her bag. 'Let's go.'

They headed downstairs, through the reception, and outside to Roag's car.

He drove off, casting a smile over at Fyona.

Excitement bubbled up inside her. She hadn't imagined that after the waltzing they'd be off for an evening outdoors. But these were the best types of fun, spur of the moment adventures. She hadn't felt like this in a long time, and relished the extended evening with Roag.

Within a few minutes, they reached the waterfall, following the glow from the spotlights through the trees to where it was situated in a setting that was like a scene from a fairytale.

Lights from the waterfall illuminated the night as Roag parked the car and they stepped out into the lush grass. They were the only ones there.

'I thought a few guests would be here,' she said.

'The restaurant still seemed busy with guests having dinner.'

'Or maybe we're the only ones venturing out from the castle for a wild night at the waterfall.' Though she wasn't sure how wild it would be. Neither of them had their swimwear with them.

Sparkling water cascaded down from the rocks into a natural pool of clear water. The new solar lights were tucked into the flowers around the edges of the pool, and the air was filled with the scent of the flowers and greenery. The pretty forget–me–not flowers were asleep for the evening, but the night–scented stock flowers, jasmine and other night–blooming flowers were scattered around.

'The water looks tempting.' Roag ran his fingers through it, testing the temperature. 'Nice and cool, but not cold.' After all the work in the kitchen, then dancing in the afternoon and evening, the natural pool of clear water looked soothing and refreshing.

'We've no swimwear,' Fyona reminded him. Then she kicked off her shoes. 'But I'd love to go for a paddle.' Tucking the ends of her skirt into the waistband, making it knee–length, she went to step into the natural pool.

'Careful you don't slip.' Roag offered her a steadying hand.

But both her hands were occupied holding up the hem of her skirt from trailing in the water that was slightly deeper than she'd anticipated.

'I'm fine,' she said, looking at the colourful lights illuminating the crystal clear water. The stones on the bottom acted as a natural filter, keeping the water fresh. The gentle flow of the water falling into the pool was mesmerising, and she dared to walk over to where it was creating bubbles as it hit the surface.

'It's like standing in sparkling champagne,' she enthused.

Roag took off his shoes and socks, deciding to join her, but before he could, Fyona stepped on a moss–covered stone, slipped, and tumbled into the water.

She jumped up, squealing, completely soaked but unharmed.

Roag reacted instantly, reaching over, lifting her out of the water and standing her down on the grass at the side of the waterfall.

'Oh, my goodness,' she said, gasping.

'Did you hurt yourself?' he said, looking concerned.

'No, but I'm soaked.' She wrung the water from the ends of her skirt, and swept her wet hair back, sending untold feelings through Roag at her natural beauty.

'Come on, I'll drive you back to the castle to get dried off.'

Fyona hesitated. 'I'll soak your lovely car.'

He shrugged off her comment. 'It doesn't matter.'

'It does matter,' she insisted. 'Maybe I could walk back. It's not that far.'

'Don't be silly. You're not walking through the forest at this time of night.' Then he started to unbutton his shirt and took it off. 'Here take your skirt and blouse off and put this on. It'll be long enough on you, like a shirt dress.'

Roag's suggestions made more sense than her ideas, and she accepted the dry shirt, trying not to gaze at his lean–muscled physique.

He turned around and looked away while she took her wet clothes off and put his shirt on.

While she folded up the sleeves that were far too long for her, he wrung as much water out of her skirt and blouse as he could.

Roag took her clothes and put them in the boot of the car.

She'd kept her briefs on, and stepped into her shoes.

'Are you dressed?' he said.

'Yes.' She wrung more water out of the ends of her hair.

When he turned around and saw her standing there, backlit by the lights of the waterfall, he scolded himself for thinking how sexy beautiful she looked.

Her heart thundered seeing Roag's bare–chested physique. His broad shoulders tapered down to his six–pack, and his lean–muscles arms were the type that made her imagine what it would be like to be held close to him.

Blinking away such thoughts, she looked flustered as she got in the front passenger seat of his car.

He pulled the seatbelt across his bare chest, and she tried not to look over at him as he drove them back to the castle.

His strong, dancer's physique was hard to ignore. There he was, sitting beside her, all lean muscles and masculinity.

Her heart reacted and she scolded herself again.

Calm down, she told herself firmly. You're just having a night–time adventure with one of the most handsome men you've ever known. No. Big. Deal.

'You can get dried off in my turret before driving home,' he said.

By now the lights shining from the castle windows were in view, and Roag parked the car.

They stealthily approached the front entrance and peered into the reception. Murdo was at the desk tending to a couple of guests.

'It's busy,' she whispered. 'I don't want Murdo or anyone else seeing me like this.'

'We'll go round the back,' he suggested. 'The patio doors should still be open. We can go in through the function room.'

This seemed like a reasonable plan, and Fyona followed Roag round to the back of the castle, keeping to the shadows.

The lights were still on in the function room and the glow poured out into the night, illuminating the two stealthy figures.

Roag tried to open the doors and shook his head. 'They're locked,' he whispered.

Fyona sighed heavily. 'Maybe I should just drive home as I am.'

'No, I want to make sure you're okay. Delayed shock, whatever, and there's no need to mess up your car too.'

'Sorry about dripping all over yours.'

Roag brushed this aside, genuinely concerned for her, and thinking he could easily sort the situation. If only he could get them up to the turret without being seen. The gossip would be fierce if anyone saw them. He didn't care for himself, only for Fyona. It was his fault for suggesting they go on an adventure.

'We can go in through the kitchen,' he whispered, and hurried along to peer in through the window and the glass door. The lights were on, but no one was inside.

'See anyone?' she whispered.

'No.' He glanced round at her. 'I don't know why I let you talk me into all this trouble.' His tone was teasing.

Fyona gasped and then tried not to giggle. 'You're the one who suggested an adventure.'

'You bring out the rascal in me,' he said.

Fyona swiped at him playfully. 'You're the scallywag!'

Roag ducked, and then Fyona took another giggling swipe at him. He side–stepped, and for a moment they laughed, and then he stealthily opened the kitchen door and led her inside.

There was no sign of anyone. The kitchen was closed for the evening, but the lights were left on so that the night porter could make tea or whatever the guests wanted during the night.

They were halfway through the kitchen, heading towards the door that would lead to the stairs, when a deep voice resonated across to them from the chocolatier area.

'If anyone was taking bets, my money would've been on Fyona,' said Innis, referring to the playful challenge he'd seen between the two of them.

They turned to see Innis standing working in his part of the kitchen, preparing boxes of chocolates to restock the cake shop.

'So would I,' Roag agreed, going along with the joke.

Innis smirked, seeing the state of the pair of them. Fyona's bedraggled wet hair, wearing Roag's shirt, and Roag's bare–chest appearance. 'I didn't know it was raining outside.'

'We were at the waterfall,' said Roag. 'Fyona took a tumble into the water.'

'Ah.' Innis looked like he wasn't buying Roag's explanation.

'I'm just going upstairs to Roag's turret to get dried off, and then I'm heading home,' she said.

Innis smiled. 'I'll not keep you then.'

Fyona and Roag smiled tightly and hurried away.

'I can imagine the gossip in the morning,' she whispered to Roag as they made a stealthy bolt for it up another set of stairs that the kitchen staff sometimes used to take meals upstairs.

'I'll explain to everyone that you have a wild streak in you that you're trying to tame,' he said.

Fyona gasped, and then chased Roag up the stairs as he laughed and made a bolt for it up to the turret.

# CHAPTER FIFTEEN

Fyona showered in Roag's en suite bathroom, taking him up on his offer of this and some dry clothing.

He'd left another clean white shirt and a pair of black jogging trousers on the bed for her, and went through to the living room to give her privacy.

Stepping out of the shower, feeling refreshed, she grabbed a large, soft clean towel and dried off.

Padding through to the bedroom, she put the shirt on, wearing it like a mini–dress, and folded the cuffs up to make the arms a better fit. She eyed the joggers, then put them on. They were obviously too big, but better than driving home wearing just his shirt.

She ran a brush through her wet hair, untangling it, making it look less wild, though the adrenalin from all the excitement of the night was still coursing through her.

Putting the brush back in her bag, she stepped into her pumps, and went through to the living room.

'Don't laugh,' she warned him before he'd opened his mouth. 'I know I look silly and these clothes are far too big, but they're fine, and I'm happy to borrow them.'

'I was going to say you look...*glowing*.'

'Considering I feel like I've been through a waterfall washing machine, and then spun dried, I'm not surprised.'

Roag laughed, and yet his heart melted just looking at her.

'Can I use the same furtive route to get back to my car?' she said, going through to the bedroom and collecting the bag containing her ball gown and dance shoes.

'Yes, I'll go with you to make sure the coast is clear.'

With Roag leading the way, they retraced their steps down the stairs that led to the kitchen.

'Innis has gone,' Roag whispered, waving her in. 'There's no one here.'

Considering they'd been caught off–guard the last time, Fyona kept a lookout as she scampered through the kitchen and out into the back garden. With Roag accompanying her, she continued round to the front of the castle where her car was parked beside his. They deftly transferred her wet clothes from the boot of his car into hers.

'Thank you, I think, for a memorable evening,' she said, smiling at him through the window as she got ready to drive away.

'One for the archives.'

'Oh, yes.'

Roag waved her off, walked into reception, nodded to the night porter, and then went upstairs as if he hadn't been up to a night of triumph and trouble with Fyona.

'I haven't heard one word of gossip about us,' Fyona whispered to Roag in the kitchen the next day as she continued to ice the wedding cake.

'Neither have I.'

'Is there the wildest chance that Innis won't clipe on us?'

Roag considered the odds and gestured with his hand that it could tip either way.

'Maybe we scored a few gold stars for teaching Innis and the others the wedding waltz,' Fyona suggested

'Tarnished now after your wild behaviour last night,' Roag said with a teasing smile.

Fyona lifted up her icing spatula. 'Any more nonsense from you, and I'll show you wild.'

'Everything okay, Fyona?' Nairne called over to her as he whisked egg whites for the meringues.

'Yes, I was just airing my icing,' she lied.

Roag smirked and got on with plaiting the puff pastry for the potato and cheese slice he was making for the lunch menu.

Nairne then piped the meringues on to a tray and put them in the oven.

Fyona whispered again to Roag. 'I brought a change of clothes for our dinner date. Not date. Dinner, just dinner.'

Roag's smirk turned into a smile. 'Do you want to get changed later in my turret?'

'Yes, and it's the last time I'll probably need to take my clothes off in your turret again. Not take them off. You know what I mean.'

'I do. And you're welcome to use the turret anytime you need to. It's obviously handier than driving up and down to the cottage.'

'Thanks, and I might bring my ball gown with me and change for the wedding and summer ball. But that will definitely, maybe, be the last time I encroach on your turret.' She shook her head as she piped icing on to the edge of the one of the cake tiers. 'At this rate, I'm using your turret more than you do.'

Roag pretended to agree. 'You're right. Maybe we should change accommodation. I'll stay in the cottage down the shore, while you commandeer the turret.' He ended with a quip. 'After all, you're in it more often than me at the moment, and it's looking like you'll take it over to get ready for the weddings and the summer ball.'

Fyona was about to wield the spatula again, when she saw Nairne glancing over, and instead smiled sweetly and whispered at Roag. 'You're determined to get me into trouble.'

Roag guffawed at the suggestion. 'I think you're making a fine job of that on your own.'

Finlay came into the kitchen as Roag finished plaiting his pastry.

'Have you got a couple of minutes?' Finlay said to Roag.

'What's wrong?' He wiped his hands, ready to help.

'I'm flummoxed by the fleckerl. Merrilees is busy writing her book in the cottage, so I don't want to disturb her. I was practising upstairs, but I can't get the dance steps in the right sequence. Could you show it to me again?'

Roag nodded and led Finlay out the back door of the kitchen on to the patio. No one else was around, but Fyona and Nairne positioned themselves so they could nosey out the window.

'I've seen it all now,' Nairne said to Fyona, smiling as he watched Finlay get himself into a fankle with the fleckerl.

Not quite, she thought to herself, picturing the previous night's fiasco and stealth moves through the kitchen.

'Crossing your right foot in front of your left...' Roag began to show Finlay what to do.

'Ah, that's where I was going wrong,' Finlay realised. 'I was starting off on the wrong foot and turning the wrong way.'

After a few practise steps Finlay got the hang of it again.

Before Roag went back into the kitchen, Finlay took a note from his pocket.

'This is a list of the songs we're planning for the summer ball,' said Finlay. 'But we all liked the music you chose for the waltzing last night. Could you write down the songs you used? We'd like to include them for the ball.'

Roag read the list. 'I'll add the songs I used, and suggest a couple of extras that I think would be suitable.'

'Great,' said Finlay.

Fyona and Nairne made themselves busy as Roag came back into the kitchen to get on with the cooking.

By the end of the day, Fyona had finished icing the wedding cake, and it was carefully put in storage.

Tidying up their work in the kitchen, Fyona and Roag then headed upstairs to get ready for dinner.

While Fyona used the bedroom, Roag messaged Finlay with an updated list of songs.

Finlay, his brothers and their fiancées, were having a private dinner in the function room to discuss and finalise the details for the weddings. Finlay read the message on his phone while they were all deciding what to order from the menu. He discussed the song list with the others, and they agreed to the song ideas that Roag suggested.

'Roag says he's added music that he danced to during some of his stage performances,' said Finlay.

'I loved the music last night,' Merrilees remarked.

'I know most of these songs, and I think they'll be great for the dancing,' Skye added, smiling as she sat next to Innis.

'Ailsa and I were practising our waltzing upstairs,' Ean told them.

'I enjoyed Roag's dance lesson,' said Ailsa.

'Roag gave me a refresher on the fleckerl,' Finlay revealed.

'We'll practise it together later,' Merrilees said to Finlay.

And then they ordered dinner, and discussed the plans for the weddings, the ball, and the honeymoon.

'Nairne says that Fyona has finished icing the wedding cake,' said Finlay. 'I thought we could all take a look at it after dinner. She's even added turrets.'

'I had a look at the cake,' Innis told them. 'It's excellent sugar craft.'

'We're fortunate that Fyona gets along well working with Roag,' said Finlay.

'They seemed friendly last night when they were waltzing,' Ean commented.

Innis said nothing about Roag and Fyona's mischief, not wanting to stir up gossip.

Roag escorted Fyona downstairs to the restaurant. He wore a suit, shirt and tie. She wore a classy tea dress and heels.

They were seated at their table and handed menus.

'I should've checked the menus in the kitchen earlier,' said Fyona. 'But it was such a busy day I didn't have time. I didn't even have lunch.'

'I'm running on the fumes of cups of tea. I've got quite an appetite for dinner.'

Fyona looked across the table at Roag. 'I purloined one of the Abernethy biscuits you baked today. But you'd made two trays full of them, so I didn't think you'd mind.'

Roag pretended to scold her. 'Shocking!'

Fyona smiled. 'It was tasty. I've never made them before. I must try baking them.'

They studied the menus.

'Everything looks appealing,' said Roag.

'Nairne made roast pepper and tomato soup, and I'd like that as a starter.'

'I'll have the split pea broth.'

Finlay decided on his main course. 'I know it's a warm evening, but I see that Nairne's traditional stew is on the menu. It's a favourite of mine.'

'Mine too,' said Ean, ordering the same as Finlay.

'Make that three servings of Nairne's stew,' Innis told the member of staff taking their order.

'Four servings,' Merrilees chimed–in.

Ailsa and Skye opted for pasta dishes.

While they ate their stew, they spoke about the route to sail during their honeymoon.

'I've plotted a route out on the map,' said Finlay. 'But it's flexible, and we can go wherever the wind blows us.'

'What's the weather forecast for the west coast?' Merrilees said to Finlay.

'Wonderful, like the past few days,' Finlay replied.

'The time has sparked so fast,' Ean remarked. 'It'll be our big day soon.'

The thought of this sent a shiver of excitement throughout the party.

'Is there anywhere in particular you'd like to see?' Finlay threw the question open to all of them.

'The Isle of Skye is lovely,' Skye said, and having been born there it was a favourite of hers.

'The Isle of Skye is one of our stopping off places,' Finlay told her.

'Tiree,' said Merrilees, having done interviews there and other islands on the west coast of Scotland during her journalist years.

'Another tick–box on the planned route,' Finlay assured his fiancée.

'The scenery is beautiful up at the Summer Isles,' said Innis.

'We'll certainly sail around the Summer Isles,' Finlay told Innis. 'And over to Loch Roag at Lewis.'

Ean agreed with the locations and added another. 'Morar is lovely.'

'What about you, Ailsa? Any locations you'd like to see?' Finlay said to her.

'All the places you've planned sound wonderful,' Ailsa told him. 'The islands off the west coast are beautiful. I want to enjoy the azure seas and white sands, like paradise.'

'We will,' said Finlay. 'And we'll be stopping off at wee towns and villages on the mainland coast and the islands. I've checked several locations, and we'll stay overnight in local hotels. We won't be sleeping on the yacht, unless it's one of us nodding off and relaxing in the sun while we're sailing.'

'As long as it's not you,' Merrilees said to him playfully.

'Ean will be spelling me during the trip, and I expect you to try your hand at the wheel,' Finlay teased Merrilees.

She laughed nervously. 'You're joking,' she said to him.

Finlay continued to eat his stew and wind her up.


'Everyone says that Nairne's stew with dumplings is one of his specialities,' Roag said, selecting the main course from the menu. 'I'll have that with Ayrshire tatties.'

'The stew looked delicious when Nairne was making it, so I'll join you,' said Fyona.

Their stew was served with the small, boiled, Ayrshire potatoes.

'This is delicious,' said Fyona.

221

'Nairne is an excellent chef,' Roag remarked.

Enjoying their stew, they chatted about baking cakes.

'Will we tackle making the sheet cake tomorrow?' Roag suggested.

'I was going to make a start on it, but two hands would be better.'

'We'll bake the sponge cake in the morning, and then ice it. We could have it done by the end of the day.'

'That would be the two main cakes for the weddings done,' she said.

They were discussing this when Murdo approached their table.

'There's dancing on in the function room later,' Murdo told them. 'Waltzing and ceilidh dances. When you finish your dinner, you should go through and join in. Finlay, Innis, Ean and the ladies are having their dinner and then taking part.' Smiling, Murdo continued on his way back through to the reception.

Roag looked across at Fyona. 'Do you want to dance after dinner?'

'Yes, but only a couple of dances. I really need to get some sleep.'

Roag nodded. 'We'll have a waltz and a ceilidh dance, then call it a night.'

'I'm not attempting a fleckerl while the guests are dancing,' Finlay said to Merrilees as they waltzed around the dance floor.

'We'll practise in private later,' Merrilees agreed.

222

The music suited the romantic waltz that couples were dancing to.

The song continued to play as Roag and Fyona walked into the function room. But as they began to waltz, the music changed to a lively tune for a ceilidh dance.

Murdo was up on the small stage, making the announcements and in charge of the music.

'And now, for a ceilidh reel,' said Murdo.

Roag clasped Fyona's hand. 'Come on, let's dance a reel.'

'I'm not sure of the steps.' Despite this, Fyona stood beside Roag as the lively reel began.

Fyona started laughing as she was whirled around the floor by Roag, Innis, a couple of strangers, and Ean, then finally circled back to Roag.

Somewhere in the next hour of lively ceilidh dancing, Fyona and Roag's plan was scuppered as they joined in the reels, jigs and ceilidh waltzes.

But the lively and fun–filled atmosphere energised Fyona and Roag and they stayed until the chandeliers were dimmed for the last dance of the night — a slow, romantic waltz.

'Take your partners for the final dance,' Murdo announced.

Roag wrapped Fyona in his arms and they slow–danced to the popular song.

Fyona wasn't dating Roag, and still had no plans to get involved in a summer fling, but feeling him hold her in his arms melted her heart.

He felt a spark charge between them as he pulled her closer.

She looked up at him, and for a moment they both knew there was an unmistakable spark of attraction between them. But neither of them mentioned it, and continued to dance until the song finished.

Under the glow of the lights, Ean held Ailsa in his arms and whispered loving words that made her smile.

Skye snuggled into Innis as the last note of the song hung in the air, and having her arms around his neck, he leaned down and kissed her.

Finlay and Merrilees were lost in each other's world, and then he kissed her before they walked off the floor together.

Surrounded by romance, Fyona felt the chill of realisation drift past her as she stepped back from Roag. No romance for her.

'That was fun,' Fyona said, making polite conversation.

She quickly collected her things from upstairs in the turret, and then Roag walked her outside to her car.

'I enjoyed our dinner, and the dancing, especially the ceilidh dancing,' she said, getting ready to drive off.

'So did I. Dinner was delicious, and the dancing was an unexpected bonus.'

Smiling, Fyona drove off with a cheery wave. She could still feel the gentle strength of his arms around her, and hear his laughter as they'd whirled around joining in the ceilidh dances.

Roag watched her car tail lights disappear out through the entrance to the castle, and then he turned and walked back towards the reception. The air was so still and clear that he overheard Finlay bidding goodnight to Merrilees as she stood beside her car...

'It was a great night,' Finlay said, gazing down at her as he held her hands, as if reluctant to let her drive back to stargazer cottage. But with the wedding day almost upon them, she was on a tight deadline to finish writing the last chapter of her romance novel.

'I'm going to work all day tomorrow to finish writing the book,' said Merrilees.

'I won't disturb you,' he assured her. 'Phone me if you'd like to have dinner.'

'I'll do that,' Merrilees agreed.

Finlay kissed her, and then waved as she drove off through the forest to the cottage.

On the opposite side of the car park Ean kissed Ailsa goodnight.

Ailsa's comment sounded clear. 'I've closed my craft shop. That's it until we get back from the honeymoon...'

Roag walked into the reception, passing Innis and Skye on their way out.

Skye chatted about the ball gowns. 'Customers collect the last of the ball gowns from the dress shop in the morning. I can't believe it's now so close to the wedding! Ailsa and I are bringing the three wedding dresses up to the castle tomorrow, so no peeking!'

'I won't.' Innis' deep voice resonated in the reception, and then he kissed her as they headed outside.

Roag walked up the staircase to the turret and stood gazing out the window, rewinding having dinner with Fyona in the restaurant, and then enjoying the ceilidh dancing and waltzing with her.

He looked at the sea shimmering in the distance, and felt the tiredness start to wash over him.

Getting ready for bed, he kept the windows in the turret open, and fell asleep with the scent of the sea, the forest, and the flowers from the castle gardens, soothing his restless heart.

Skye and Ailsa arrived at the castle the next morning with the three wedding dresses. The dresses were suitably covered to hide them from prying eyes.

A guest bedroom had been allocated upstairs, in the private area of the castle, for the use of the brides to store their dresses and other items for their big day.

It took two trips down to Ailsa's car to transfer everything upstairs.

Skye flopped down on one of the two single beds. The room was used for friends and relatives to stay in while visiting the castle. It was just along from Finlay's suite. Now it was being used for the brides to get everything ready.

Skye, Ailsa and Merrilees planned to help each other on the day of the weddings with their hair, makeup, and putting on their bridal gowns. Holly had promised to help too. Skye, Holly and Ailsa's modelling backgrounds would come in handy, and between them they were confident to help each get ready for their special day.

'I could hardly sleep last night for excitement,' Skye confessed to Ailsa. She stretched out on the plush bedcover. 'Don't let me fall asleep.'

Ailsa went over, clasped Skye's hand and encouraged her to get up. 'Come on, sleepyhead. There's work to do. Help me hang up the dresses and check that every seam and sequin is sewn.'

Skye bounced up, her ponytail whipping with renewed energy when she thought about the wedding dresses.

They'd brought padded hangers with them, and each dress was carefully hung up in front of the two wardrobes and inspected for flaws.

They found none.

'All sorted.' Skye jokingly flopped back down again on the bed. Then she jumped up when there was a knock on the door.

'Don't come in,' Skye shouted.

'It's just me,' Geneen assured them.

Ailsa opened the door and let her in. Geneen had seen the dresses in the vintage dress shop, so they didn't need to hide them from her.

'Oh, the bridal gowns are beautiful,' Geneen enthused. 'Wait until your grooms see you.'

'Every time I think about it, my heart starts fluttering,' said Ailsa.

'Mine too,' Skye chipped–in.

'And mine,' Geneen agreed. 'The staff are adding wee bits and pieces to the function room, and Murdo is erecting the bough outside on the patio ready for the ceremony. Flowers will be entwined around the bough on the morning of the wedding, and the flowers for the bouquets fresh picked too.'

Skye dug into her bag. 'I brought a roll of white ribbon to tie the bouquets.'

'Give the ribbon to me,' said Geneen, taking charge of it. 'I'll give it to the staff who are making the bouquets and flower displays.'

'Thanks, Geneen,' said Skye, happy that another important task would be dealt with.

'I came to see if you want a cup of tea and something to eat?' said Geneen.

'Tea please,' Ailsa replied.

Skye nodded too.

'I'll bring it up myself,' Geneen assured them as she left.


Roag and Fyona were busy in the kitchen, preparing the sheet cake. The large, vanilla sponges were sitting on racks ready to be iced.

They'd mixed the icing, and started work on the cake.

Geneen bustled around, chatting to Nairne, and making a tray of tea for Skye and Ailsa.

Nairne added two shortbread petticoat tails to a side plate and put it on the tea tray, along with a small bowl of fresh strawberries and raspberries.

'The lassies are keyed–up with excitement,' said Geneen. 'And so am I.'

'Aye, you can sense it bubbling throughout the castle,' Nairne remarked. 'Finlay, Innis and Ean had their breakfast as usual outside on the patio, but I could sense the anticipation in the air. The traditional ceremony is in many ways easier, but with the three couples getting married at the same time, and then the summer ball, everyone is buzzing.'

Geneen took the tea tray away, leaving Nairne to get on with his cooking.

Roag and Fyona iced the cake, and discussed the preparations for the weddings.

# CHAPTER SIXTEEN

A cobalt blue sky arched over the castle on the day of the weddings and there was a sense of excitement in the warm summer air.

The flowers for the bouquets had been picked from the gardens. Each bouquet was a different confection of flora and greenery, tied with white ribbons.

Ailsa's bouquet combined blue cornflowers, thistles, white cosmos and white roses.

Pink and white roses, pink peonies, thistles and pink cosmos formed the perfect bouquet for Skye.

Merrilees opted for yellow and white roses, thistles and white peonies.

The three brides were upstairs in the guest room getting ready. Their hair and makeup was done to all their satisfaction.

Ailsa wore her hair up, pinned with floral diamante clasps. The clasps secured a wisp of a veil. Her classic chiffon and silk dress looked like a bridal ball gown.

A sparkling tiara adorned Merrilees' hair. Her hair fell in silky waves to her shoulders. A short veil trailed down the back of Merrilees' satin dress, and the bodice glittered with beadwork.

Skye wore her hair down, and a chiffon veil was attached with diamante clasps. The look suited the design of her white satin wedding dress. And she wore the diamond bracelet Innis had given her at Christmastime.

Holly was there helping them, and wearing the lovely pale yellow chiffon dress.

Fyona and Roag were busy in the kitchen preparing the last few items for the buffet.

Nairne had organised everything well, and although all the staff in the kitchen were busy, the catering for the buffet was going to plan. But he welcomed Roag and Fyona's help to maintain the smooth–running of the whole event.

The buffet tables were being set up in the function room, and included a chilled table for the ice cream that Brodrick had provided. Lyle had delivered the cakes and pastries Nairne had ordered from him, including a white cake and other specialities.

'The buffet is coming together well,' Roag said to Fyona as they worked in tandem preparing some of the fresh cream mini–cakes and puddings.

Fyona balanced miniature fairy cakes and butterfly cakes on a tiered cake stand. She'd already prepared two stands with mini wedding cakes, and these had been taken through to the function room by members of the catering staff.

Roag layered glasses with vanilla sponge cake, fruit, custard and whipped cream and set them on trays that were picked up by staff and added to the buffet.

The wedding cake was arranged in the function room on a silver cake base, and the traditional skean dhu was placed ready for the newlyweds to cut the first slices.

The sheet cake sat on another table, along with lavish chocolate cakes, and a selection of Innis' chocolates and truffles.

Savoury dishes ranged from mini quiche and dainty sandwiches, to cheese puff pastries, lattice slices, and flans.

The buffet included a bar serving a variety of drinks.

Tea and coffee were available, and catering staff were there to help serve the guests whatever they wanted.

With time wearing on, the afternoon sunlight cast a golden glow over the castle and the garden patio where the three couples were due to stand under the flower–covered bough.

Nairne had changed out of his chef's clothing into his kilt and jacket, ready to watch his niece tie the knot with Ean. Now, he was continuing to whiz around the kitchen organising the last few bits and pieces before everyone attended the ceremony.

'Let's check the buffet and then we'd better get dressed for the weddings,' Roag said to Fyona.

'Yes,' she agreed. She'd taken Roag up on his offer once again to use his turret. Her red chiffon dress was hanging up in his bedroom ready to put on.

They went through to the function room and were satisfied that everything was in order, and then hurried upstairs to the turret to get changed.

Having become accustomed to sharing the turret for the purpose of changing their clothes, they manoeuvred efficiently around each other. Roag gave Fyona priority in using his bedroom to put on her dress.

When she stepped from the bedroom into the living room, Roag couldn't hide the effect her vibrant beauty had on him.

'You look gorgeous,' he said, admiring her red chiffon and silk ball gown. And Fyona.

She lifted the dress hem a fraction and showed him her pale gold dance shoes. 'I'm all set for the ball.'

Roag hurried past her into the bedroom to get changed and cast a comment to her. 'I expect to dance the first waltz with you.' He made his claim clear.

She pretended to tick her dance card. 'Accepted.'

Fyona checked her hair and makeup, and then stood at the open window taking a calming breath. The sound of voices chattering wafted up in the warm air as everyone started to arrive for the ceremony.

'I think we'd better get a wriggle on,' Fyona called through to Roag.

Moments later, he emerged immaculately dressed in a dark suit, white shirt, tie and the vintage red waistcoat.

He was fussing with his tie, and Fyona went over and straightened it for him.

'There, very handsome,' she said, and then tried to rewind her remark. 'Classy suit and waistcoat.'

Roag smiled. 'I preferred the first assessment. But I'll take both.'

The sound of bagpipes in the distance signalled that the weddings were about to begin.

Fyona held up the hem of her dress as they hurried down the staircase.

Roag kept a grip of Fyona making sure she didn't tumble.

The reception was buzzing with guests heading through to the function room, and in the midst of them they saw Geneen wearing her ball gown, and Murdo kilted and all set to join the throng in the garden.

Family and close friends of the couples were gathered outside on the patio awaiting the brides. Other guests were in the function room, but the patio doors were open wide so they could participate in the happy event.

Roag and Fyona wound their way through the guests in the function room and took their place beside Nairne, Geneen, Murdo, Holly and Lyle as the bagpipes began to play. Lyle wore his blue tartan kilt and clasped Holly's hand, a gesture that Roag felt inclined to do with Fyona, but resisted.

Nearby was Elspeth from the knitting shop and her husband, Brodrick. His staff were taking care of his cafe bar. Innis' cake shop was closed to allow Rosabel and Primrose to attend the weddings.

Finlay, Innis and Ean stood in their traditional kilted finery, each of them wearing their matching dark grey and black tartan kilts, sporrans, tartan flashes and skean duhs tucked into their socks, and thistles in their buttonholes.

Their father, the laird himself, was there wearing his kilt too, and Fyona noted the likeness of the tall, silver–blond, handsome laird to Finlay in particular. Their mother was elegantly dressed in a grey, full–length gown, worn with a grey and black tartan sash. Her auburn hair was swept up in a chignon. Ean was the closest in likeness to her. Innis appeared to the be lone wolf of the family.

The laird was in charge of the six gold wedding rings, and beside the laird and his wife stood Merrilees' parents. They were staying overnight at a friend's farmhouse near where they used to live when the island was their home.

Gasps and murmurs sounded from the function room, hinting that the brides had arrived.

Merrilees, Skye and Ailsa walked through, holding their bouquets, smiling, excited, nervous.

As they stepped outside, the three grooms glanced round for their first look at the brides, and it was clear to everyone present that they were taken aback by their loveliness.

Each bride stood to the left of their respective groom.

Lyle squeezed Holly's hand, seeing her start to be overcome with happiness for Skye, and her friends.

Holly gladly accepted Lyle's strength and kindly assurance as they stood together near Roag and Fyona.

As Fyona admired the bridal gowns, Roag admired Fyona. Her hair looked like amber fire in the afternoon sunlight, pinned back at the sides with diamante clasps, and falling softly in waves to the shoulders of her dress.

The exchanging of vows was heartfelt. And although the setting of the castle was magnificent, the ceremony itself was small and intimate.

Wearing their wedding rings, the couples kissed under the floral bough.

The bagpipes sounded the conclusion of the happy event, announcing that the couples were now married.

Photographs were taken outside in the garden, and with the castle in the background. Individual couples, group pictures, and the entire proceedings continued to be filmed by the man in charge of the video recording.

Roag and Fyona stepped to the side, allowing the couples and their nearest and dearest to take centre stage, but were soon waved over to join in, and were captured in the golden light of the late afternoon sun along with the others.

The laird came over and shook hands with Roag, and his wife gave Roag a kiss on the cheek.

'I hear you've helped enormously with the buffet, Roag,' said the laird. 'I want to thank you for that, and hope that you won't be a stranger to the island from hereon in.'

'Yes,' his wife added with a smile. 'And bring Fyona with you.' She smiled at Fyona. 'The design of the thistles and turrets on the wedding cake is marvellous. We appreciate your fine work, and assisting Roag with the waltzing.'

The laird's face lit up with a knowing smile. 'We received a copy of your recent late night performance, Roag. And your elegant ballet dancing, Fyona.'

Fyona felt a blush begin to form across her cheeks.

'We don't wish to embarrass you,' the laird assured her. 'We were extremely impressed with your dancing skills.'

'Thank you,' said Fyona.

'I'm pleased the wedding ceremony went well,' Roag said to them.

The laird and his wife were then swept into a special family portrait, leaving Roag smiling at Fyona.

'Which brings me to another matter,' Roag said tentatively to her.

'About what?' She sensed it didn't have anything to do with the wedding or the ball. And she was right.

'Our videos have been released into the wild, so to speak,' Roag began. 'A dance show producer I used to work with phoned me earlier, but we were up to our elbows in baking cakes. I was going to wait until tomorrow to tell you—'

'Tell me what?' Fyona cut–in.

'He wants me to perform at weekends in Glasgow and Edinburgh for their forthcoming dance show tour. The dates are arranged, theatre tickets are selling well, and he wants me to be one of the guest performers. To dance two showpieces. With you as my partner.'

This news took Fyona aback, but before she could respond an announcement was made to the guests.

'Will everyone now decant into the function room for the cutting of the cake,' Murdo announced.

As people poured past them, Fyona stood in the garden, wide–eyed, looking at Roag. 'To perform two dances on stage to live audiences?' She needed to clarify this.

Roag nodded. 'I was part of the show last season, so I'm familiar with the choreography. The tour was so successful that the dance company want to do another run of it later this summer and in the autumn.'

'I've never been involved with a stage show.' Part of her was excited. Part of her in panic mode. 'What sort of routines would we be dancing?'

'A romantic waltz routine,' he said. 'And a showpiece. Whatever we want. Though I suggest we

237

utilise your ballet in the routine. Spins, leaping around the stage, plenty of lifts and catches.'

Her eyes widened further.

'I'll do all the lifting and catching,' he added with a smile.

His smile made her see the playful side of things, the chance to perform on stage as part of a successful dance show. Something as a young girl she'd often dreamed of.

'We could start rehearsing here at the castle,' said Roag. 'And then practise with the dance show producer when we get back to Glasgow. From the details he gave me, I think it's feasible to fit the stage shows into my work at the restaurant. The performances are only in the evenings at weekends. It would be fun, a challenge, exciting, all those great things. A time in our lives to look back on and say — yes, we did it!'

'A challenge, with bells on!'

'Speaking of bells,' Roag ventured to add, 'he did mention about performing during the Christmas show tour. But that's waaay down the line.'

'Christmas!' she exclaimed.

'Come on, Fyona. Be wild, take a chance, accept the challenge, dance with me during the show nights.'

In her heart she felt the surge from her past, that daring streak she'd long since tamed. She knew she should refuse as it would upset all her plans, but then she heard herself say, 'Okay.'

Roag reacted instantly, lifted her up in a huge hug and swung her around.

Fyona's squeals turned a few heads, and he put her down again.

'Just practising for those lifts,' Roag said with a grin.

Fyona laughed, and then they headed inside to see the cutting of the wedding cake with the skean dhu.

The first slices of the cake were cut by each of the three couples, and then Nairne took charge of slicing it into pieces for the guests to help themselves.

There were whisky and champagne toasts all round, and then the three couples stepped on to the dance floor for their first waltz.

Their chosen song began, and everyone stood around the edges of the floor watching their waltz routine, and were surprised when each couple performed a different move during the chorus.

Finlay and Merrilees performed their pivots well, and then added the fleckerl.

The guests were impressed and cheered them on.

Innis and Skye's underarm turns looked great, as did Ean and Ailsa's face–to–face and back–to–back movements.

As the song finished, and another song began, guests joined the three couples on the dance floor.

Roag held his hand out to Fyona. 'I believe you promised me a waltz.'

'I did,' Fyona confirmed, accepting his hand. They began to dance together, waltzing past Finlay and Merrilees and exchanging smiles with all the newlywed couples.

Fyona felt as if she was dancing in a fairytale, and loved the feeling of wearing her ball gown.

Innis held Skye close as they waltzed, and whispered lovingly to her. 'You look so beautiful.' Skye smiled up at him as they danced on.

No one, except Ailsa, heard Ean telling her that he loved her, and her reply that she loved him too.

Finlay hadn't let go of Merrilees since they'd danced their first waltz, and kissed her while they continued to sweep around the floor.

Amid the heart of the busy dance floor, Roag waltzed with Fyona. She kept thinking about agreeing to perform on stage with him, feeling waves of excitement mixed with trepidation.

'You'll love the choreography,' Roag assured her, feeling the tension in her, sensing her thoughts. 'The moves will follow the romance theme of the show, and be similar to what audiences enjoyed before. But with your ballet expertise, I'll be able to add to the choreography. And I expect input from you.'

Fyona laughed. 'What have I let myself in for?'

'Excitement, drama, wearing wonderful costumes, and stepping into the world of dance for a few special nights.'

'You're a hard man to resist,' said Fyona, and then reworded her comment. 'Hard to refuse.'

Roag swept her around the floor in a flourish of spins. 'I preferred the first version.'

Breathless from the spins, Fyona couldn't resist enjoying herself with Roag.

He finally slowed down as the next song changed to a romantic melody.

'You'll love the costumes.' Then he looked thoughtful as he admired her dress. 'Maybe the dress you're wearing would be perfect. It suits you, and you dance so well in it.'

Before Fyona could consider this, Roag danced them over to the patio doors that were open wide, letting the early evening air flow in. The amber twilight cast a golden glow over the scenery behind them.

Roag took his phone from his pocket, and with an outstretched arm, tried to take a photo of them showing as much of Fyona's red chiffon ball gown as he could.

Merrilees was standing at the buffet with Geneen, while Finlay danced with his mother. Seeing Roag struggle to extend his reach, she went over to take the photo for him.

'Let me help,' said Merrilees.

'Thanks.' Roag handed her his phone.

The professional photographer in her advised them to adjust their pose and move to the most advantageous angle for the background. She took a few pictures, highlighting the full effect of the ball gown. And then advised Roag to take his jacket off for the last two pictures to show his classy red vintage waistcoat.

Merrilees showed them the pictures on the phone. 'I think this one is a winner.'

Roag and Fyona agreed. It showed his waistcoat, the angle of his body as he held Fyona in a waltz pose. The colours of their clothes made them look like a perfect match. And it captured the flow of the chiffon of her dress.

It only took a couple of minutes for Merrilees to do this, and then she went back over to the buffet in time to be joined by Finlay.

'I'd like to send a couple of the pictures to the dance show producer,' Roag said to Fyona. 'And confirm that you'll be part of the show.'

Fyona nodded, and her heart raced with excitement, but nothing in her wanted to change her mind.

Roag sent two pictures. One where he wore his suit jacket, and the winning shot they'd all liked best. His message was succinct.

*Fyona said, yes! We're at the castle dancing the night away at the summer ball.*

Tucking his phone in his pocket, Roag led Fyona inside and over to the buffet.

'I can recommend Fyona's cheddar and caramelised onion mini quiche,' Roag said to her.

'I think I'll try one of Roag's savoury lattice puffs.'

Picking these up, they smiled and enjoyed the other's delicacies. Then they had tea and pieces of the wedding cake.

'Remember, we won't tell anyone about the dance show performances,' Roag reminded her. 'It'll look like we're trying to steal the newlyweds' thunder.'

'Certainly not,' Fyona agreed. She bit into the cake. 'Nairne's fruit cake is delicious.'

'The icing is not bad too,' Roag teased her.

As they indulged in the sumptuous buffet, they listened to snippets of gossip and chatter all around them.

Geneen and Murdo were chatting excitedly to Nairne.

'The laird has given all the castle's staff a substantial bonus for their hard work in preparing for the weddings and the ball,' Geneen said to Nairne.

'Really?' Nairne sounded delighted.

Murdo nodded. 'Tell the catering staff.'

Rosabel and Primrose were eating ice cream at the buffet when Innis came over to them.

'Come on, Rosabel,' said Innis. 'Waltz with me. You can't come to my wedding without giving me a dance.'

Rosabel beamed with glee.

'You're next, Primrose, so finish your ice cream and get ready to waltz with me,' Innis added and then led Rosabel away.

Elspeth wanted to try a piece of the sheet cake, and Brodrick joined her, as they took a break from the dancing.

'The wedding cake was lovely, but I like this light vanilla sponge and the icing,' said Elspeth.

'Nairne told me Roag and Fyona made it,' Brodrick revealed. 'I must try making a sheet cake for the cafe bar.'

'This white cake is so tasty,' Merrilees said to Finlay as he helped himself to another square of Scottish table from the sweetie display.

'Thank you, Merrilees,' Lyle commented as he walked by holding hands with Holly.

A message popped up on Roag's phone. He read the reply from the dance show producer and shared it with Fyona.

*Wonderful! You both look marvellous. Love the pics! Enjoy the ball. Chat soon.*

Roag clicked his phone off and tucked it in his pocket. They finished eating at the buffet and then waltzed around the dance floor again.

As the evening came to a close, couples danced the last waltz. Roag danced with Fyona to the romantic song, finishing in close hold as the music came to an end.

'We'll practise our choreography soon,' said Roag, releasing her from his arms. 'I'll send you clips from the previous shows.'

'Great, I'd like to watch those.'

Guests started to filter out of the function room, and the newlywed couples wished everyone goodnight at the front entrance of the castle. The laird and his wife had already left to catch the last ferry back to the mainland so that the laird could continue his business meetings.

Nairne was organising the staff to clear away the remnants of the buffet, and Murdo and Geneen were on hand to help deal with the guests.

Roag accompanied Fyona upstairs to the turret and she quickly changed out of her ball gown. Folding it into a bag, she picked up her shoes and other belongings and was set to leave.

'I've sent you links to the dance clips,' said Roag.

Fyona checked her phone. 'I'll watch them tomorrow, or probably when I get back to the cottage as I'm curious to see the dancing.'

'Try to get some sleep,' he advised. 'We've got a busy day ahead. I'd like to start planning the dance party nights.'

'I'm up for helping you with those,' she said, and started to leave. 'I'll see you in the morning.'

Roag walked downstairs with her and outside to her car. Most of the guests had gone home, and the newlyweds had retired upstairs to their private accommodation.

Fyona breathed in the night air. 'The weddings were wonderful, so romantic.'

'The summer ball was a success,' said Roag.

'When do the couples sail off on Finlay's yacht?'

'They don't want any fuss, and plan to set sail very early tomorrow morning.'

'Well, I'd better go and try to get some sleep.' She got into her car, smiled and drove off.

Again, Roag watched her drive away, then headed into the castle and upstairs to his turret. His mind was whirring with ideas for the show dance choreography, and as he got into bed, he wondered if Fyona was watching the video clips.

Grabbing his phone from the bedside table, he sent her a message.

*Did you watch the dance clips?*

Moments later she replied.

*Yes, you knew I couldn't resist.*

*What did you think?*

*The routines were dramatic, romantic, and filled with great choreography.*

*We'll add our own special moves. But we'll chat in the morning. Get some sleep, Fyona.*

*You too.*

The messages ended there, and Fyona settled down, gazing out the bedroom window at the starry night sky, wondering what it would be like to perform live on stage with a professional ballroom dancer like Roag.

# CHAPTER SEVENTEEN

Finlay's yacht sailed off from the island early in the morning sunlight, heading out into the aquamarine sea. The light breeze blew through Finlay's open neck white shirt, as he stood behind the wheel, steering his brothers, and Merrilees, Skye and Ailsa off on their three–week honeymoon.

None of the shops were open yet for business, and there was no fanfare, just the three couples themselves disappearing into the distance under the bright blue sky.

They were all on deck, some looking outwards to the far away islands that their sailing trip would take them past. Others, like Skye and Ailsa watched the shops disappear from view, and the coastline's white sand glisten in the distance.

Skye stood up from where she was sitting at the rear of the yacht with Ailsa and Merrilees, and pointed towards the island.

'Look! I can see the castle's turrets peering over the forest,' Skye exclaimed, causing them all to glance back.

As the sea deepened, in depth, and in colour, to hues of rich aquamarine, Finlay steered the yacht away from the island and out into the wide open water where the blue sails, that matched the sea, billowed in the breeze.

Merrilees cupped her hand to shade her eyes from the sunlight glinting off the sea. Then she dug her phone from her bag and took a few pictures of Finlay,

Innis and Ean at the front of the yacht, standing on the deck and gazing outwards at the seascape. And she included pictures of Skye, Ailsa and herself sitting at the rear of the boat against a backdrop of vibrant blue water and the last glimpse of the island.

She'd finished writing her book and it was now in the hands of her editor. But that wasn't the only thing she'd completed writing.

'I sent the pictures of the wedding dresses away late last night to Celia at the fashion magazine,' Merrilees told Skye and Ailsa. 'I didn't want to send them before the wedding day. I added bridal pics, and us waltzing at the summer ball.'

'When will these be in the magazine?' Skye sounded excited.

'In the next printed edition,' Merrilees explained. 'But Celia intends to put the vintage wedding dress feature up on their online edition, so I'll check soon to see if it's been added. I wrote the editorial to go with the pictures, describing the dresses in detail, and the alterations, embroidery work, and upscaling that was done at the vintage dress shop.'

'It'll be an interesting feature,' Ailsa remarked.

'And a great promotion for the shop,' said Skye.

They all wore vintage summer dresses for their going–away outfits, and continued to chat about the magazine feature while Ean spoke to Innis.

Ean wore classic neutral tones, and Innis wore expensive dark casuals, and they studied the first part of the route on Finlay's map.

'The beaches along the coast on this island are ideal for swimming,' Ean remarked.

Innis looked up at the bright cobalt sky. 'And it's a fine day for taking a dook.'

'We'll do that,' Finlay agreed. He'd hoped the weather would be as warm as predicted, and had scheduled their route accordingly to include swimming and exploring along the way.

'Tell me when you want a break from the wheel,' Ean said to Finlay.

'It's fine,' Finlay said, trying not to smile. 'Merrilees is keen to learn how to sail the yacht.'

The chatter from the women stopped, and Merrilees looked worried for a moment, before Finlay laughed.

Relieved that he was teasing her, Merrilees retorted, 'Be aware, I might decide to take the wheel and learn the ropes. Goodness knows where we'd end up though. I'm rubbish at reading maps.'

Finlay looked at his brothers. 'I don't mind an off–map trip to the continent.'

Innis lifted the lid on their picnic basket. 'If I'd known, I'd have packed more sandwiches and extra flasks of tea.'

Finlay shrugged playfully at Merrilees. 'Ah, well, your plan is scuppered.' He smiled at Ean. 'I'll have to rely on you to spell me on the wheel.'

Merrilees laughed, and the light–hearted mood continued as the yacht headed out further into the sea off the beautiful west coast of Scotland.

Holly walked down the hillside to open the vintage dress shop earlier than usual. As promised, she hadn't been there to wave Skye and the others off on their honeymoon. No tears, even happy ones to taint them sailing away. She'd wished her sister well the previous night, but waking up early, even after the late night, Holly decided to head down to the dress shop and start her day with some sewing and mending.

But as she walked towards the shop, she couldn't help but notice that Finlay's yacht was no longer anchored at the harbour. They'd gone, as planned, but a wave of emotion washed over her.

The lights were on in Lyle's tea shop. He'd been busy in the kitchen baking fresh bread, scones and other tasty treats, ready for opening up later in the morning.

Holly was so steeped in thoughts that she didn't notice him approach her. Lyle had seen her from the front window of his tea shop, and sensed she might be a little bit upset. It had been a wonderfully emotional time recently, culminating in the weddings and waltzing.

'Morning, Holly,' he said as he got closer.

She turned to see the warm smile and caring expression on Lyle's face, and her heart squeezed just looking at him.

'Are you okay?' His tone was steady, reliable, as was Lyle.

'Fine.' Neither the truth or a lie. Somewhere in her unsettledness.

He could tell that she wasn't quite fine.

'Come and have your breakfast with me,' he offered. 'I'll make us a full, tasty breakfast. Fresh bread and butter, scrambled eggs, tattie scones, tomatoes, the works.' His offer was exactly what she needed.

Beckoning her, he started to walk away, thinking she'd follow, but instead she called out to him.

'Lyle!'

As he stopped and looked back at her, Holly ran towards him, threw her arms around him and kissed him full–on, almost knocking the breath out of him.

'What was that for?' he said, beaming at her as she stepped back.

'Nothing.'

Lyle smiled at her. 'I'll have to do nothing more often.'

He put his arm around her shoulders, and she leaned into him as they walked together to the tea shop and disappeared inside.

Feeling the warmth and comfort of Lyle's world, and his cheery company, Holly enjoyed the tasty breakfast he cooked for them, while they chatted about the cakes he planned to bake for the forthcoming dance party nights at the castle.

'When is the first dance party night?' said Holly, sitting in the kitchen with Lyle.

'Soon, according to Roag. He said last night that he'll phone me today with the exact dates. We're invited to attend, so you'll need nice dresses for the dancing. I hear the vintage dress shop has a lovely selection.'

Holly smiled. 'So does my wardrobe at home. It's filled with vintage dresses, many that I haven't even worn.'

'That's you sorted for the party nights.'

Holly buttered a slice of still–warm, thick–cut bread. 'It is.'

'Roag mentioned that he'd like to keep to the current schedule that had been planned for the guests. There's supposed to be a dinner dance on tomorrow evening.'

'So soon after the weddings and the summer ball?'

'That's the whole idea, to keep the fun nights going with plenty of dancing, and great buffet food.'

Holly was glad to have the party to look forward to, and the knitting bee that evening.

Elspeth pinned a notice on the front window of the knitting shop.

*The Knitting Bee is on tonight. Crafting, cakes and chatter!*

She'd changed the date to suit the hurly–burly of the weddings and the ball.

Elspeth had spoken to Fyona at the ball and invited her to come along to the knitting bee. Fyona agreed she'd be there. As did Rosabel and Primrose. And Geneen. The only members missing would be Skye, Ailsa and Nettie. Plus, her Aunt Morven was still away gallivanting around Scotland with her boyfriend, Donall.

But there would be plenty of members buzzing at the bee, knitting, sewing and doing all sorts of crafts. Elspeth had no doubts about what the main topics of their conversation would be — the weddings, the brides' dresses, waltzing, and romance.

Holly and Lyle had looked closer than ever. And Roag and Fyona showed promise of having a summer romance on the island. Everyone had noticed the sparks igniting between them.

Rosabel and Primrose were on their way to open up Innis' cake shop, and saw the notice in the knitting shop window. Elspeth waved out to them as she added pale blue and pink yarn to the window display.

They gave Elspeth the thumbs up that they'd be there at the knitting bee. Elspeth nodded, and they continued on to the cake shop.

The shops in the main street started to open up, as the sun shone along the harbour road, and the bunting fluttered in the warm summer breeze.

'Let's do it.' Nairne sounded keen as he spoke to Roag and Fyona in the kitchen. They were having a brief meeting about the dance party nights. 'A dinner dance is scheduled for tomorrow night anyway. We'll serve a buffet rather than a dinner for the guests.'

'I'll sort out the music for the dancing,' said Roag. 'There will be waltzing, other ballroom dances, popular dances, a great mix for the guests to enjoy.'

Fyona had a copy of the wedding buffet menu, with notes on variations. 'The buffet could be a variation of last night's buffet. Obviously, not as lavish, but with really tasty pastries, puddings and cakes.'

'The main emphasis is on the dancing, and creating a classy, fun party atmosphere,' said Roag.

'I'll tell Murdo to print a note for the guests to let them know that the dance party is on tomorrow night,' said Nairne. And off he went, through to the reception, leaving Roag and Fyona in the kitchen.

253

'We'll organise the second dance party night for the following week,' said Roag.

'Yes, and vary the buffet selection.' Fyona tucked the copy of the buffet menu away.

'Are you busy this evening?'

'I'm going to the knitting bee night. Elspeth invited me.'

Roag looked thoughtful. 'What time does the knitting bee finish?'

'Around nine o'clock.' Fyona didn't want to ask why he wanted to know. She sensed it involved late night dancing.

Roag confirmed her suspicion. 'Would you be up for some midnight dancing with me?'

Her heart reacted, and although she knew he meant it for work, she couldn't help the feelings he stirred in her.

'Yes,' she said brightly. 'Who needs sleep?'

Roag laughed, but acknowledged she was right. 'After we get this first dance night under our belts, we'll make an effort to get ourselves into bed.'

Fyona blinked and smirked, seeing the instant embarrassment show on his face.

'Separate beds, not together,' Roag explained, as she started to laugh at his faux pas. 'I wasn't suggesting you jump into bed with me, Fyona.' His voice was louder than he'd intended, causing the kitchen staff to pause and glance over at him, before getting on with their work.

Fyona tried not to giggle as she got on with baking cheese and potato lattice pastries.

'I know what the topic of gossip is going to be at the knitting bee this evening,' Fyona said under her breath.

'What was that?' Roag said, knowing fine well what she'd muttered.

'I'll make a start on your Christmas scarf at the bee,' she lied.

Roag shook his head, and relented with a smile. 'Perhaps I should fan the flames of the knitting bee gossip by showing Geneen and others the promotional picture that's up on the dance production's website. I was going to show you later, but you seem to be in a playful mood so...'

He sent her a link to the website.

Fyona checked the link on her phone, and gasped when she saw the latest news post and the picture of her posing with Roag, wearing her red dress. He wore his waistcoat. The dance show producer had picked that photo to promote their guest spot on the website.

She read the bold caption and brief details.

*Enjoy an evening watching our popular dance show.*

*Special guests, Roag and Fyona, will perform two spectacular show dances live on stage during the tour.* Dates were included.

There was a clip of them dancing that included Fyona's ballet leaps and spins, and the two of them waltzing together.

*Tickets are now available.*

Fyona gasped. 'They've announced me as if I'm like you, a professional ballroom dancer.'

'Can you tango?'

'A little bit. I'd need to practise.'

'No rest for the wicked, Fyona.' Roag smiled and went to prepare the lunch menu.

'I'll come up to the castle after the knitting bee tonight,' she relented with a smile.

The knitting bee was buzzing with chatter as Fyona arrived to join in. She'd brought a tote bag filled with yarn she'd picked from Nettie's stash, scarf patterns, and knitting needles. And a strawberry and cream sponge cake she'd baked at the castle to contribute to the gathering.

Fyona followed the sounds of the activity through to the back of the knitting shop. Tables and chairs were set up, and the ladies were unpacking their knitting and sewing ready to enjoy an evening of cheery chatter and crafting.

The patio doors at the back of the room were open to allow the evening air in, and the sounds of teacups and plates being set up filtered through from the kitchen where Rosabel and Primrose were helping Elspeth.

Holly smiled when she saw Fyona and waved her over to sit next to her. 'I'm working on a hat and scarf set,' Holly said to her.

Fyona started to unpack her patterns. 'I've brought yarn from Nettie's stash, and patterns. I want to knit a scarf for myself, and one for Roag's Christmas.'

The chatter in the room notched down a few pitches, and the ladies looked at Fyona.

Primrose peered in from the kitchen. 'Knitting a scarf for Roag. You two are getting quite cosy.'

'It's only a Christmas present for him,' said Fyona. 'I promised I'd knit it.'

The giggles and knowing glances from the women showed they weren't completely buying Fyona's explanation.

Elspeth came through to welcome Fyona, and was pleased to accept the cake. 'I'm glad you could come along tonight. I know how busy you are at the castle.'

'And due to get even busier.' The comment was out before Fyona could curtail it.

The chatter stopped, and everyone looked at Fyona.

'I thought things would quieten down a bit now that the weddings and the summer ball are by with,' said Rosabel, joining in the conversation.

Fyona explained about Roag's plan to hold two dance party nights at the castle, and that the first one was scheduled for the following evening. 'Guests staying at the castle will take part. But the invitation to join in is extended to those living locally. It's short notice, but Roag said that if any of you want to come along, it'll be a fun night of dancing and a delicious buffet.'

Primrose and Rosabel nodded to each other. 'We're up for that.'

'Oh, yes,' Holly agreed. 'Roag phoned Lyle earlier and invited us to go. Lyle is baking cakes and pastries for the buffet.'

'Brodrick has a special night at the cafe bar, but maybe we could go to the second dance party,' said Elspeth.

'The dinner dances at the castle are popular with the guests,' said Geneen. 'But I like Roag's idea to have a buffet instead of a full dinner, and lots of exciting dancing. I think the guests will really enjoy it.'

Several ladies were keen to join in the dance party, and after discussing this, the conversation turned to the weddings.

'The brides looked beautiful. All the wedding dresses were lovely,' said Primrose. 'I loved the fabric, the satin and silk.'

'The glittering beadwork on the dresses was wonderful,' Fyona commented.

'They looked like fairytale brides,' said Elspeth.

'Murdo says we'll get to view the video after Finlay and the others come back from their honeymoon,' Geneen told everyone.

'They'll all be sailing up the coast by now,' Primrose remarked.

One of the other ladies sighed. 'How romantic.'

'Have you heard from Skye?' Rosabel said to Holly.

'No, I told her to relax and enjoy her honeymoon, and not feel that she needs to keep me updated,' said Holly. 'But Merrilees said to me a few days ago that she was sending pictures of the wedding dresses to Celia at the fashion magazine. I meant to check if the feature was up yet on the magazine's website.' Holly checked the website on her phone, not expecting to see that it was listed as headline news. 'It's up!' Holly squealed. 'Take a look.'

The ladies gathered round, and others, like Fyona, checked the magazine feature on their own phone.

'The pictures show the dresses so well,' said Fyona. 'There are close–ups of the embroidery work.'

Holly read snippets of the feature out loud.

'*The three brides chose to wear vintage gowns for their fairytale weddings at the castle. From 1930s satin sheath styling, to fabulous forties fashion, and 1950s classic couture...*'

During the evening, Elspeth advised Fyona on what patterns and yarn to use to knit a scarf for herself, and one for Roag.

'I picked several different colours and textures of yarn from Nettie's stash.' Fyona showed Elspeth the colours. 'Nettie has four large balls of this classic grey yarn that I thought would suit Roag. But I'm not sure what pattern to choose.'

Elspeth read the patterns. 'This one would knit up well with the grey yarn.'

Fyona was grateful for Elspeth's expert advice.

'I like this pale blue, double–knit yarn for my scarf, or perhaps the pink,' said Fyona.

'The blue is lovely, and I'd use it with this pattern,' Elspeth advised.

Fyona was happy with the colours and patterns they'd picked, and cast on the stitches to start knitting Roag's scarf.

The evening continued with plenty of chatter, tea, cake and crafting.

As the bee night finished, Fyona packed up her knitting and drove up to the castle. She'd worn a casual dress that would be suitable for dancing, and brought her dance shoes with her.

It was only just after nine in the evening when she arrived at the castle, and went up to the turret.

Roag welcomed her in. He was smartly dressed in dark trousers and a cream shirt.

'How did the knitting bee go?' he said, offering her a cup of tea.

'Great. I made a start on your scarf.' She'd brought the tote bag with her.

'Can I have a peek?'

Fyona opened the bag and let him look at the several rows she'd knitted, hoping he liked the colour.

'I love the colour.' He picked up the knitting.

'Careful, don't drop any stitches off the needles.'

Roag handed it back, and Fyona tucked the knitting safely into the bag.

'Thank you for knitting this for me,' he said, and continued making the tea.

'I found it quite relaxing. Though I imagine I'm in for a lively night of dancing now with you.'

He poured two cups of tea and handed one to her. 'We can't use the function room until very late, so I thought we could practise here tonight. I've moved the couch and chairs to clear the floor. I want to go over some of the dances for tomorrow night. We'll dance a traditional waltz first, and encourage the guests to join in. Then I'd like to include a tango. Add a bit of drama. I think the guests will enjoy it.'

'I've danced a tango at functions, just for fun, and probably got the technique and steps all wrong.'

Roag put some music on. 'I've lined up a selection of songs. This is classic tango music.' He held out his hand to her.

Fyona put her tea down and let Roag take her in hold.

'When dancing a tango, think of being passionate and powerful.'

Passionate was the last thing she wanted to feel when she was here with Roag. It could lead to all sorts of trouble.

'Keep your core strong,' he instructed. 'That's excellent. There should be beauty in your posture, tempting me, drawing me in.'

Fyona felt his strength, holding her close and connected to him.

They began to dance, slow, staccato moves, and Fyona followed his lead, concentrating on the steps, the hold, the posture.

The music filled the turret with a sense of drama and even though the windows were wide open, the heat from their simmering passion burned deep.

Fyona pretended it was the warmth of the evening causing her cheeks to glow.

'You dance the tango well,' he said, feeling his heart thunder from the feelings she stirred in him.

'Are we teaching the dances to the guests at the party?'

'No, just prompting them,' he explained, changing the music for the next dance. 'Since I got the go–ahead to organise the party nights, I've been planning to use three main dances. The waltz, tango, and salsa.'

261

Fyona heard the lively beat of the music. 'I've done salsa, but only on a social level.'

Roag came over and clasped her hands. 'Then let's start moving to the rhythm of the song.'

They spoke while they danced, letting themselves dance freely, enjoying the music and each other's company.

'Between the three main dances there will be other popular songs that the guests can dance to,' he said. 'And all we need to do is give them a prompt by dancing each one.'

'Most of them will be able to waltz,' she agreed. 'And I suppose during a party night atmosphere they'll try to tango.'

'It'll be fun, especially the salsa.'

Roag didn't have to instruct Fyona how to salsa, and they danced until the song ended.

Slightly breathless from the dancing and the excitement they stirred in each other, they stepped back, putting some space between them, and discussed the buffet for the party night.

An hour sparked in and Fyona got ready to leave.

'We'll use the function room in the midnight hours to rehearse our show dance routines,' he said.

'I didn't tell anyone at the knitting bee about us being guest performers on the dance tour.'

'Now that the information is on the dance tour website, it's not a secret.'

'Let's wait until after the party night,' Fyona suggested.

Roag agreed.

Fyona took her dance shoes off and put her flats on. 'I'll see myself out,' she insisted, and headed downstairs and out to her car.

As she put her bag in the car, she glanced up at the turret. Roag was standing at the window, lit by the glow of the lights. He waved down to her.

Fyona waved back and then got into her car and drove away from the castle.

From the turret, Roag watched her leave, and something in his heart ached, a longing he knew could lead to more heartache, even more so than in his past. Stepping away from the window, he put upbeat music on and began to dance, burning off the feelings and excess energy coursing through his entire body.

He was adamant not to overstep and cause trouble for himself and Fyona by venturing into a romance that could go so wrong when everything else in their lives was doing well.

There was no one else on the private floor to hear the music, and he danced well into the late hours without disturbing anyone.

Finally, he stripped off, took a shower, then went to bed, hoping tiredness would help him sleep.

Fyona was determined to go for a swim the next morning before starting work at the castle. Before breakfast, she drove down to the shore. The sea sparkled under the summer sky, and apart from a couple of other people further along the coast, she had it all to herself.

Wearing her red and white polka dot swimsuit, Fyona walked towards the sea and waded in, wondering how cold the water would be, and finding it pleasantly refreshing. There was barely a breeze.

Her hair was pinned up in a ballet bun, and when she was waist deep in the sea, she started to swim, enjoying the feeling of swimming along the shore of the beautiful island.

This was the type of day she'd pictured when she'd agreed to come to the island for a working holiday. Once the dance party night was over, she'd have more time to enjoy things like this. She planned to explore the castle's estate, go back to the waterfall, and take another trip to thistle loch.

Swimming back to where she'd left her towel on the sand, she sat down for a few minutes to enjoy the warm sunshine and the view of the glistening blue sea before driving to the cottage to shower and get changed.

Fyona told Roag about her morning swim when she arrived at the castle kitchen and began to prepare the pastries and cakes for the evening buffet.

'I plan to enjoy the castle's scenery, and go for a sail on thistle loch,' said Roag as he rolled out the pastry for the caramelised apple pies.

'I'm going back to thistle loch when I have a chance,' said Fyona. 'I didn't know you could sail,' she added.

'There used to be two small rowing boats tied up at the edge of the loch for people to use,' Roag explained. 'Murdo says the boats are still there, and so I'm going to row across the loch like I did years ago. It's not as grand as Finlay's yacht, but I remember how much fun I had.' Then he looked thoughtful. 'You're welcome to come with me, if you fancy a wee boating trip.'

The idea instantly appealed to her. 'Yes, I'd like to go, but I've never rowed a boat before.'

'I'm happy to do all the rowing, unless you'd like to take a turn. I'll show you how to use the paddles. It's easy.'

This suggestion appealed to her as well. 'Okay, I will.'

'We'll go soon,' he promised. 'Once the dance party night is over.'

Nairne came bustling over to them, wielding a copy of the buffet menu. 'We're going to have to bake more pastries and cakes for tonight's buffet. Murdo says lots of guests have been discussing it over breakfast in the restaurant. It'll be a wee bit busier than we'd planned to cater for.'

Roag and Fyona had copies of the buffet menu.

'I'll rustle up more mini quiche, sausage rolls, and cheese whirls.' Roag listed off the cakes he'd bake too.

'I'm baking extra lemon drizzle cakes, chocolate eclairs and meringues,' Nairne told them. 'There will be plenty of salads, bread, fresh fruit and scones.'

Fyona checked the menu. 'When I finish these pastries, I'll bake trays of cupcakes and swirl them with vanilla, strawberry and chocolate buttercream.'

Between them, they organised the extra items.

'Did you bring your dress for tonight, and your dance shoes?' Roag said to Fyona as they worked alongside each other in the kitchen.

'They're in the car.'

'Put them upstairs in the turret. The door isn't locked.'

'Maybe I should move half of the clothes in my wardrobe into your turret,' she joked.

Roag laughed. 'Only half?'

Fyona smiled at him and then got on with her baking.

The morning went in quickly, and before her lunch break, Fyona took her dress and shoes up to the turret while Roag was in the kitchen.

Even though she was nosy to see the turret while Roag wasn't there, she wasn't the type to pry or rummage through his wardrobe. But his accommodation was tidy, his bed made, clothes tidied away, presumably by him and not the staff. He was a tidy worker in the kitchen, and it seemed this extended to his private life too.

Roag himself was always well–dressed, something she admired about him.

Fyona hung her shades of blue tulle evening dress on the outside of his wardrobe. She'd packed a few dresses to bring with her to the island, knowing she'd need them for social events at the castle. This dress was soft and fluid, with a ruffled hemline and shoestring straps. She thought it would suit the waltzing, and particularly the tango and salsa dancing.

Taking a moment to look out the window, she admired the view. This would be one of the memories she'd take back with her to Glasgow when this fairytale summer was over.

Lyle drove Holly up to the castle. The windows were aglow with lights against the inky blue evening sky.

He parked the car and escorted her inside. He wore a smart, dark suit, white shirt and tie.

Holly had selected a deep pink, vintage evening dress that flattered her figure.

'You look lovely,' Lyle said, giving her hand a squeeze as they walked through the busy reception and into the function room.

Music played in the background, and guests were milling around and helping themselves to the buffet.

Holly and Lyle saw Fyona and Roag and went over to them.

'It's busier than I thought it would be,' Holly said to them.

Lyle's cakes were part of the buffet, and he noticed the change in the menu from the wedding selection. 'A temping array at the buffet again.'

'We had to rustle up extra,' Roag confided. 'More guests wanted to join in the dancing.'

Murdo made the opening announcement. 'Good–evening. I hope you will enjoy the buffet and dancing tonight. The dances include popular numbers, and waltzing, tango and a wee bit of salsa.'

The guests glanced at each other in pleasant surprise, and Roag and the others heard the murmurs of *tango and salsa dancing*!

'We're starting the night with a classic ballroom waltz,' Murdo announced. 'Please take your partners on to the dance floor.'

The introduction to the music began, and as the floor started to fill up with couples eager to dance, Roag and Fyona, and Lyle and Holly, joined in.

As Roag and Fyona danced around, they saw one or two familiar faces, including Rosabel and Primrose waltzing around with a couple of men who'd invited them to dance. Geneen was up dancing too, though she was still on duty to help Murdo and the staff.

Nairne peeked into the function room, checking on the buffet, and then hurried back through to the kitchen.

Roag had given Murdo a rundown of the music to be played for the dances. Murdo was also in charge of using his phone to video the dances, and the buffet. Roag had promised Finlay there would be clips to put up on the castle's website.

Two popular songs played after the first two waltzes, and then the tango was announced.

'Take your partners for the tango!' Murdo said from the small stage.

Excitement erupted through the function room, and although most of the guests weren't capable tango dancers, they were willing to give it a go.

'Come on, Fyona,' Roag said to her, and took her in hold.

As the music kicked in, so did Roag and Fyona, using bold, staccato moves, encouraging the guests to follow their lead.

There was laughter from the guests, and exaggerated moves, as the majority of them had an impression of what a tango entailed. The evening wasn't about being an expert dancer. It was about having fun, dancing to great music on the well–sprung floor of the function room. And it was all part of their stay at the castle.

From the stage, Murdo filmed the tango dancing, and guests had been advised that this would happen, though no one objected to being included in the footage. Quite the opposite. Most hoped to see themselves on the website.

Roag dipped Fyona in a dramatic move during their tango, causing others to try this.

Laughter erupted as the guests enjoyed the fun of the dancing.

Fyona gasped as Roag clutched her body close to his in the final part of the tango, and ended with him holding her in a passionate pose.

Roag's firm lips were a breath away from hers, and for a moment, she thought he would kiss her, and knew she wouldn't have resisted.

They blinked from their intimate moment as the guests applauded their performance.

Fyona smiled and tried not to blush.

Roag acknowledged their applause with a grateful nod.

Then the dancing continued with a popular song, and Roag led Fyona over to the buffet for a refreshing break.

'I've scheduled the next dance party night for the following week,' Roag told Fyona. 'That will be the last one before I leave.'

'It should encourage Finlay and the others to include this in the castle's activities.'

'Yes.' He looked around. 'People are enjoying themselves. It's a lot livelier than the dinner dances, and those can still be on the itinerary.'

'You've added something new and exciting,' she said.

'With your help, Fyona.'

The salsa music began, and they finished their cold drinks and headed on to the floor.

'Ready to salsa?' said Roag, holding her hands and giving her a sexy grin.

'Nope,' she joked.

'Too bad.' And he whisked her around, prompting the guests to join in.

And they did. So too did Lyle and Holly.

'No, Lyle! It's too fast,' Holly shrieked.

'Nah! It's salsa!' Lyle gyrated. 'Come on, Holly. Give it laldy.'

Holly could barely dance for laughing, but then realised, this was always what happened when she was with Lyle.

Even those with no experience in salsa dancing were really giving it a go.

The evening finished with a slow dance, and Roag waltzed with Fyona, before being pulled into conversations with the guests wanting to talk to him about his dancing.

Fyona slipped upstairs to the turret to pick up her things. She kept her dress on, but changed into her pumps for the drive home.

When she came back down, she found Roag deep in conversation with some of the guests at reception.

Murdo was there, and she nodded to Roag on her way out, eager to get home to relax.

She was about to drive off when Roag came running out of the castle and smiled in the window.

'Thank you so much for all the dancing this evening. I couldn't have done this type of party night without you,' he said.

'I've enjoyed learning even more dance moves from you.' She smiled at him. 'But it's late, and I thought I'd get back and try to get some sleep.'

Roag nodded, smiled and waved her off.

Fyona had fallen asleep as soon as she went to bed, and woke up half an hour early, feeling refreshed. So she put her swimsuit on, pinned her hair up in a ballet bun, grabbed a towel and drove down to the shore.

The morning sunlight already cast a summer glow across the sea, and she had the shore all to herself.

Kicking her shoes off, she was surprised by her own exuberance as she ran into the sea, and started playfully splashing about, and twirling around in the sunlight, arms extended, a bathing ballerina.

Diving smoothly into the sea, she began to swim the route she'd taken the previous day, knowing the length suited her.

On the way back she suddenly had an overwhelming sense of Roag, and slowed down, and looked around, half expecting to see his handsome face bob to the surface, smiling at her. But no, there was no sign of him, or anyone. She still had the shore all to herself, so she swam on, heading back to where she'd left her towel.

Roag was fresh from the shower and stood at the open window buttoning up his shirt collar while gazing out at the view of the glistening sea and white sand shore in the distance. Deep thoughts occupied his mind, and he breathed in the sea air, hoping to clarify the things he was planning. And in the heart of those thoughts was Fyona. Beautiful Fyona, the one woman he'd ever known who constantly challenged him in ways he cherished and admired.

There were plans he had in mind, but hadn't quite moved the pieces around the mental chess board to make them the correct moves. Gazing far out at the sea he thought about Fyona. Once he had the last pieces set, he wanted to talk to her in private, where their conversation wouldn't be easily disturbed. Certainly not in the kitchen during stolen moments having a tea or lunch break. Or during the dance chorography he'd planned for their stage performance. No, he needed somewhere else, and then an idea came to mind.

Deciding to invite her to join him on an excursion one afternoon to thistle loch, he headed downstairs to the kitchen to cook himself breakfast and make an early start to the day. She'd already agreed to a trip to the loch, but they hadn't set a date. He planned to check her rota in the kitchen.

Fyona shook the water from her face as she emerged from the sea. She sat down on the sand for a few minutes, again enjoying the early morning sunlight.

The work day at the castle was pretty jam–packed as she'd agreed to help Nairne make a large batch of shortbread, chocolate cakes covered in ganache, and decorate a fruit cake with royal icing.

She was officially off from work in the afternoon and evening, having not taken any breaks since she'd arrived. And she aimed to relax in the cottage until it was time to head back to the castle for her midnight dance rendezvous with Roag.

Roag already had a chunk of the morning's menu underway when Fyona arrived.

'You look bright and breezy,' he commented.

'I went swimming again at first light. I had the shore all to myself. It was sheer bliss. I'll certainly miss doing this when I go home to Glasgow.' She shrugged off any wearying thoughts, and shrugged on her chef's jacket.

The large fruit cake was set on a stand waiting to be iced.

'I'll work on the first layer of royal icing,' Fyona called over to Nairne. 'Then make the chocolate ganache cakes while it sets.'

Nairne stirred a large pot of summer vegetable soup and gave Fyona the thumbs up from across the kitchen.

Roag used a pastry cutter to make the leaves on the top of a shortcrust pastry leek and potato pie. He popped the pie in the oven to cook, and on his way back to where he was making another pie, he paused to talk to Fyona.

'I noticed on the rota that you have a full day off tomorrow,' he said.

Fyona sensed that it was about to be taken up with something Roag was brewing.

'I do.' She continued to mix the ingredients for the chocolate cakes.

'I wondered if you'd like to accompany me to thistle loch. I'll pack us a picnic lunch. We could go for a sail on the loch.'

All of this appealed to her, but she sensed he had something else to add. 'And?' she said, boldly.

No fooling Fyona he thought, even though this wasn't his objective. 'And, I'd like to talk to you, in private, where we won't be interrupted.'

'Talk to me about what?'

'I'd prefer to tell you in private.'

'Okay. But you do the rowing. I don't know how to wield a paddle.'

'You could learn. I could teach you. It's easy, and you're a fit young lady.'

'If this is a ruse to get me to row you around the loch, you're going in the water.' She lifted her bendy spatula and gestured firmly.

Roag held up his hands in mock surrender. 'The thought never crossed my mind.'

Fyona shook her head at him and smiled.

'And are we still on for our late night dancing this evening?' he ventured to check.

'We are. But I'm off this afternoon and going to relax in the cottage. So I'll arrive dressed for the dancing. Is there something special I should wear? Leggings and a vest top? A dress? A ballet wrap skirt?'

'The wrap skirt. We're going to utilise your ballet skills this evening as part of the routines.'

'I'll bring my low heel ballet shoes. They're very flexible and comfortable, and I like them for various dance moves.'

'Bring your ballroom shoes too.'

'I will.'


The afternoon sun flickered through the trees as Fyona drove down the forest road to the cottage having finished all the baking and other tasks for the day.

Making herself a cup of tea, she sat outside in the garden under the shade of an umbrella and unwound from the recent activity. The flowers were wafting in the light breeze blowing up from the shore, and filling the air with their fragrance. She wished she could bottle the scent of this summer by the sea and take it back to the city with her. But the memories of this time would linger for ever.

In the late afternoon she decided to be sensible and went inside and relaxed on the couch, inadvertently falling asleep. She woke up in the glow of an amber twilight streaming into the pretty living room, highlighting the stash of yarn on the shelves that she still found so tempting to knit with.

Padding through to the kitchen, she made herself a light dinner of Scotch broth, bread, and a side salad. She ate it in the kitchen with the door wide open, taking advantage of the warmth of the summer evening.

There were still a few hours before it was time to drive up to the castle, so she relaxed and made a start on her scarf, casting on forty stitches and knitting a few rows with the lovely blue, double–knit yarn. She thought if she knitted the scarves in tandem, she might have both of them finished in time for Christmas.

Later, she refreshed her makeup, brushed her hair, and tucked the gold ballroom shoes in her bag, along with a white, crossover wrap top to wear on the drive home.

Then she put on her pale blue leotard and matching maxi–length chiffon ballet wrap skirt. She wore her low heel ballet shoes, and used her barre to stretch in readiness for the dance practise with Roag.

Finishing her warm–up routine, she picked up her bag, and headed out. The stars twinkled in the night sky as she drove up to the castle, parked her car, went inside and up to the turret.

Roag was ready and waiting for her, and his smile warmed her heart. He wore his black dance trousers with an open–neck white shirt.

He admired her outfit. 'You look like a ballroom dancing ballerina. The perfect combination for what we're going to practise tonight.' He gestured over to where he had his laptop set up, paused at a video showing clips from the dance show's previous tour. 'But I'd like to show you this before we go down to the function room. The clips were put up today on the show's website.'

Fyona stood beside him and watched the three clips. Roag was in two of them.

There was stylishness and strength in his routines.

'The new choreography will give a nod to the previous routines from last year's tour,' he said. 'But I really want to use your ballet skills to create a fresh take on our performance.'

She understood and agreed with this, but as he went to close the laptop, she noticed that a couple of the venues were booked solid. Sold out signs were emblazoned next to the two theatres.

'It could be a coincidence, but tickets sales have increased again since the producer put our picture and details on the website,' said Roag.

Fyona blinked. 'These are fairly large venues. And they're sold out!'

'This happens, especially when the guest dancers are announced, and extra venues are going to be added. There's a lot of interest in the show, and it's being promoted to include our performances.'

The excitement stirred in her. She should've been equally nervous, but instead she felt eager to take part in the show.

He studied her. 'You look relaxed. Did you enjoy your afternoon off.'

'I did. I sat in the garden, then relaxed inside and started knitting my scarf. After making dinner, I did a ballet barre routine to get ready for this evening, then I drove up here.'

Roag smiled to himself. Her relaxing time sounded quite busy in its own way.

He checked the time. 'It's extremely late, so that means we now have the function room all to ourselves.'

Fyona laughed and they went downstairs to the reception. Murdo was on duty and gave Roag the thumbs up that the security cameras were switched on to record their dance practise.

Roag nodded to Murdo, and then led Fyona into the function room and closed the doors so as not to disturb the guests.

By the light of the chandeliers, Roag played the first song. 'It's upbeat but dramatic. It's great for an opening number. I've got other songs and I'll let you hear them too. But let's try dancing to this one first.'

Fyona straightened her posture and got ready to learn the choreography.

'We'll start together in a romantic embrace,' he began, pulling her close to him. 'Then when the music changes, we'll be thrown apart, as if something has come between us.'

Fyona went along with the choreography, pleased that she was able to pick it up.

'Great,' he said encouragingly. 'Now we dance apart. I'll perform steps that are similar to the ones I used before.'

'What do you want me to do?'

'I'm throwing you in at the deep end, Fyona. Dance what you feel. Interpret the music, the heartache, longing and drama. Use your beautiful ballet skills.'

Come on, she urged herself, feeling the energy of the music. She'd done interpretive dance as part of her modern stage training, though that was years ago, but the feelings flooded back.

Roag danced while being in awe of what Fyona was doing, covering the floor with strong but elegant moves, leaping into the air when the music hit a crescendo, and interpreting the heartache as if it was real. Maybe it was. They'd both been unlucky in love.

He danced towards her during the second verse, expecting her to fold into his arms as he reached out to her.

Instead, Fyona spun away at speed. Her multiple pirouettes took her to the other side of the dance floor. The look she gave him across the room burned through him.

'Yes!' he said, unable to contain his enthusiasm. 'This is wonderful.'

He danced towards her again, and this time she fooled him by letting him think she was in his grasp, but as they went into a waltz movement, she made her escape, spinning away again.

Roag hoped that this was being captured on video, because if they could perform this powerful and romantic routine, he knew audiences would love it.

'I'm coming to capture your heart now, to make it mine,' he said, prompting her.

'Do I give in to you?' she said, dancing around him, flitting like a fairytale ballerina.

Roag reached out, and his strength could not be resisted as he pulled her into his loving embrace.

'Do you want to?' His voice was deep with passion and longing.

Was he acting? Was this part of the routine? Or was this a flicker of how he felt about her?

'Yes,' she said breathlessly, revealing the truth that bolstered her and troubled her, for how could there be a happy ever after ending for two people like them. The flames of their characters both burned bright, and seemed to come to life particularly in the midnight hours when they were alone, dancing, romancing... But like anything that burns so fierce, there's a danger of one or both of them having their feelings scorched.

His heart already bore too many scars from the battlefield of love. So did Fyona's, though less so. But that didn't make it any less harsh.

'Take a chance with me, Fyona,' he said, dancing her across the floor, almost in a tango hold, with his body pressed hard against hers.

She could feel the lean muscles of his entire body, and tried and failed to hide the effect his potent masculinity had on her.

Roag caught the look in her eyes as she gazed up at him, and as the music ended on a dramatic note, so did their dance.

He held her for a second too long, revealing his passionate and growing love for her.

His lips were a breath away from hers, but then he stepped back and applauded. 'That. Was. Magnificent.'

Breathless from the feelings he ignited, rather than the dancing, she smiled at him. 'Will it do?'

'It'll more than do. I think we've just nailed one of our routines tonight. We won't dance another routine. Let this one sink in and linger. Sleep on it. We'll both remember it better.'

Fyona agreed.

Roag switched the music off, and led Fyona upstairs to collect her things, and then he escorted her back down to her car.

The night air was hot, offering no breeze to cool his ardour.

As she got into her car, he leaned down and spoke through the open window. 'That's one of the best routines I've ever danced.'

Fyona smiled at him. 'Send me a copy of the video. I'd love to watch it again.'

'I'll go and get a copy from Murdo.' He stepped back from the car.

'What time should I come up here tomorrow for our trip to thistle loch?' she said before driving off.

'I'll pick you up at eleven tomorrow morning,' he said. 'I know where the cottage is.'

'I'll be ready.' She smiled at him and drove off, wondering what was so important that he wanted to talk to her in private. Something to do with the next dance party night? The catering for the buffet? She was still thinking what it could be as she pulled up outside the cottage and went inside.

Roag sat in the turret watching the video on his laptop. He'd sent a copy to Fyona. Murdo had it ready fast.

Seeing them dancing together, Roag saw the potential in their partnership. Dance partnership, he reminded himself, though he had other thoughts in mind.

Fyona would've had an earlier night if she hadn't been so excited to watch the dance video several times.

But she woke up anticipating a lovely day at thistle loch.

She was all set to go, wearing a blue chambray summer dress and pumps, and when she saw Roag's red car drive up, she grabbed her bag and hurried out into the bright sunny day.

'I've packed a picnic basket for us,' Roag said as she got into the car.

It was on the back seat.

'I love picnics,' Fyona said, relaxing back to enjoy the drive along the shore, up through the forest and onwards to the loch, set in the heart of the rolling countryside.

They chatted about the dance video and laughed when they both confessed they'd watched it several times.

'All we have to do now is learn it, so our performances are confident,' he said.

'Should we learn this routine before we start the choreography for the second show dance?'

'No, we'll nail the second routine and then practise both of them. So, if you're free for another late night of dancing...'

'I am.'

Roag smiled over at her, and then navigated the car through the forest until the road opened out to reveal thistle loch and the surrounding countryside.

'I expected others to be here enjoying the beauty of the loch,' she said as he parked the car and they stepped out into the lush grass scattered with wildflowers.

Roag wore black trousers and a classic, collarless white linen shirt that had a vintage quality to it. A remnant from his dancing days.

He looked around, holding the picnic basket. 'We're the only ones.' He strode over to where two small rowing boats were tied up at the edge of the loch. Putting the picnic basket in first, he clasped Fyona's hand and helped her sit down at the stern of the boat, facing him as he sat at the front and took charge of the oars.

Reaching over, he untied the rope that secured the boat to the edge posts, and used the oars to push them off into the loch.

'The water is so calm,' she remarked, looking at the sky and surrounding scenery reflected in the smooth surface.

Before revealing what he wanted to talk to her about, he rowed the boat across the loch, and then offered her a chance to take charge.

Giggling, Fyona changed seats with him, being careful not to topple into the loch, and gripped the oars. She'd seen how he'd handled the boat, and tried to emulate this.

'Row us back across to the other side,' he suggested. 'Unless you'd like to stop halfway for a cup of tea or hot chocolate.'

Fyona blinked. 'Hot chocolate on a summer's day!'

'Why not?' He lifted the lid of the picnic basket to show her the two flasks.

'I'm struggling to think of a reason other than it's a hot day, but...' She grinned at him.

He poured two cups of hot chocolate, and made her laugh when she saw he'd brought mini marshmallows for the topping.

'Anyone would think you were a chef,' she teased him, setting the oars down, and accepted one of the cups. 'Cheers.'

'Cheers.' He relaxed and sipped his drink, enjoying being out on the loch, and her company.

They chatted about their dancing while finishing their hot chocolate, and then he put their empty cups back into the basket.

Fyona smiled at him. 'So, there was something you wanted to discuss with me in private. It could hardly be more private than this.'

Roag took a steadying breath. If he said this wrong, it could affect their friendship, and their dance partnership, so he needed to do this right.

Fyona sensed the struggle in him, but sat calmly, waiting on what he wanted to discuss.

Finally, he spoke up. 'There's something I want to ask you.' He took another deep breath. 'I want to propose—'

Fyona reacted instantly, gasping, surprised, elated, and totally taken aback. And in that moment, she accidentally knocked against the oars.

Roag stood up, making a grab for the oars, and in the meleé, Fyona managed to whack him with an oar, sending him toppling backwards into the loch with a huge splash.

She shrieked, hoping he'd bob back up to the surface. And he did, spluttering water.

Reaching out her hand, she offered to try to pull him into the boat, but it threatened to capsize, so he stayed where he was, swimming behind the boat while

Fyona floundered around, trying to handle the oars and row the boat as quickly as she could back to the edge.

Surprising herself, she managed to do this, and clambered out, holding the rope and tied it to the post.

Roag was now in the shallows, wading out, drenched from head to toe. His white shirt clung to every muscled contour of his body, and the fabric hid nothing, having become almost transparent. His trousers showed his long, lean thighs to full advantage.

Shame on her for taking in the sexy, gorgeous man that Roag was. Double handsome? Right now, she'd triple that score.

'Step back from the edge,' he warned her. 'We don't need both of us taking a dive into the loch.'

Fyona took his advice, for her heart was thundering and her senses were cast to the breeze.

'I'm so sorry,' she apologised. 'I didn't mean to hit you with the oar when you proposed to me.'

Roag frowned. Now her reaction made sense. 'I wanted to propose a *business idea. A business proposal.*'

His clarification flipped her world upside down again. She wasn't sure what was the most exciting or disappointing. Roag didn't want to marry her. He wanted her to get into bed with him for business.

Leaving her wondering what type of business proposal he had in mind, he went over to his car, stripping his wet shirt off along the way. The muscles in his broad back glistened in the sunlight, throwing her senses again.

Calm down, she scolded herself. And then failed as he called over to her.

'I'm going to take everything off.' He had a change of clothes in the boot of his car, not because he expected to tumble into the loch, just a habit from his dancing days. He always had something spare to wear.

Don't peek, she scolded herself yet again, as he took his trousers off and stood for a moment in his briefs while digging out dry clothes to put on.

What a physique, she thought, clearly not taking a telling off from herself. And then looked away as he was about to strip everything off.

Fyona lifted the picnic basket from the boat and sat it down on the grass.

Then she heard him walking towards her, and turned to see him wearing another pair of black trousers, dry shoes, and he'd flung a white shirt on, but it was unbuttoned, exposing his lean six–pack.

Her heart took another hit as his shirt wafted in the breeze as he walked closer and ran his hands through his wet hair, pushing it back from his face.

She assessed his expression. Grumpy, accusing, displeased with her? None of these fitted.

'It's my own fault,' his deep voice told her. 'I should've waited until we were on dry land before talking to you.'

'Do you want to tell me now?'

He shook his head. Water droplets trickled down his sculptured features. 'We'll talk under less stressful circumstances. I'll drive you back to the cottage.' He dumped the picnic basket in the car.

Fyona got in, and during the drive they barely exchanged a word, except a couple of polite remarks as he said they'd chat some other time.

Roag dropped her off at the cottage, and then drove away. She felt the heaviness trail behind him. Sighing wearily, she went inside and closed the door on their disastrous trip to the loch.

He muttered to himself as he headed along the shore road and then up through the forest to the castle. What a mess of a day! He should've waited until they were having their picnic to talk to her about his plans. But more than anything, he couldn't stop thinking about Fyona's reaction when she thought he was going to propose marriage. She was surprised, shocked, but then smiled.

The more he thought about the situation, maybe there was something even better to be found than he'd intended. Did Fyona like him? Really like him? And not just as a friend.

His mind was still in a whirl as he trudged up the stairs to the turret. Everyone was too busy to notice him. He looked ruffled, but his clothes were dry.

Upstairs he jumped in the shower and emerged feeling less tense. Wrapping a towel around his waist he sent a message to Fyona.

*Have dinner with me tonight.*

A few minutes later she replied.

*Okay. Will I come up to the castle?*

*No. I'll bring dinner down to the cottage. If that's okay.*

*It is.*

*See you around seven.* Roag finished the messages between them. This was the only way he could think of to salvage the situation. Surely he could talk to her in private at the cottage.

287

At five minutes to seven the red car pulled up outside the cottage. Fyona had changed out of the blue chambray, into a floral print dress that was light and airy. Nothing to remind them that he'd taken a dook in the loch.

She opened the front door and welcomed him in. 'I've set the table in the kitchen. I thought we could have dinner there.'

Roag nodded, and carried through another picnic basket that was larger than the last one. He set it down on the old–fashioned dresser and began to unpack the dinner he'd brought. Scottish cheddar pie with light as air pastry, roast potatoes, salad with cherry tomatoes and greentails, and a selection of relishes including bramble chutney.

Roag took charge of the oven. 'I'll pop these in to heat.' He put the pie and potatoes in and set the timer.

The kitchen door was open to let the air in.

Roag thumbed through to the hallway. 'I noticed all the colourful yarn in the living room as I came in.'

His interest prompted her to show him through while the dinner heated.

'This is my Aunt Nettie's stash.' Fyona gestured to the shelves that were filled with balls and skeins of yarn.

He nodded, impressed, and then stepped back into the hallway, intending to go through the kitchen. But he paused seeing Fyona's bedroom door was open and noticed her barre.

'Is that the infamous ballet barre?' He walked towards it.

'It is.'

'Mind if I take a look?'

'Not at all.'

The barre was set just inside the bedroom door, and he ran his hand along part of the barre feeling how sturdy it was for something so lightweight.

Fyona stood watching him from the doorway. 'Try it out if you want.'

Roag took little persuasion. He was wearing a pair of black trousers, the dance version that had a stretch in them, and a cream shirt with the sleeves rolled up to reveal the corded muscles of his lean forearms.

Holding on to the barre like a ballet professional, Roag surprised her by going into first position and then doing a perfect plié. Then he stretched one leg along the length of the barre displaying his strength and flexibility. He wasn't parading himself, and watching him up close, she felt the power and years of dance training in him.

Stepping back he nodded as he looked at the barre. 'I think I'll get one of these for my house. I use the back of a chair to do my warm–up stretches before dancing at night after a long day at the restaurant.'

The picture he conjured up was of a man with two talents that were hard to fit into one life.

'It must've been difficult to step away from your dancing career,' she said. It was a subject they'd touched on briefly, but she wanted to discuss it further.

There was a silence in the bedroom before he replied. 'It was,' he said finally, before revealing more than he had before. 'They say that a dancer never really stops being a dancer, even when their performing days are done. For some, like me, it's over when they're still in their thirties, but I'd been dancing for almost thirty years, since I was a wee boy. That's not a bad run at it.'

Fyona continued to listen to him.

He ran his hand along the smooth white finish on the barre. 'I love my restaurant and being a chef. But there are times when all it takes is to hear a song play and I'm cast right back to a time when I danced to it, remembering every step, the rhythm of the routine. I actually feel it in my arms, my legs.' He took his hand off the bar and smiled round at her. 'Muscle memory.'

'I know what you mean. I often hear a piece of classic ballet music and remember dancing to it when I was a wee girl in the dance classes.' She shrugged. 'The feelings never really go away. Though it must be more intense for you having performed on stage to audiences. I imagine the atmosphere was incredible.'

'It was.' His deep voice resonated in the quietude of the bedroom.

The shared understanding seemed to deepen the feelings between them.

'Do you dance often when you're at home?' she said.

He nodded. 'I use the polished wooden floor space in my living room and leap about to the music, on my own. We can use the floor to practise our show routines, once we decide on the choreography.'

'Promise we won't squabble over the dance moves. We haven't had any artistic differences yet, but...' She shrugged.

He stepped closer, and those blue–green eyes of his gazed down at her. 'I've no desire to squabble with you, Fyona.'

The word *desire* and her name jumped out at her. She startled herself from the intensity of the feelings he stirred in her. A blush rose up across her cheeks.

The timer sounded on the oven.

'Saved by the bell,' she said, chirpily, and ran away through to the kitchen.

Roag strode after her. 'Saved from what?'

'Nothing.' She smiled tightly, grabbed the oven mitts and lifted out the tray of piping hot pie and roast tatties. Putting it down, they busied themselves serving it up on the plates while the kettle boiled.

'You look hot,' he observed.

Fyona blinked.

'Your cheeks,' he clarified.

'Ah, for a moment I thought you were paying me a compliment about my dress.'

'All your dresses are very nice. I like your style. I see the dancer in your couture.'

'Oooh! I'll take that compliment,' she said. 'Recently, I've had a love for vintage fashion. I plan to stock up from Skye and Holly's shop before I leave the island. And I'll probably buy from them online when I'm back on the mainland.'

'I like the designs from the past, classic, traditional. Maybe they'll have another vintage waistcoat I can buy before we go.'

Fyona glanced at him. There was something in the way he included her in his leaving. She shrugged off

291

the notion as the kettle boiled. 'Would you like tea? Or do you prefer hot chocolate?' Her smile teased him.

'Tea,' he said, smiling, and garnishing their dinner with salad and relish.

They sat down at the kitchen table to enjoy their meal.

'I'd like to talk to you about a business proposal,' he said.

Fyona cut into a roast potato and nodded to him.

'Have you found a job yet in Glasgow, or Edinburgh?'

'Not yet.'

'Would you be interested in working with me?'

Fyona was taken aback. 'At your restaurant?'

Roag shook his head. 'No. Unless that's what you'd prefer. But I have another suggestion. Did you see the coffee shop next door to my restaurant?'

'Vaguely, when I walked past it. A wee coffee shop,' she recalled.

'Since the New Year, I've been wanting to expand my business. I know the coffee shop owners. They're moving to larger premises. I've spoken to them, and to the property owners about taking on the lease. Everyone is amenable to this. I was in the throes of discussing the deal when the laird phoned and wanted my help to oversee the castle. So I put the plans on ice to come here. But when I get back, I fully intend to take on the shop lease. The owners of the coffee shop haven't found suitable premises to move to yet, so the timing has worked out nicely for all of us.'

'You want to own a coffee shop? Or expand the restaurant premises next door?'

'Neither,' said Roag. 'I want to run it as a vintage tearoom.'

Fyona's eyes showed her surprise. 'And you want me to...?'

'Help me run it. Make it a success. Work with me, not for me,' he emphasised.

The idea of running a vintage tearoom in Glasgow filled her with excitement. 'I have some money to invest, but it's not much and—'

'I'm not looking for you to invest any money, but again, you can if you wish. I want your expertise, and seeing your skills in the castle's kitchen, I couldn't wish for someone better than you, Fyona. I trust you.' He smiled. 'And we seem to get along.'

'Even when I topple you into a loch?'

'There are no lochs near my restaurant, so I think I'm safe.'

She smiled warmly at him. 'A vintage tearoom. I've long wanted to open one, and planned to when I had the finances.'

Roag tucked into his dinner. 'I think it would be a great business venture for both of us. But think it over. Oh, and I wanted to show you this.' He took his phone from his pocket and held up a message from the dance show producer. 'This is the deal proposed by the producer for your dance tour performances.'

Fyona read the sum of money and blinked. 'Really?'

'Guest performers for this show are well–paid. Each performance is quite lucrative in earnings. And according to the producer, sales of tickets were great, but they've definitely increased again since we were promoted as part of the performances.'

'Audiences know you, but they don't know me.'

'But they will, and apparently people have enjoyed seeing the clips of us dancing. So ticket sales are up. A win for everyone. It'll be a great show, an entertaining night out at the theatre. Live dancing, music, guest performances. I'd be sitting in the audience enjoying it if I wasn't one of the dancers.'

Fyona smiled at him, and he grinned across at her.

'Eat your dinner,' he said. 'We've been doing more talking than munching. Nairne made this pie and it's tasty.'

'So are the roast tatties.'

'Thank you,' he said, indicating he'd cooked them.

'A vintage tearoom in the city,' she mused.

Roag gestured to her plate. 'Get your dinner down you. And think it over before you say yes.'

'It's a *yes* from me.' She threw him a mischievous smile, and then tucked into her dinner.

Roag revealed another piece of news. 'Murdo spoke to me as I was leaving the castle. He couldn't help but see our latest dance routine on the video, and he wondered if it was something we were planning for the next dance party night. So I told him about us taking part in the tour, and gave him a link to the show's website. He saw the picture of us.'

'I expect the gossip will circulate soon.'

Roag nodded. 'But let's keep the tearoom news to ourselves for now.'

'Agreed.'

After dinner, they cleared the plates away together and packed them in the basket. Roag took it out to his car and put it in the boot.

Gazing out at the burnished seascape as the sun refused to give way to the twilight, he took a deep breath.

'Want to go for a meander along the shore, to walk off that dinner,' he suggested.

Fyona nodded and closed the cottage door, and got into Roag's car.

He drove them down and they got out and walked down on to the sand.

'The sea is dazzling.' Fyona shielded her eyes.

'Are you going swimming in the morning?' he said, walking beside her.

'Probably. I've got the shore more or less all to myself really early in the morning.'

'Want company?'

'Okay.'

'I'll drive down early.' He took a deep breath of the warm sea air, and continued to walk beside her as they discussed their plans for the dance tour, the tearoom, and the final dance party night at the castle.

During the next few days, Fyona and Roag spent a lot of time together, swimming, going back to the loch and not tumbling into the water, dancing, baking and organising the buffet for the party night.

On the evening of the last dance party night, the castle was lit by the glow of the fading sunlight after another warm summer's day.

The patio doors in the function room were open, the buffet was set with a delicious selection of food, and music played in the background as the guests arrived.

As it was their last special dance party, Fyona wore the sparkling evening dress that was more like a fairytale ball gown, and Roag was elegantly suited.

The dancing began with a waltz, and Roag led Fyona around the floor. Others living locally were invited, and Primrose and Rosabel were there, along with Elspeth and Brodrick, and Holly and Lyle.

Murdo and Geneen were on duty, but joined in the dancing too.

Roag repeated the success of the previous week's dance choices, and guests enjoyed another lively and fun night at the castle. Clips from the previous dance party night had been posted on the castle's website, and Murdo captured more clips to help promote the castle's dance nights.

'You look beautiful in that dress,' Roag said to Fyona as they waltzed under the chandeliers during the last dance.

'It's one of the designs I bought from the vintage dress shop.'

'This evening is another success,' Nairne said to Roag and Fyona as he went by. 'I think Finlay will want to include dance parties like this from now on.'

They nodded to Nairne as he hurried away to the kitchen.

Roag wrapped Fyona in his arms as they slow–danced to the final song.

As she smiled up at him, the main lights dimmed, creating a romantic atmosphere lit by sparkling chandeliers. And for the first time, Roag leaned down and kissed Fyona.

She didn't resist, feeling the warmth of his sensual lips press against hers. And for a moment, they were lost in each other.

The lights gradually turned back up, signalling the evening was over, and guests cheerfully filtered out of the function room.

'I'm sorry, Fyona. I let the atmosphere get the better of me. I shouldn't have overstepped,' Roag apologised.

'It's okay. I think we both got a bit carried away.'

Neither of them spoke about it again, and Fyona drove back to the cottage, still feeling the loving kiss from Roag on her lips.

From his turret later that night, Roag stood gazing out at the star–filled sky, and the sea glistening in the distance. And he thought about Fyona. He'd overstepped, but she hadn't resisted him. And for the first time he thought there was hope that she felt as strongly about him as he did about her.

In the quiet of the night, standing there, he was truthful with himself. He was falling deeply in love with Fyona. But he wasn't sure how this would end. In the meantime, there was work to do during the last week of his stay at the castle. He planned to concentrate on that, rather than romance.

The last week at the castle was busy, fun and exciting. Roag and Fyona managed a few nights of midnight dancing in the function room, working on their choreography. A meeting had been arranged for them with the dance show producer as soon as they got back home to Glasgow. They were due to sail off on the ferry, the day the honeymoon couples arrived home, and meet with the producer that evening. Everything was planned.

But Murdo received a call from Finlay, changing the honeymoon schedule.

Murdo beckoned to Roag at the reception.

'Is something wrong?' Roag said to him.

'I've had a call from Finlay. They're extending their honeymoon trip by one day. They've been having a wonderful time, swimming nearly every day, enjoying their visits to the islands and wee towns. And they want to stop off at the Isle of Arran on their way back.'

'I can't change my plans, Murdo. Fyona and I have booked the ferry for tomorrow afternoon. I thought we'd have lunch with Finlay and the others, and then we'd leave for Glasgow. We're meeting the dance show producer that evening. And my staff at the restaurant are expecting me back on time. It would upset everyone's schedule.'

'I told Finlay that you and Fyona are due to leave, and he understands, but says he hopes you'll come back to the castle for a visit soon,' said Murdo.

'We will,' Roag assured him. 'You haven't seen the last of us. I'll be bringing more trouble to your castle in the future.'

'Ach, you were no trouble at all. Quite the opposite. We've all had a great time with you and Fyona being here. You'll be sorely missed.'

For their last night on the island, Roag invited Fyona to have dinner with him in the turret. He wore a dark suit, white shirt and tie.

When she arrived, wearing a lovely floral dress, he guided her over to where he'd moved the table to the window so they could dine while admiring the view. He'd set it with white linen and a candle lamp.

Staff kindly brought their dinner up, and Fyona sat opposite Roag, expecting them to reminisce about their time on the island.

But Roag had something else he wanted to talk to her about.

'I wanted to talk to you in private,' he began.

'Another business venture?'

'No, nothing to do with business.'

She ate her dinner and looked across at him. He looked handsome, but slightly serious.

'Since I met you, I've been fighting against my feelings for you. Romantic feelings. I know that neither of us was looking for romance this summer, but...I can't hide my feelings any longer.'

Fyona's heart began to thunder excitedly, in hope.

'You should know that I've been falling in love with you,' Roag continued. 'And seeing your reaction at the loch, the way you smiled at me, gave me hope that you have feelings for me too.'

Fyona couldn't deny that she had. 'I feel the same, but I've tried not to, because I didn't want to end this summer with a broken heart.'

Roag looked at her lovingly. 'I'll never break your heart, Fyona. I was concerned that you would break mine.'

She shook her head. 'Never.'

Roag stood up, clasped her hands and pulled her close to him. He smiled at her, causing a rush of emotions to surge through her, and then he kissed her softly, and then with passion and love.

Fyona melted into him, feeling that everything was going to work out the way she'd hoped, never thinking her dream of a future with Roag would come true.

Secure in their romance, they sat down to their first dinner as a couple.

She gazed out at the thousands of stars sparkling in the night sky, and seeing the North Star shining bright, she remembered making a wish. She'd wished for happiness and to one day find romance.

After dinner, Roag put on some music and they danced together in the turret, finishing with a romantic waltz.

The sun shone in the cobalt sky, and the fresh breeze blew through Fyona's hair as she stood on the deck of the ferry.

Roag stood behind her, wrapping her securely in his arms. Their cars were parked below deck, and they'd come up to enjoy the warm summer's day as the ferry's bow cut through the sea.

'I love you, Fyona,' he murmured, gently holding her close.

She turned her face round to him and smiled. 'I love you too.'

His kiss assured her that their future together would be an exciting and happy one.

The mainland was far in the distance, but the towns and cities would soon become clear along the coastline.

'Do you notice something?' Roag said to her as she leaned back against his strong chest.

'Notice what?'

'The way we're facing,' he said. 'We haven't even glanced back at the island disappearing as part of our past. We're looking ahead to the mainland, where our future is. Going home to Glasgow, to the city, exciting new ventures, the dance tour, and our happy future together.'

End

# About the Author:

De-ann Black is a bestselling author, scriptwriter and former newspaper journalist. She has over 100 books published. Romance, thrillers, espionage novels, action adventure. And children's books (non-fiction rocket science books and children's fiction). She became an Amazon All-Star author in 2014 and 2015.

She previously worked as a full-time newspaper journalist for several years. She had her own weekly columns in the press. This included being a motoring correspondent where she got to test drive cars every week for the press for three years.

Before being asked to work for the press, De-ann worked in magazine editorial writing everything from fashion features to social news. She was the marketing editor of a glossy magazine.

She is also a professional artist and illustrator. Embroidery design, fabric design, dressmaking, sewing, knitting and fashion are part of her work.

Additionally, De-ann has always been interested in fitness, and was a fitness and bodybuilding champion, 100 metre runner and mountaineer. As a former N.A.B.B.A. Miss Scotland, she had a weekly fitness show on the radio that ran for over three years.

De-ann trained in Shukokai karate, boxing, kickboxing, Dayan Qigong and Jiu Jitsu. She is currently based in Scotland.

Her 16 colouring books are available in paperback, including her latest Summer Nature Colouring Book and Flower Nature Colouring Book.

Her latest embroidery pattern books include: Floral Garden Embroidery Patterns, Christmas & Winter Embroidery Patterns, Floral Spring Embroidery Patterns and Sea Theme Embroidery Patterns.

Website: Find out more at: www.de-annblack.com

Fabric, Wallpaper & Home Decor Collections:
De-ann's fabric designs and wallpaper collections, and home decor items, including her popular Scottish Garden Thistles patterns, are available from Spoonflower.
www.de-annblack.com/spoonflower

Also by De-ann Black (Romance, Action/Thrillers & Children's books). See her Amazon Author page or website for further details about her books, screenplays, illustrations, art, fabric designs and embroidery patterns.

Amazon Author page:
www.De-annBlack.com/Amazon

**Romance books:**

Dance, Music & Scottish Romance series:
1. Romance Dancer

Quilt Shop by the Seaside
Embroidery Bee

Scottish Loch Romance series:
1. Sewing & Mending Cottage
2. Scottish Loch Summer Romance
3. Sweet Music
4. Knitting Bee
5. Autumn Romance
6. Christmas Ballroom Dancing
7. Scottish Highlands New Year Ball
8. Crafting Bee: Crafts & Romance in Scotland

Music, Dance & Romance series:
1. The Sweetest Waltz
2. Knitting & Starlight
3. Ballroom Dancing Christmas Romance

Snow Bells Haven series:
1. Snow Bells Christmas
2. Snow Bells Wedding
3. Love & Lyrics

The Cure for Love Romance series:
1. The Cure for Love
2. The Cure for Love at Christmas

Scottish Highlands & Island Romance series:
1. Scottish Island Knitting Bee
2. Scottish Island Fairytale Castle
3. Vintage Dress Shop on the Island
4. Fairytale Christmas on the Island
5. Summer Ball Weddings & Waltzing

Quilting Bee & Tea Shop series:
1. The Quilting Bee
2. The Tea Shop by the Sea
3. Embroidery Cottage
4. Knitting Shop by the Sea
5. Christmas Weddings

Sewing, Crafts & Quilting series:
1. The Sewing Bee
2. The Sewing Shop
3. Knitting Cottage (Scottish Highland romance)
4. Scottish Highlands Christmas Wedding

Cottages, Cakes & Crafts series:
1. The Flower Hunter's Cottage
2. The Sewing Bee by the Sea
3. The Beemaster's Cottage
4. The Chocolatier's Cottage
5. The Bookshop by the Seaside
6. The Dressmaker's Cottage

Scottish Chateau, Colouring & Crafts series:
1. Christmas Cake Chateau
2. Colouring Book Cottage

Summer Sewing Bee

Sewing, Knitting & Baking series:
1. The Tea Shop
2. The Sewing Bee & Afternoon Tea
3. The Christmas Knitting Bee
4. Champagne Chic Lemonade Money
5. The Vintage Sewing & Knitting Bee

Tea Dress Shop series:
1. The Tea Dress Shop At Christmas
2. The Fairytale Tea Dress Shop In Edinburgh
3. The Vintage Tea Dress Shop In Summer

The Tea Shop & Tearoom series:
1. The Christmas Tea Shop & Bakery
2. The Christmas Chocolatier
3. The Chocolate Cake Shop in New York at Christmas
4. The Bakery by the Seaside
5. Shed in the City

Christmas Romance series:
1. Christmas Romance in Paris
2. Christmas Romance in Scotland

Oops! I'm the Paparazzi series:
1. Oops! I'm the Paparazzi
2. Oops! I'm Up To Mischief
3. Oops! I'm the Paparazzi, Again

The Bitch-Proof Suit series:
1. The Bitch-Proof Suit
2. The Bitch-Proof Romance
3. The Bitch-Proof Bride
4. The Bitch-Proof Wedding

Heather Park: Regency Romance
Dublin Girl
Why Are All The Good Guys Total Monsters?
I'm Holding Out For A Vampire Boyfriend

**Action/Thriller books:**

Knight in Miami

Agency Agenda

Love Him Forever

Someone Worse

Electric Shadows

The Strife Of Riley

Shadows Of Murder

Cast a Dark Shadow


**Children's books:**

Faeriefied

Secondhand Spooks

Poison-Wynd

Wormhole Wynd

Science Fashion

School For Aliens


**Colouring books:**

Summer Nature

Flower Nature

Summer Garden

Spring Garden

Autumn Garden

Sea Dream

Festive Christmas

Christmas Garden

Christmas Theme

Flower Bee

Wild Garden

Faerie Garden Spring

Flower Hunter

Stargazer Space

Bee Garden

Scottish Garden Seasons


**Embroidery Design books:**

Floral Garden Embroidery Patterns

Floral Spring Embroidery Patterns

Christmas & Winter Embroidery Patterns

Sea Theme Embroidery Patterns

Floral Nature Embroidery Designs

Scottish Garden Embroidery Designs

Printed in Dunstable, United Kingdom